TO MELT A SNOWDRIFT

READY TO GO?
BOOK TWO

LISA HATFIELD

To Melt a Snowdrift

Copyright © 2023 by Lisa Hatfield

Published by High Plains Wordsmith LLC

Paperback ISBN 978-1-7368941-4-9

Hardback ISBN 978-1-7368941-6-3

Ebook ISBN 978-1-7368941-5-6

Audiobook ISBN 978-1-7368941-7-0

This is a work of fiction. Names, characters, places, and incidents either are the product of the author's imagination or are used fictitiously. Any resemblance to actual persons, living or dead, events, business establishments, or locales is entirely coincidental.

In addition to telling a story, the book aims to provide information and to stimulate action. The author and publisher make no claim to provide any type of professional advice. The author and publisher hope the contents of this volume will be helpful to readers. But readers must take responsibility for their own choices, actions, and results.

Published by High Plains Wordsmith LLC
First edition September 2023
Cover and book design by Gordon Saunders
LisaHatfieldWriter.com

This book is dedicated to:

Emma Jennifer Hatfield a.k.a. Bryngeror Deotrichsdottir

Books in the 'Ready to Go?' series by Lisa Hatfield

To Starve an Ember
   To Melt a Snowdrift
   (coming next...hurricane novel!)

Subscribe to my newsletter at LisaHatfieldWriter.com, and I'll send you a short story (PDF, Epub, or MP3). The intermittent newsletter will tell you about in-person and on-line events for the **Ready to Go?** series, including when the next book will be completed.

Write a review of this book on the site where you bought it or at:
   www.goodreads.com/book/show/195233885-to-melt-a-snowdrift

TUESDAY, NOVEMBER 26, 2019, PIONEERSBURG, COLORADO 7 P.M.

Anna needed to know why it took her husband two hours to make the ten-minute drive home. She wanted so much to welcome David home from his freight hauling trip, but she was mad and scared. It was cliché to say, "What took you so long?" but she had to ask it. He reached out to give her a hug in the apartment doorway, but she fought her wish accept it.

David shrugged and lowered his eyebrows with seriousness. "I know where we live, babe. I just took a little unplanned detour." Cold November raindrops made dark splotches on his unruly blond hair and dripped down his scruffy chin. "After a trip of 3,000 miles, what's a few more?" Since Anna still blocked the doorway, he directed this comment over her shoulder to their twenty-six-year-old daughter Jessie and her boyfriend Prentice who stood behind her.

It took all Anna's emotional strength not to step aside just yet.

Jessie rested her hand on her mom's shoulder and said, "Dad, we were just worried. We thought you'd be here pretty soon in the Pete after you dropped off the trailer at the storage yard."

The Pete was David's nickname for his Peterbilt tractor cab, used to haul his semi- trailer.

He looked from face to face. "Aren't you gonna let me in?"

Anna stood her ground, still blocking the doorway, desperate for an answer. *He's not used to me confronting him like this,* she thought. She frowned and looked up at him, waiting.

David laughed. "Okay, so I have to explain where I was. That's my ticket in. All right," he said. "After I dropped off the trailer, I drove the Pete up to Garnet, going home the way I always go." He tried to step inside, but she wouldn't let him.

"Why would you — David, we haven't lived there since the fire —" Anna said. Three months ago, a wildfire had burned through their Garnet neighborhood while he'd been on the road. Little things seemed to be slipping his mind lately, but losing their house in a fire was not a little thing. She looked up into his blue eyes, searching for an answer.

"The fire, yeah." He sounded sheepish. "I remembered that when I got there tonight. The house was all dark and smoke-stained."

Anna tried to soften her grim expression but couldn't make herself smile. Was he trying to tell her that he drove ten miles toward a home that he forgot wasn't livable? And then he didn't get here to the apartment in Pioneersburg until two hours after he texted her from a few miles away? She crossed her arms over her chest, fighting panic. Where had he really gone?

"The second I saw the house, I remembered that you're

not there, you're here at Jessie's!" He grinned. "Anyway, it wasn't a total waste driving up there, babe. You'll be glad to know that they finally ripped off the front porch, so that's something, right? A little progress, but it's still a pit." His laugh this time faded, and Anna saw signs of fatigue settle over his face. "Hey, how about a smooch, babe?"

Anna stepped into her husband's arms and buried her face in his chest, inhaling his familiar smell, a mix of damp road grime and sweat. If only the worried muscles in her neck would relax. He was a cross-country trucker. He always knew where he was. But today he'd gone to the wrong house and driven out of his way to do it?

She tilted her chin up to give him a genuine kiss, and he bent to meet her halfway. They might have seemed mismatched: a tall Nebraska trucker who'd grown up on a dairy farm, married to a petite Chinese-American artist who'd been raised by her strict mama in San Francisco. But they were perfect together, Anna thought, a rare but perfect match in every way.

They stepped back from each other. "Anna, babe, I'm sorry you're mad. I didn't mean to worry you." His winning high school grin lit up his forty-five-year-old face, and he squeezed her hand as they walked inside. She squeezed back, taking in the twinkle in his eyes that hinted more fun for later that evening... However, this highlighted the very close quarters of their living arrangement. Ever since the fire had forced them from their house, Anna and David had been sleeping in Jessie's spare room in her apartment. Even as Prentice and David shook hands and mumbled greetings, Anna caught her daughter's glance, smiled faintly, then looked at the floor. *Awkward!*

"Tell us about your trip," Jessie said, hugging her dad

and then pulling him into the living room. "You're all wet. Where's your raincoat?"

"Yeah, I'm pretty chilled, Jes. Can't seem to warm up these days," was David's only answer. He sat down in the middle of the sofa.

Anna and Prentice followed in their wake. Anna remained standing but gave Prentice a friendly look as he sat in the armchair next to the sofa, thanking him for his presence and patience. She got along well with Jessie's boyfriend.

Jessie tossed her dad a fresh shirt from the living room coat closet where he and Anna were storing the few clothes they owned. He pulled the rain-dampened shirt off over his head, replacing it with the dry one.

"Boy, this rain is miserable." David said. After using the damp shirt to dry off his hair, he wadded it up and tossed it to Jessie, who put it in the bathroom hamper and returned to sit next to him. "Wish it were summer again. This cold weather really takes it out of me. Can't seem to warm up these days."

Doesn't he notice he's repeating himself? Anna wondered, still standing in the living room. But he was exhausted, under pressure. They were evacuated from their own home. A string of excuses ran through her mind, a thin covering for a nagging feeling she could not pinpoint. "At least you're dried off now," she said with more brightness than she felt.

"Oh, Dad, do you want me to go out to the truck and get the groceries?" asked Jessie with a smile. "I didn't see you bring a bag in."

He gave her a questioning look.

"Did you pick up the sour cream and chips to go with the chili?" Jessie clarified.

He looked at her, his face blank. "Sour cream?"

"But David," Anna couldn't help saying. "When you texted me from the storage yard, you said you were stopping at the store—"

"You said you had to get some things for your truck." Jessie sounded as puzzled as Anna felt.

He slapped his hands together and shook his head. "I forgot, that's all. Okay?" David's voice was sharp.

Jessie and Anna exchanged a look, and Prentice focused on a spot on the carpet. It was unlike David to be so gruff. As much to break the tension as anything else, Anna turned on the radio on the pass-through counter and went into Jessie's galley kitchen, pondering the miscommunication. She would have gotten the few things they needed from the store herself, but when he texted them two hours ago, David had said he needed to stop to restock the supplies in the Pete and he'd be home soon.

Something felt off.

"I'm glad to be off the road," David said to the group, as if he'd forgotten his annoyance of a moment ago. Jessie leaned her head on her dad's shoulder.

David, more in true form again, chimed in with the radio playing in the background, a classic rock song by the Electric Light Orchestra. "Ooooh, rain is falling..." He repeated that part of the chorus a few times but stopped abruptly, looking up at the ceiling as he failed to remember the rest of the lyrics. To Jessie, he said, "Speaking of rain, wasn't it great when you and I got to hang out on a dad-daughter weekend while we both happened to be in Maryland this summer? No rain then." He smiled at his daughter.

"Yeah Dad. Hiking Sugarloaf Mountain was great, but I felt so guilty—"

"I know." David glanced at Anna in the other room. "At

the same time we were having a good visit, your mom was back here in Colorado, alone in your apartment."

Anna had been forced to evacuate Garnet because of the August wildfires, and so she'd gone to Jessie's place in Pioneersburg, ten miles south of there, with their yellow Lab, Casey. From the kitchen, she said, "I told you then, there was nothing either of you could have done but pray whether you were here or there, and you already knew I was safe here. So I'm glad you had fun while you were both working in Maryland." She added, "And, Casey was with me."

Prentice spoke up at last. He'd gotten his fill of those Garnet wildfires since he was part of the fire crews that tried to do structure protection against the ember storms. "We did what we could, but with two fires, it was dicey. We couldn't control the weather. Better for civilians to evacuate and not rush back into the danger zone." He smiled over at Anna. "You did the right thing to get out of there as quickly as you did."

Anna nodded back at Prentice across the pass-through counter. "I met you briefly that night you fixed Jessie's car, the week or so before the fires, but I hadn't really talked with you until you showed up here that day looking for her."

"And I found you here instead of Jessie!" He laughed. "She'd told me she was going out of town, but with all the chaos, I'd forgotten. And here you were, hunkered down in a safe place, with your loyal dog." He looked around for Casey but didn't see him.

"He's here in the kitchen with me. He's not your ordinary knucklehead," said Anna. She turned off the radio so she could hear better.

"Nope," said Prentice. "And he was right there under my

feet when you showed me how to make wontons that day, too. In case I dropped something."

"That was surreal, when you think about it," said Anna. "I was still numb. Trying not to worry about what was happening with the houses in Garnet. I'm glad you showed up, even if it was by accident. It was a good distraction."

"And of course, you could see why Jessie had been talking about me so much already," he joked. "I was covered in soot and sweat and had a wrecked ankle."

From the sofa, Jessie said, "Mom called me in Maryland as soon as you left that day, Prentice. She told me all about you appearing here, and about the wildfires up in Garnet too. Then I knew she was really safe."

"And I was totally no help, I'm sorry to say," David said. He steered the conversation back to Maryland and away from the fires. "Remember playing miniature golf, Jes? We got three rounds for the price of one."

"Yeah, by skipping the last hole that would have captured our golf balls." Jessie laughed.

"We didn't stop playing until it was dark," David said, and looking over at Anna, who was still listening from the kitchen, he said, "You lost out, babe. It was a great trip." He looked away, looked back, suddenly somber. "Why haven't you come along with me on a truck run lately, Anna? We always have such a good time."

She wiped nonexistent crumbs off the counter top. "I don't know. I think the last time was last spring, wasn't it? That's not too long ago." *It feels like a hundred years ago, though.* Why didn't she go with him this summer on one of his runs? Was she waiting for him to invite her?

David joked, "Maybe you just don't love me anymore," but that wasn't funny at all. He continued with his silly stories, oblivious to her discomfort. He'd already turned back to Jessie. "And then there was that time you were working in Maryland and I got to stop in and visit you while I was on a run. That was a great dad-daughter weekend."

"Um, yeah, Dad. That's what we were just talking about," said Jessie, with a quizzical expression at Anna. "You just told that story."

Anna returned Jessie's frown.

David, looking sheepish, said, "I did? Well, shoot, it really was fun, anyway."

"Right," Jessie laughed again, and Prentice changed the subject by launching into a story about firefighters playing jokes on each other at the station, and then one about a wildfire evaluation he did that got interrupted by a flock of wild turkeys.

Anna listened without really hearing. Something was different with David, but she couldn't put her finger on it. It was as if he were missing a part of himself, but she didn't even know what she meant by that. She lifted the lid on the pot of chili that would be dinner. It had been ready for a long time, but she didn't feel like calling them in to eat it.

Out of nowhere now, though, she heard David ask Prentice, "Hey, buddy, what do you do, again?"

Anna dropped the lid back onto the crock pot with a clatter.

Jessie's laugh froze.

Prentice blinked hard but answered, "Firefighter."

Anna saw David's eyebrows lift, silent encouragement that Prentice should tell more about himself—as if David didn't know. But he did know, for heaven's sake, Anna thought. Anxiety beat in her throat.

"In Garnet," Prentice continued, and the tone in his voice reflected his bewilderment. Anna could practically hear him wondering why he was having to repeat facts David already knew.

"Dad, you sound tired." Jessie came to everyone's rescue. "How many miles did you drive today, anyway?"

He slapped his knee. "All of them!" he said, and when he laughed, after a moment, Jessie and Prentice did, too. Even Anna smiled at David's old joke. That one was worth repeating.

At least he was home safe. Maybe his memory lapses were only due to fatigue. Of course, that was it. What else could it be? Or who? But no, she told herself. He was here, wasn't he?

Outside, a blast of raindrops hit the patio window, and David asked Jessie to grab his sweatshirt from the closet.

Anna thought about how the same chilling rain was falling right now on the terrible burn scars in Garnet left in the wake of the summer fires. Unbidden thoughts of possible flash flooding sprang to her mind. And for sensitive Anna, this renewed memories of the past disasters she'd weathered...

...the earthquake that had hit San Francisco when she was in kindergarten. She could still feel it, how the earth shook itself, knocking all the kids flat onto ground that wobbled and pitched instead of staying firm.

... and years later, she, her mama, and Jessie, who was just a girl in middle school, had survived hurricane Katrina in Mississippi.

...and last summer, there had been two separate wildfires in Garnet, which she'd dealt with by running here to Jessie's, to safety.

She was still dealing with the aftermath of those fires. All the house insurance adminis-trivia was her job, not David's. He didn't even want to talk about it. But it had always been hard to discuss serious topics with him, and the additional stress of being displaced by the fires had only made it harder. Too much reality setting in.

His habit was to make a joke of everything. He'd say it was his job to earn the money and her job to spend it. If she asked for a serious answer, he'd give her a look and say, "I knew the bride when she used to rock and roll!" reminding her that they both used to be more fun when they were young.

But someone had to be responsible, and she was the lucky one with more time. Lucky her. Lucky him.

She stirred the chili and thought about how much she missed hiding out in her art studio. That's when she was the most fun and could relax, when she gave herself time for being creative. But here at Jessie's, it was impossible to make her painting a priority. There wasn't room in the apartment for her to buy new supplies to replace the ones that had gone up in smoke, and anyway, how could she goof off and paint when they had so many insurance and construction forms to complete?

The best way for me to deal with chaos is to stay away from it, she decided. *I'm not strong enough to hit it head-on.* She pondered as she washed a few stray dishes in Jessie's kitchen. *I don't want to think about anything serious ever again. But I have no choice.* She yearned for some R & R with David where they could both relax.

He's right. I'm no fun right now.

8 P.M.

Casey sat on the floor in the kitchen. He stuck with Anna always, whether she was at home alone or on the road with David. Looking down at him, she said, "You're a Good Dog." He wagged his tail. "Want a treat?" she asked as she unwrapped a green dental chew bone. He gobbled it up, and she gathered the ingredients to make pumpkin pie, although it was still two days before Thanksgiving. She mixed the filling, poured it in the crust, and slid it in the oven.

Moon cakes. She wished she'd remembered to order the special ingredients to make snow skin moon cakes filled with purple yam paste. In her childhood, she obsessed over treats like moon cakes that her mama wouldn't let her buy. As an adult, she enjoyed making fun and delicious desserts for celebrations, but she hadn't written it on her jam-packed to-do list, so it didn't happen. *Oh well.*

She was now out of reasons to stay in the kitchen, and Anna joined the gang in the living room, where the conversation was centered on how bizarre it was to have rain in Colorado in November. This was more than unprecedented; it was almost impossible, so late in November. Anna settled on the sofa on the other side of David, and as the rain continued, Prentice got on his wildfire soapbox, explaining how severe fires like the ones a few months ago damaged the soil to an extent that would surely lead to flash flooding next spring. "People need to build hillside erosion barriers above their homes. No one's going to do it for them."

David said, "That sounds like a lot of work."

Prentice agreed. "But it's easier work than dealing with flood damage after the rain."

"Isn't Garnet's public works department doing storm drain improvement work?" Jessie asked Prentice.

He shook his head. "Bixby and I have been helping them find funding to get the culverts ready before next spring when the rains really pour, but the town's done no work yet." He glanced at the window.

"I'm sure people don't want to do erosion control when they're trying to replace their house that they lost in the fire." Jessie said. "Especially if they're still making mortgage payments on an empty lot where their house used to be," she added. "Sorry, Prentice. Like Mom says, prophets are not without honor except in their hometown."

Prentice's earnest face fell. "And Garnet's my hometown. But I hope someone will listen before it's too late, next spring."

David switched on the TV with the remote. The expanded weather forecast focused on unlikely late-fall rain in this part of Colorado. All four of them watched the report.

"I was hoping this rain might turn into some nice, early snow on the ground, not a flood," Anna said as she watched the screen.

Since it was Thanksgiving week, the regular forecaster was gone, maybe on vacation with her family. Her substitute was the retired full-time forecaster. He'd put on weight, Anna noticed, and his hair was white now, but she found his gravelly voice and well-documented reports reassuring.

He explained how today's extraordinary late-season rains were flowing down the ruined hillsides. The video showed a burned neighborhood in the little town of Garnet running with water and debris. It accumulated into scouring tangles as it ran down the slopes and roads, removing more topsoil as it went.

Anna looked at Prentice. "This is what you've been talking about. But I thought this kind of flooding wouldn't happen until spring."

"It shouldn't be," he muttered, shaking his head.

The meteorologist said, "The super-hot fires in August made the ground impervious to water, and the changes to historic drainage patterns mean water is flowing into places that have never had water flows before." The camera aimed at another home that had survived this summer's fires but was now in peril of flooding. Residents piled sandbags, trying to keep water out of the window wells.

He continued in his raspy, deep voice, "Flooding affected other homes in Garnet, both near the mountains and east of the interstate today." Video of water-filled basements and living rooms confirmed this statement.

Unable to listen any longer, Anna turned off the TV, and they all sat staring at the dark screen.

"This was all because of today's little rain?" Jessie said.

"It's rained pretty steadily," Prentice said. "When the vegetation's gone, the soil can't slow it down." He demonstrated with his hands. "It picks up sediment and branches and it becomes a demolition force. Water can take out the supports for a bridge." He made a swooping motion with his arm. "Or it picks up a wad of trees and pushes them right into a house."

"Just like it showed on the news?" As worried as she was of the answer, Anna had to ask. "Did anyone see that house they showed with the flooded basement? Do you think that was our house?"

"What, Mom?" Jessie looked surprised.

"On the news?" Prentice shook his head. "Nah. It didn't look like your place, Anna."

David added, "When I was up in Garnet earlier, I did notice more water than usual in the streets, now that you mention it. I was busy looking at the fire damage, though." He shook his head. "That's part of the reason it took me a while to get back here."

Anna asked. "You had to drive through water near our house?"

He nodded. "Yeah, it was a mess. I was a few blocks away. I had to take it easy in the Pete since it throws up so much spray with the big wheels." He smiled. "Drenched a car going the other way—"

Anna straightened. "But David, was our house okay?" *We cannot afford any additional damage.* As it was, she didn't know if the insurance was going to pay for all the fire damage. She felt like it was taking forever to get replacement figures to the insurance company and get the house fixed, and meanwhile, here they were, taking up space at Jessie's. *I hate being in charge of all the paperwork and finances. I'm so afraid I'll miss something.*

David had the nerve to laugh. "Like I said, babe, our house wasn't flooded when I saw it. Boy, that would be awful, though, wouldn't it?" His blue eyes shone at her. "Good thing it's taking so long to get all the wildfire repairs done, huh?" He really meant this to be funny.

"I'm working on it," she said in a strained voice. "You're stuck with doing it at my speed, I guess."

Their whole marriage relationship had evolved without a plan. It didn't matter much to David where they lived or what Anna did, as long as his ladies, his wife and daughter, were safe and happy. He loved to drive the long-haul miles and be the provider. So, Anna was left to handle the money, and she had to learn through trial and error. They never fought about it or even talked about finances. It just worked out that way.

And ever since they first met as high schoolers during spring break, she couldn't stay mad at him, even now when he made her worry and just blew off their current crisis as a joke. The fact that he would always look at the bright side was why she loved him. And why she went along with his joke now, even when it made her feel uncomfortable. "You're a goofball, David DeGroot," she told him.

8:30 P.M.

David wiggled down into the sofa, getting ready to tell another story; Anna knew the body language. But she took note when he pulled the bright knitted afghan up over his legs. Usually, he was too warm. She kept her smile in place long enough to get back to the kitchen to check the pumpkin pie. A moment later, glancing up, Prentice startled her, appearing across the kitchen pass-through.

"Anything I can do, Anna?" he asked. "I haven't been much help tonight."

"Thanks Prentice. I don't know why I don't just serve this." She gestured at the crock pot full of chili.

"Well, I'm starving," said Prentice with his crooked grin. "I'll start taking stuff out there, okay?"

"Here you go." Anna handed him the silverware from the drawer, though he knew perfectly well where it was since he was at Jessie's all the time. "Thanks," she added, not taking her eyes off David on the sofa. *He's right there, but he feels so far away from me.* The troubling thought whispered through her brain.

Prentice took the silverware and then set up the TV trays while he was out in the living room, and Anna set four bowls of chili on the pass-through for him to grab when he came back.

"Do you have any corn chips?" Prentice was asking. She took a half-full bag out of the cupboard and handed it to him. Those had been on the grocery list.

He made more trips and then returned to the armchair. Anna squeezed in beside David and Jessie on the sofa. Eating in the living room, instead of sitting at Jessie's dining room table, was supposed to make it feel like a fun welcome home party.

David said, "Don't we have any sour cream?"

He was not joking. No one answered him.

"Well, fine, I'll just have chili without it," he said.

Anna pondered. *Even though we've spent a lot of time apart from each other, we've helped each other get through so much together... My mama moving in with us when Jessie was little. The hurricane while he was gone on a run, and us bailing out to Colorado right after that. Mama dying a few years later. Then came the fire. We'll figure this out too. He'll stick with me like he always has, in his own goofy way.*

David moved on to another trucking story they'd heard before. It ended with, "Can you believe that? The tumbleweeds had blown in overnight and jammed up my motel room door. I couldn't get down the walkway! I spent forever trying to untangle the stupid tumbleweeds and throw them over the railing into the parking lot."

Jessie said, "Did you know tumbleweed's the same plant as knapweed? It's an invasive weed that came from Europe in some ship ballast."

Prentice laughed. "Even for a computer systems expert, you really are a nerd."

"Thank you," Jessie said. "I'm a lifelong learner, even on my days off."

"You tell us that knapweed story every time your dad tells his tumbleweed story." He reached over to rub her shoulder, and she leaned into it, looking contented.

David's smile didn't fade when he said, "Oh, have I told that one before?" Unfazed, he launched right into another one, a story that was actually new to them. "What about the time this summer—there I was, heading down the interstate with an 18-wheel dry van loaded full of..." He paused before saying, "Full of what, I had absolutely no clue!" Slapped his hand on his knee and looked around with a grin.

Anna stared at him and was about to question him about not knowing what he was hauling. To a long-haul trucker, that could mean life or death.

"What do you mean?" Jessie asked before Anna could. "You honestly didn't know, Dad?"

"I just couldn't remember, that's all," he said.

"Where were you taking it?" She took a spoonful of chili.

"That's what made it even funnier," David said. "I couldn't remember that either."

Anna's heart dropped. *And why does he think that not remembering all this is funny?* She noticed Jessie and Prentice, a smart network IT professional, and a college-trained forester and experienced firefighter, exchanging worried glances. *I know I'm not imagining things here*, she thought.

"What did you do then, David?" Prentice asked. He scooped chili onto a corn chip, shoving it all into his mouth.

"Aw, you know," David said. "I had the destination keyed into my truck GPS, so I just followed Janet Bossy's directions."

"Janet Bossy, who's that?" Prentice asked.

"What Dad calls his GPS lady," Jessie answered, then looking back at David, she said, "So, you dropped your load in the right place after all?"

"Yep, it worked out fine. It always does."

Anna's stomach was in a knot, and she wished to run away from this chaos, so she changed the subject. "The voice in my GPS is called Lee from New Zealand," she said.

"Should I be jealous? He sounds cute." David wiped his mouth with his napkin.

She patted his arm. "No, honey. Your voice is all I need." She leaned sideways and looked up to give him a kiss, but he didn't notice.

Instead, he started another story. "Then there was the time I couldn't remember if I was going for a haircut or going to pick up something at the store..."

"When was that?" Anna demanded.

He flapped a hand. "I don't know. It was no big deal."

She looked away. How could he say that when it was one memory lapse after another? And he sat there making jokes? Anna felt she might be sick. David was always telling stories, but until recently, he'd never mentioned not remembering things.

She gathered their bowls and took them to the kitchen, then without any warning, she crouched down, out of the view of the others, trying to stop the frightened tears that burned her eyes.

"Mom, are you okay?" Jessie came into the kitchen and sat on the floor next to her.

"Oh Jessie," said Anna, sniffing, wiping her eyes. "It's nothing. Don't worry."

"C'mon. You've taught me better than that. You're not okay."

Anna sniffed again. "Thanks, my sweet girl." But even as she spoke, she wondered whether she'd been expecting too much from him when his mind was overloaded with practical trucking matters. At the same time, she felt burdened with all she had to do with the finance tasks that recently seemed worse than ever, though David was working just as hard.

She needed to vent.

Jessie asked, "Wanna talk in my room?"

Anna nodded and followed Jessie down the hall. Sometimes she felt like the daughter instead of the mom, she thought, sitting beside Jessie on her bed. Out in the living room, Prentice and David talked and laughed.

Jessie took Anna's hand as they sat on the bed. "What's up?"

Anna said, "Wow. I guess your dad's stories about forgetting things are upsetting me."

"Me too, Mom. He's our rock." Jessie laughed at her nerdy pun. "Our rock, but not our *Rock*. You know what I mean?"

Anna knew. "We love him, and he loves us, and he always takes care of everything."

"No, he doesn't, Mom. You run the show at home, even when you're living at my home," she joked. "Besides, I am an independently wealthy college graduate."

They both laughed. It was a running joke in the family that Anna's art sales were a hobby that made hardly any money. Jessie was recently out of college, doing network and systems work for a government contractor, and still paying off debt, though at an increasingly rapid pace.

Anna looked at her wise daughter. "Your dad is my awesome guy. But he's acting differently lately. Do you agree?"

"Yes. He's always been a free spirit, but he always pays attention to the important things. Like where he's headed in the Pete," said Jessie.

Anna agreed. "He's always been my life of the party, but how could he joke about getting so confused while driving a fully loaded tractor-trailer?"

Jessie smiled. "When my friends used to ask what my

dad's job was, and I said 'O-O,' they didn't get it 'til I explained it was 'owner-operator.'"

"I think it's a good thing he already had his truck to escape to when my mama showed up to live with us in Mississippi."

Mom and daughter laughed quietly together with their own memories from the years when Jiexen left San Francisco and moved in with the family when Jessie was in first grade. They had a common enemy then.

"Tiger Grandma," Jessie said simply.

"Whenever I was around my mama, I just felt like such a dummy." Anna shook her head.

"Yeah, I saw that," Jessie said, "But I didn't know until I was older that not everyone had their ferocious grandma living with them. I know my own answer, but what was it about her that scared you so much?"

Anna cleared her throat. "Well. I've thought about this a lot since I left home after high school. She was a perfectionist. But for good reason." She looked up as she remembered. "She and my dad — I called him Baa, and she called him 'the husband' you know — had to fight to leave China and then fight some more to make it work when they got to San Francisco. They opened their noodle shop..."

"And then one day 'the husband' just took off?"

"We never found out what happened." Anna shook her head again. "I have this feeling like it was my fault, but I can't figure out why that would be." They stayed quiet for a few minutes. "Mama wouldn't talk about it."

"How old were you then?"

"About six," said Anna. "She was a force of nature, wasn't she? I wish we could have weathered that storm better."

"Now stop," Jessie said, "Focus, Mom. She was a fighter. Like you said, she just wanted us to be better off."

Anna nodded. "She told me once that America was better than she ever imagined, even though her husband had vanished in San Francisco, and after we'd been through Hurricane Katrina. Compared to her growing up in China, we are living like kings and queens every day of our lives."

"So," Jessie prodded in the way she did so gently, "why do you seem so spooked today?"

Anna's tears started again. "What happens if he disappears on me just like my baa did?"

"What are you talking about? Dad's not going anywhere." She patted Anna on the back. "And even if he did, you could handle it. Hey, what's the advice you always give me?"

"Do as I say, not as I do?" She laughed weakly.

"No." Jessie sounded exasperated. "Mom, give yourself more credit. I mean, about remembering you're beautifully and wonderfully made. You're beautiful inside and out."

Anna smiled and sat up straighter. "The Bible verse is actually, 'I am fearfully and wonderfully made; marvelous are Your works, and my soul knows it very well.' But thanks, Jessie. I needed that."

"Oops. Well, you're welcome either way," said Jessie with a smile and a shrug.

Anna said, "There's a Chinese saying: 'Beautiful women will have difficult lives.'"

"I'm surprised to hear you quoting any Chinese sayings," Jessie smiled. "I thought that was Tiger Grandma's job. Generally, you stick with the American rock lyrics."

"No, you're right, my dear girl," said Anna. "And you know I'm not a fatalist. I just have trouble getting into gear sometimes. That's when I need to pray more."

They hugged, and Anna went to the restroom to wash her face and reapply the smudged eyeliner. She liked to accentuate her narrow eyes above her delicate cheekbones. She gave herself a smile in the mirror. *Come on Anna, this is supposed to be a welcome home party. Be fun.*

Back in the living room, the guys had quit telling stories and switched on the TV again to watch the news. Jessie and Anna sat on the sofa on either side of David. The anchorman was talking football, which Anna couldn't have cared less about. David leaned back and stretched his arms over his head, then put one around Anna's shoulders and the other around Jessie's. "My two super ladies."

Anna relaxed with her head on his chest, enjoying just being near him. He'd always had a calming influence on her, though tonight she still felt an undercurrent of worry she didn't know how to deal with. It was more than the current housing situation or his unexplained delay.

Whatever it was, she didn't know how to bring up her concerns without it sounding like an accusation. *It's not like he'll leave me just because I don't laugh at his jokes. But why is it so hard to ever discuss serious things with him?*

2

FALL, 1979, ANNA'S
KINDERGARTEN MEMORY,
CHINATOWN, SAN FRANCISCO,
CALIFORNIA

PART 1

In the depths of San Francisco's Chinatown, foghorns echoed, and little Anna darted to the edge of the narrow alley as fog boiled up from the bay. A man pushed a cart piled with cardboard boxes, but he didn't see her as he grunted along. If she hadn't pressed herself and her blue plastic backpack against a metal door, he would have run her over. The tears burned. She stayed pressed to the wall, waiting in the thick fog long after the man was gone. Fearful because she couldn't remember the way home, to the noodle shop where she, Mama, and Baa worked and lived.

Yesterday, her first day of kindergarten, Mama had walked her to school and picked her up again. "You walk this way," Mama had said in English, her third language. "Walk at side of road, no problem. See tall white tower, you here."

Anna nodded and ran to keep up.

"You lucky girl to go school, learn English," Mama had continued. "The husband and I—we swim across water to get be safe. Anna just walk to school. Eight blocks. Easy."

Mama always called Anna's father 'the husband.' Anna called him Baa.

Anna had never quite understood that story about swimming across the water. Mama mentioned it a lot, how she and the husband ran away from something evil, far from America. They ran, Mama had said, then swam, then begged for passage on a boat across the ocean—all so Anna could walk to school. Anna often wondered if there wasn't an easier way to get to school. But if she asked questions, her mama would say, "You listen. You work hard. Not talk so much."

The alleys and streets were always full of activity. Yesterday, Mama and Anna had to walk around a group of men unloading pig meat from a truck. So many people squeezed in such a few square blocks. Red lanterns on strings between the buildings blew in the breeze.

And yesterday was special, because after her first day at school, Mama served Anna a little plate of sweet almond jello: white gelatin cubes tossed with orange and red fruit cocktail. Such a sweet surprise. But yesterday, no man with a cart had almost run her over. No fog had obscured the sun. No little girl had to walk alone.

Today, in the fog, Anna couldn't run. She pressed her back against the unlabeled metal door and couldn't even move. She couldn't remember how to get back to the noodle shop. People flowed by in both directions, carrying bags and boxes and babies. Under her thin cotton dress, her skinny legs felt cold from the mist.

But abruptly now, a short, round lady with crinkly, wrinkly eyes materialized out of the fog. "You lost?"

Anna peered at her, recognizing her. It was the lady who sold ducks! She remembered the window of the lady's shop, full of hanging, roasted ducks with long necks. Brown and crackled, they smelled so good.

She nodded at the lady, and taking hold of the hem of her sweater, was led along the many blocks to Mama and Baa's busy noodle shop. Stepping inside, Anna inhaled deeply. She loved the smell of soy sauce and fried delights.

Customers stood in line to buy food, and Baa put the money in the cash register with his long, slender hands. Whenever he held an ink pen, his hands moved with grace, and the words looked like artwork to Anna, though she could not read them.

She wondered where all the money from the customers went. Mama asked Baa about it a lot, but he never said. But then, he didn't say much of anything to Anna. Mama said the husband was a professor when they lived in China. *That means professors are very quiet people*, little Anna reasoned.

The duck lady nudged Anna inside and went on her own way without a word. She took a few steps farther into the noodle shop, with the room above it that was their home. Baa stood at the counter with a customer, giving him change and a plastic bag of white cardboard food containers. He nodded at Anna and pointed his chin toward the kitchen to see Mama.

Anna froze when she saw Mama's flat black eyes evaluating her.

"Why you late?" Mama said to Anna. "School not so far. Go wash hands."

Anna did as Mama said. She wasn't old enough yet to chop vegetables or make dough, but she could stand on a stool and wash a tub full of vegetables or a sink of soapy dishes. No almond jello for her today.

They worked in silence for a long time, interrupted by conversations in the front as Baa greeted customers and sold steamed pork dumplings, vegetable dim sum, sweet sesame rice balls, Double Happiness, Hong Kong crispy noodles. He and Mama exchanged a few words when he came in back to the kitchen to pick up plates of food.

Mama finished filling a tray of spring rolls, then loaded a plate of noodles and stir-fried vegetables for Anna and sat her down at the wooden table. "What you learn in school?"

Anna's head swam with questions. *What is the right answer to that?* The teacher talked a lot. So much English. *Did we learn something I should tell Mama?* She wanted to sing the alphabet song in English, but after just hearing it once, she couldn't remember how it went.

So, she just looked at Mama and blinked her narrow, black eyes.

Mama shook her head and moved her eyes away from Anna to a new batch of dough. "You not smart. Go up to room."

Anna climbed the narrow steps from the kitchen to the one-room apartment above. She played with her cloth doll, talking to her, dancing with her, putting her to bed, and waking her up again. She sang what she could remember of the alphabet song.

She and the doll climbed up on her cot to look out the window at the alley below. If she craned her neck to the side, sometimes she could glimpse the mysterious blue water many blocks away. But today with so much fog, all she could see was the dim outline of buildings in the grayness.

TUESDAY, NOVEMBER 26, 2019, 8:45 P.M.
Pioneersburg, Colorado
The timer went off in the kitchen and Anna got up.

"I love the smell of pumpkin pie," said Prentice from the armchair. "My mom made it for us when I was little."

Jessie said, in her penetrating way, "You don't have a lot of memories of your mom, do you?" When he shook his head, Anna heard her tell him, "Well, it's good to have that happy one, right?"

She liked the way Prentice and Jessie could tackle absolutely any subject head-on.

In the kitchen, Anna grabbed two hot pads and opened the oven door, letting the delicious aroma of cinnamon, nutmeg, and ginger waft throughout Jessie's small apartment. "Well, I hope this will live up to your mom's memory, Prentice," she announced, setting the pie on a rack on the counter and walking back into the living room. "I hope you guys don't touch this pie tomorrow. I'm baking ahead for Thanksgiving, so we'll have enough oven space on Thursday. Tomorrow's Wednesday, and I'll make the mashed potatoes and honey-hoisin sweet potatoes for Jessie. Buttermilk cornbread for David. And of course, the wontons for Prentice!" She grinned sidelong at him. Teaching him that wonton recipe in August had been their bonding moment.

David said, "What? Thanksgiving? Oh wow, babe. Why are you cooking all the food a whole week early?"

Anna, Jessie, and Prentice all turned to stare at David with furrowed brows.

"What?" he said. "Man, you three are acting really weird tonight."

Anna exchanged glances with Jessie and Prentice before saying, "David, Thanksgiving's in two days."

He smiled and slapped both hands on his knees. "Not next week? Are you sure?" They shook their heads at him in unison.

"Well, too bad, 'cuz I picked up an extra run for tomorrow and Thursday."

"Tomorrow?" she said. "So you'll return Thursday?" She stepped closer to him, where he sat on the sofa.

"Yeah, I had a chance for this extra load, and I thought it would help with our finances," he shrugged. "I was sure Thanksgiving wasn't until next week," he said under his breath.

"Well, yes, the money would help. But how far is it? When do you get back?"

"Oh, probably by late Thursday afternoon. It's only about 350 miles between Pioneersburg and Durango." He grinned his handsome grin and looked around as if to gather his thoughts. "I'll get up super early to get back. We could have Thanksgiving dinner at night instead of the afternoon. How about that?"

Anna walked away, going over to sit at the dining table. Her face felt frozen. She could still see the others in the living room, but at least she had some distance from them in the small apartment.

"Anna?" David raised his voice. "Maybe you could come along with me again? You haven't been with me on a run for months."

She wanted to say yes without hesitation. It would be fun. She and David could get some alone time. They could get reconnected. So why was she hesitating?

Jessie spoke up. "Sure Mom, why not? Since you and Dad and Casey moved in with me, we're always together. The only way I'll be able to tell anything's different on Thanksgiving is by the sheer quantity of food, not because you're company coming for dinner." She laughed, but her eyes were serious and never left Anna's.

"Oh honey. Of course, you must need some space." Anna

shook her head. "It would be fun to go on a run again," she said, but her heart didn't agree with her wistful thought. What if her concern about David's lack of attention was right? What if they were growing apart? And she had more insurance phone calls she ought to be making...

Jessie said, "If it would help, we could even delay Thanksgiving dinner until Friday. I've got the day off on Friday, and so does Prentice, right?" When he nodded, Jessie caught Anna's glance. Looking at Prentice, Anna thought he seemed confused and no wonder. There was too much unspoken conflict in the air, too many back-and-forth looks to keep track of.

Anna said to David, "You're going to Durango, you said? That's two mountain passes tomorrow and then back again on Thursday, right?"

"Yeah." David smoothed his hands on his thighs through the vintage blue and pink afghan. "Look, I'm sorry I forgot to tell you about this one, Anna. I already accepted the run off the log board, and I've gotta leave early tomorrow morning."

"Even though..." she stammered.

He got up from the sofa, joined her in the dining room, and took her hand. "Will ya' come with me, Anna? We could use some time for ourselves."

Anna looked into his blue eyes that she adored, the ones she'd melted into as an eighteen-year-old in San Francisco. Fine wrinkles crinkled around them now as they did hers.

"Oh, I wish I could."

~

9 P.M.

"Go, Mom," said Jessie. "I can work on the cooking

myself tomorrow night and Thursday morning, and by the time you and Dad get back, we'll be set. It won't taste like it does when you cook, but..."

"It's not just that," said Anna. "That picture we saw on the news tonight... I'm still afraid that was our house under water." Her head buzzed.

"If it is, it is," said David. "But it seemed okay when I was up there today. Except for the burned parts...."

"You told us, honey." She shuddered, and getting up from the dining table, she paced, thinking out loud. "You must be exhausted. I should have gotten a proper job again after the fire, so you wouldn't have to over-do it, but I've been sitting here like I'm on vacation."

David and Jessie both said, "No, you haven't!"

"If I'd gotten the insurance claims done sooner, we might already be back home, and Jessie could have her apartment back."

"It's not all under your control, Mom," Jessie said.

A new accusation popped up in Anna's head to confuse itself with the others whirling around her head. "It's hard when you're gone so much," she said. "You weren't there during the hurricane in 2005, and the fire." She caught herself making all these excuses. Why? What was she afraid of?

David said, "Hey, I'm sorry, babe. I was working."

She paused. Hadn't his job for the last two decades taken him away? This trip now was nothing new. But she couldn't stop. She kept ranting, "and you've been gone so much since the fire, trying to earn more money...."

Jessie and her dad exchanged a wondering look, while Anna noticed Prentice was trying to become invisible in the armchair and stay out of the family discussion. He was uncomfortable with her emotion, Anna thought. Probably all three of them were. She didn't care. She was tired of keeping her feelings buckled down. Couldn't remember the last time she'd spoken up for herself. Maybe not since her mama was in the picture and Jessie was a little girl, when her mama's bullying would set off Anna's fight-or-flight reflex to overtake her logic. Even then, sometimes her arguments had made as much sense as this one totally did not.

Still, she couldn't keep it inside. She looked at him and said, "I'm tired of being alone, David," she blurted. "Why don't you quit this over-the-road business altogether? Why aren't you ever home with us? I wish I could see you more, every day! We got married so we could be together..." She broke off, eyes brimming, teary. She didn't know where her clingy emotions were coming from, unless she would admit she was worried about David, and she couldn't do that.

"Babe, where's this coming from?" David asked, his grin dimming. "When you come along with me, we get to spend tons of time together. It's like a vacation together every day."

But she hurtled on with this desperate new plan. "If you were a dispatch guy, or a mechanic, you could sleep at home every night. And you wouldn't have to worry about finding a place to park the Pete and store the trailer." She took a breath, keeping her eyes on him. "But maybe you don't even want to spend time at home, when we don't even have a home of our own right now. Maybe there's someplace else you'd rather be?"

David's golden smile disappeared altogether. "No babe, there's nowhere else I'd rather be than right here." His eyes on hers were loving but somber. "But I've gotta get up at 4 a.m., so I'm going to bed now. 'Night Jessie. 'Night Prentice. See you in bed, Anna." He kissed Anna, and his long strides took him out of the dining room in just a few steps. The bedroom door closed behind him.

"I better get home." Prentice got up and leaned down to give Jessie a quick kiss. "See you tomorrow," he told her.

"Thanks for spending your day off with me," said Jessie. "Mom might want you to help cook."

"That's okay. She's taught me a lot already." He made his exit out into the icy rain which was unimaginable in late November.

"Jessie," Anna said, "I'll clean up in here. Why don't you go to bed?"

"Oh Mom." As if Jessie hadn't heard her, she followed Anna into the kitchen. "This is tough. I can't believe Dad forgot about Thanksgiving." They worked in silence for a few minutes, loading the dishwasher and putting away the food, then going back into the living room. Anna shut off the floor lamp, leaving the room dark. She sat on the sofa, and Jessie joined her.

Anna was grateful for Jessie's presence and her lack of questions. She broke the silence with, "Well, I don't know if he forgot, or if he's worried about the money." She trailed off.

"When was the last time you went with Dad on a run, Mom?"

"Lemme think. This spring, when he did a run to Florida. We got some beach time in on that trip. But you're right, in the last year I haven't gone with him as much as I used to. Not sure why. Well, especially not since the fires."

After a moment, Jessie said, "I noticed that."

"It wasn't like he didn't want me along. I just stopped inviting myself, I guess."

"Hm," was all Jessie could come up with. They sat in the living room twilight. "So, are you going with Dad on this trip, then?"

"Oh, I don't know. Maybe I should, even though it's last

minute." Anna shook her head and crossed her arms, warming herself. "I really wish he hadn't signed up for this one. I could keep an eye on him." *Keep an eye on him.* The words repeated in her mind like a warning.

"You never say no to him," said Jessie.

Anna didn't answer. This was true. She never said no to David, because they usually agreed on everything, and there was no need.

Jessie switched gears. "You never have liked the cold, have you?"

"No. It was a huge adjustment for me moving from San Francisco to Nebraska when I was pregnant with you."

Jessie laughed. "You two did things out of order, as they say, but it's turned out right."

Anna said, "I really wanted to be with him even before I knew I was pregnant, but without you coming along, I might never have taken the risk to leave my mama, skip college, and go find him."

"But Mom, even then, you were doing what was right for other people's plans more than for yourself. That time you did it for me, leaving San Francisco, and I wasn't even born yet!"

"Hm," she said again. "David didn't even know I was pregnant until he picked me up at the bus station."

Jessie asked her mom to tell the story again. Anna loved to tell it.

"It was still summer when I got to the farm. After I told him we were going to be parents, David proposed to me. We were engaged for about three days and had our wedding outside under the apple tree in the yard. The pastor from the Lutheran church was there." She pictured it. The hot summer day, two teenagers getting married in his parents' backyard, and so much food at the picnic. "But by the time you were born, it was a full-blown Midwestern winter. David and I and you, our brand-new baby, living in the basement of his parents' farmhouse. That was cold, for sure, but they always made me feel welcome."

Jessie said, "They had warm hearts. I wish I could have gotten to know them better."

Anna said, "Yes, that would have been special. I'm glad you spent so much time with them when you were little."

"Me too." She rubbed Anna's arm and leaned over to give her a hug. "Okay, 'night mom."

Light from the parking lot illuminated the window. When Jessie left the room, it got too quiet. But Anna couldn't face going to bed yet. *What do I do? Do I send David on this trip alone? Or maybe I ought to go along for the ride?* She could notice if he made more flaky mistakes or was taking unusual risks. She could see if there was anything suspicious. She could just keep an eye on him.

She sat in the darkness. *God, this is nuts to go at the last minute. But David's bound and determined. So, what do I do?*

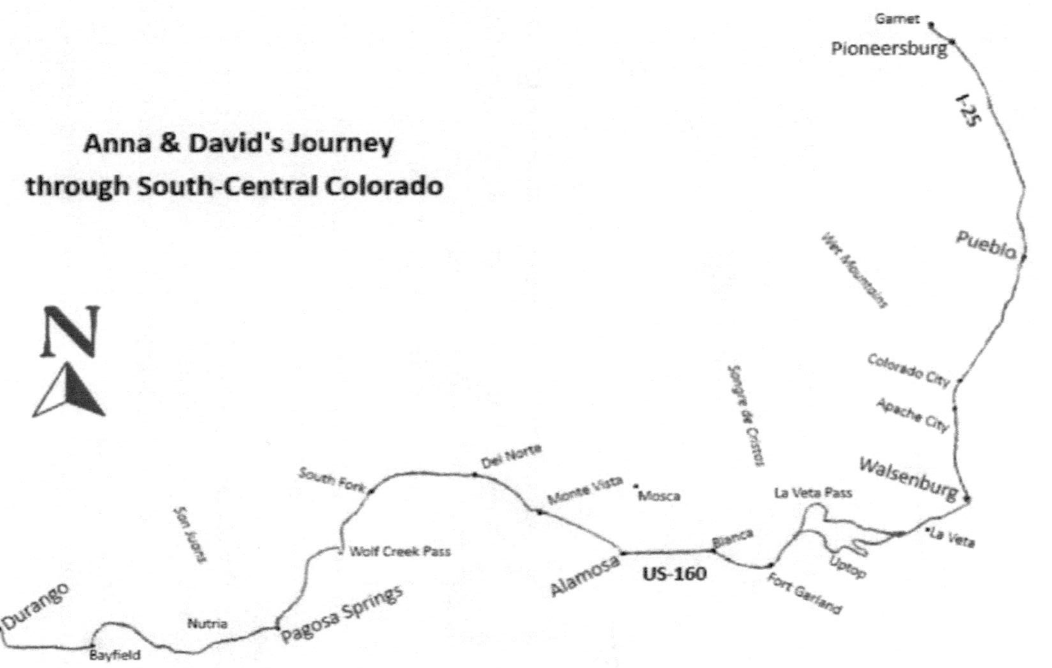
Anna & David's Journey
through South-Central Colorado
N
Garnet
Pioneersburg
I-25
Pueblo
Wet Mountains
Colorado City
Apache City
Walsenburg
La Veta
La Veta Pass
Uptop
Fort Garland
Sangre de Cristos
Blanca
US-160
Alamosa
Mosca
Monte Vista
Del Norte
South Fork
Wolf Creek Pass
San Juans
Pagosa Springs
Nutria
Durango
Bayfield

3

WEDNESDAY, NOVEMBER 27, 2019, 4 A.M., PIONEERSBURG, COLORADO

David was fast asleep on their mattress on the floor in Jessie's extra room. Anna put on her PJs in the dark and snuggled in next to her husband. He rolled toward her to put his arm over her, but he didn't wake up.

She stared at the lights from the parking lot on the ceiling, thinking she ought to get out of Jessie's way and go with David.

"It doesn't even feel like Thanksgiving," she breathed to the ceiling. "Why doesn't it?"

She prayed, finally. *Why don't I pray first instead of last?* She let her eyes focus on nothing in the darkness, then closed them and smiled a little. *God, what am I supposed to do?*

She listened to David's regular breathing.

We haven't really sat and talked in a long time. Even before the fire. We just got so distracted.

God, I've been talking about you when I should be talking to you, instead. "Why am I waffling so much, God?" she whispered. *And why is David being so stubborn?* She sighed.

Because he's trying to take care of us, like he always has. And I've always been a wimp.

"But I need to try," she whispered in the dark. "Maybe he'll listen to me and end his over-the-road career soon." But now she worried she sounded like her mother, trying to control everyone. *Or is it just that my normal self doesn't speak up enough?*

The conversations of the evening and her thoughts tangled in her head. She thought she'd never get to sleep, yet the next thing she knew, David's phone alarm sounded, and she felt him creep quietly off the mattress.

"Honey?" she said, her eyes still closed.

"Oh, I was trying not to wake you, babe."

"David," she said in a sleepy voice. "David, could I still go with you?"

Kneeling down, he covered her with warm kisses, surrounding her with his warm arms, like he had that first night long ago during Spring Break in San Francisco. That was the night that had given them their baby, Jessie. The blond stubble on his chin tickled her face. "I was hoping you'd change your mind," he said. "Let's get outta here, fast."

She giggled. "And let's drive fast, so we can continue this conversation in our own hotel room tonight. Just the two of us."

"Deal," he said. "Well, three of us. What about Casey?"

"Right. He's my loyal trucker dog."

"Okay, let's get outta here," he said again.

She turned on the light, stepped out of her pajamas, and put on some black yoga pants, wool socks, and a long-sleeve workout top. They were her usual clothes when on a run with David, as opposed to the loose artsy layers she wore when she was being creative at home, back when she had her art studio. In the bathroom, she pulled her long black hair into a ponytail and brushed her teeth.

Following David into the living room, she said, "I'll write Jessie a note and tell her I'm going with you. And taking the dog!"

"I'm sure she'll figure it out," he said as he got dressed in front of the coat closet in his usual outfit, jeans and a long sleeve t-shirt. Today the shirt was black.

Anna said, "I just realized I should borrow Jessie's snow boots. I didn't buy any new ones for myself yet." *Another thing to itemize with the insurance company claim.*

"Good idea," he said, and crossing the room, he bent down to nuzzle her neck. She nuzzled right back.

"Are you gonna wear your flannel shirt, too?" she asked.

He didn't seem to have heard and was busy now putting on his socks and work boots.

Anna got her toothbrush, some clean undies and socks, and the pajama pants and top she'd just taken off, and threw them into her backpack, hoping she'd remembered everything she'd need, since she was in a sleepy fog. She got Casey's leash and filled a zip-lock bag of food for him, tossing it into one of Jessie's cloth grocery bags she found in the kitchen. She took some snacks for the road: a can of potato crisps, a big bar of dark chocolate, a can of soup, and the rest of the kale from the fridge, which she liked to munch on raw. She tossed it all into the cloth bag.

The pumpkin pie sat on the counter, and she wondered if she should leave it, but then she wrapped it in foil and added it to the top of the bag, feeling selfish... and adventurous.

"Bye Jessie, my dear girl," she whispered. The note she left on the counter said, *I bet you'll miss Casey more than us, and it'll be good to have the apartment to yourself. Have fun with*

Prentice. Oh - that doesn't sound right. I mean, 'This is the day the Lord has made. Let us rejoice and be glad in it.' See you tomorrow night. Love, Mom.

She wanted to bring the knitting project she'd been working on the last time she went with David on a run this spring. However, now it resided in a landfill with all the other items from the house that had smoke damage that couldn't be cleaned. She hadn't allowed herself to buy more yarn yet, since she felt like she should complete her dealings with the homeowner's insurance before she got herself a treat.

She put on her new orange beanie and green parka and made sure the lights were off in the living room. Casey trotted out in front of her, down the apartment steps and across the parking lot to David. No leash needed right now; this dog knew the next adventure would be in the 18-wheeler tractor called the Pete.

Carrying her day pack, a small purse with her phone and wallet, and the cloth bag of food, she locked the door of the apartment. The rain had stopped, leaving the air damp and cold. She caught sight of David, or the shape of him—it was too dark yet to see much—as he climbed the vertical steps from the truck cab at the back corner of the parking lot. She heard the low growl of the diesel engine going, to get all the cylinders firing smoothly, since he hadn't let it run all night. He'd said once that the high amp batteries in the truck worked well in this temperature range.

Thinking she'd better get her sunglasses, she stopped by her car. She was careful, walking. The wet pavement felt almost icy under her feet. It was while she was tucking the sunglasses into her purse that she thought about grabbing that old duffel in the trunk. Soon after they had escaped Mississippi in the aftermath of Katrina and moved to

Colorado fourteen years ago, she'd taken a short emergency preparedness class at the library in Garnet. The instructor had listed possible essentials that might be necessary in the event of a forced evacuation and recommended packing them into a tote and stowing it in the trunk of your car.

Anna had thrown a few items into an old duffel, planning to stock it better later, but with so many other things going on, she'd never gotten around to that. The only thing that she'd used since was the flash drive in the side zipper pocket containing photos of their house and important papers. That work to scan documents and put them on the flash drive had really saved the day when she started filing insurance claims for the house this year.

Shouldering the bag, an image of the flooding from last night's newscast flashed through her mind. But she didn't want to think about it. There wasn't anything she could do about it, and she was going on vacation. It was time for some fun for a change.

Approaching the Pete, she saw that Casey had jumped up into the cab, taking up his usual post next to the driver's seat. Anna went around to the driver's side door and handed her backpack, the duffel, and the cloth grocery bag, one at a time, to David, who tucked them out of the way.

He grabbed her hand, helping her up the ladder-like steps, and she noticed, as her eyes passed by floor level, even in the dark, that the truck floor was filthy. David spent so much time in the Pete, it was his second home, and he normally kept it spotless, even though it was over twenty years old. There wouldn't be time on this trip, but likely on his next run, he'd stop at a truck center and vacuum the crumbs and dirt out of the carpet.

She stood in the cab's doorway next to where he sat, hand resting on his shoulder. The faded red down parka he wore used to be his dad's. Even though David hadn't gone into dairy farming, he'd had a close bond with his dad.

"I've got some snacks in the cloth bag," she told him. She considered last night's glitch, when he meant to do his grocery shopping but then, inexplicably, forgot. "But that's just what I found at Jessie's. We can add it to what you've already got in here," she said.

"They do have shops and restaurants along the way, remember?" he said.

Normally, they didn't stop at restaurants in the middle of a run, because it took too long. His usual routine was to bring food along so he could make his meals in the cab, which David kept well-stocked. She asked, "Aren't they closed on Thanksgiving?"

"You worry too much, babe."

She didn't know why she was acting so clingy again, but she changed topics and asked. "Do you have an ice scraper?"

"Anna, let's go. I do this for a living, remember?" David pulled her into his lap for a welcoming kiss, which she returned before she made her way over to her seat on the passenger side. She took her purse off her shoulder and stowed it in the cubbyhole above her head.

Casey allowed her to scratch his ears as he sat on the floor between the seats. Then he hopped onto the bed behind the driver's seat and the bulkhead cupboards behind it, separating the sleeping area from the driver's seat. She buckled herself in and took a deep breath of the chilly morning air but almost choked on the smell in the cab. David's home away from home smelled like unwashed bedding. This wasn't like him, either. Not much they could do about it right now.

"I'm all set, hon," she told her husband, trying to ignore the smell. "I hope I didn't forget anything." A wide yawn took over her entire face. She tried to stifle it but gave up and stretched her arms up as high as she could above her head. The roof of the cab was so high, her short arms came nowhere close to reaching the top. She wondered if David had just not had enough time between runs to get the Pete cleaned up, though through the years, he'd always found time before. "We should wash your bedding when we get back, honey."

"Yeah, I've been meaning to do that," David laughed at her gently. He released the brakes with a hiss, put it in gear, and eased the Pete out of the apartment parking lot and toward the street so they could go pick up the trailer at the storage yard.

Glancing at him, taking in the strong line of his jaw, she thought it felt like longer than last spring that she'd gone on the road with him. It felt like forever.

In fact, maybe because it smelled like a teenage boy's laundry hamper in the truck, it felt like they were on their first date.

4:30 A.M.

The Pete headed south on the interstate, through Pioneersburg, to an exit at the south end of the city. Until he picked up the trailer, it meant he drove bobtail, just the Pete by itself, which made the ride bumpier at highway speeds. It was better when they got back on the smaller collector streets in the city, which had stoplights and slower speed limits. A few lights glowed dimly in the pitch-dark, frosty-wet morning. The moon was new and shared no light.

"What's the load this time?" she asked, rubbing her

mitten'd hands together to stay warm. The temperature in the cab was not cozy yet, though David had the vents on.

"Durango Regional Food Bank got a big donation from, ah—" he hesitated, seeming to search for the name — "some manufacturer," he said when he couldn't come up with it. "It's good for a big tax break. They need all these canned vegetables sent to Durango, since their food ware-house is gettin' a little bare."

"That's not good over the holidays, so it's good timing," she agreed.

"It's not good anytime." He took off his earmuffs and started to put them away in the console, but then he changed his mind and put them back on.

"I wish people could buy the food they want with the money they earn," she said. "Sometimes it's not enough, I guess. We've been in times like that, when we started out. Even though your parents helped, we didn't want to lean on them."

"Yeah," he said, "fresh outta high school. But we figured it out. We learned, and we worked for wages. We didn't keep doing the same thing we were doing, and it got better."

"Yes," she said. "You worked at the hardware store in town at first. And I took Baby Jessie and worked at that daycare." Anna stretched her arms out in front of her again to warm up and wake up. "I learned a lot about babies and toddlers then, so much to learn in a short time."

David said, "Yep. Probably different from how your mama raised you, huh?"

Anna didn't take the bait about her mama's parenting. "Your parents were amazing, too. I showed up out of nowhere at your house, and they didn't even blink." She sighed. "You didn't flinch either. You all made it work."

"What were we gonna do, turn you away?" He chuckled.

"By December, your belly was bigger than the rest of you put together, little girl."

At forty-five years old, Anna always felt younger around David. Or just youthful? "You're my knight in shining armor. You didn't have to choose a short girl like me."

"But I did choose you," he said, voice deep with emotion. "You'll always be my delicious Chinese bride."

She laughed. "Hey, I'm American. It was my parents who were from China." When they were on the road, she and David loved to take turns telling their own history out loud, affirming the ups and downs and mysteries of their marriage.

"An American who grew up with a mom who spoke Cantonese and Mandarin."

"Ha ha, yeah. But I'm the girl who won your heart during your spring break in San Francisco and showed up at your parents' farm to give you your Christmas present."

"And we named the baby Jessie, after your mama Jiexen, the same lady who had just kicked you out of the house you grew up in," he recited.

Anna said, "I think that peace offering did calm her down. It only took her seven years to come and meet her namesake."

He said, "When she decided to move in with us." He grinned. "What an amazing time." He maneuvered along the quiet roads toward the storage lot. "At least I had just graduated from high school when you showed up at my door."

"Me too. I got through graduation without anyone knowing. It would have been horrible if my mama's neighbors found out. Your parents were so different. They're the ones who taught me about unconditional love." She laughed. "Well, so did you, of course!"

"And that's why we have such a smart, beautiful daughter. She has your good looks and brains, and my, well, I don't know, my big Dutch nose." He laughed.

"I love your nose. And on Jessie, it's... well, it's a smaller version of yours, but clearly not pure Chinese, you're right. She's definitely related to both of us."

"She's just our beautiful daughter. That's it." David said.

Anna glanced at him. He wasn't ordinarily talkative so early in the day, but she loved this change in him.

"You know," he said, going off on a new tack, "I'm feeling sorry for the yard jockeys at the warehouse in Durango that have to stick around to unload the cargo when we get there this afternoon."

Anna hoped the trip would go smoothly. "I bet the guys'll be wanting to get started on their Thanksgiving time off, too."

He puffed air out of his mouth. "About that, babe, getting this run scheduled right on top of Thanksgiving. Sorry I got my weeks mixed up."

She was glad for the acknowledgment but wanted to keep the weekend getaway mood going. "Things have been so crazy since the fire, David. You've been driving so much, staying on the road to make money. Thank you for keeping us afloat," she said. "I've been doing all I can with the insurance research and phone calls," she said. "Maybe I should go back to working in day care, at least, like I did when Jessie was a baby."

"Aw, babe," he said. "I don't know."

This was one of those topics they never got around to discussing, unbelievably. Life just moved along one day at a time, and they both did what they could think of doing. This was how it was when both people in a marriage were free spirits. They just winged it every day with no master plan.

He said, "I know you don't like being saddled with the insurance, but you're doing great on that paperwork. I know it."

She sighed. "You haven't even looked at any of it," she said. "But somebody's got to do it, I guess."

"Anyway," he continued as if she hadn't spoken, "it'll be easier when we aren't all holed up at Jessie's place. And then you can figure out what you want to do."

"She's been so generous to let us stay with her all this time. Well, mostly letting me stay with her," said Anna.

He glanced over at her as he pulled into the storage yard. "You know how I hate being cooped up. I'm still really a farm boy. Staying with her in that little apartment..." He shook his head. "When we get our home back, life will start to get back to normal. I miss our house. I miss being with you and no one else."

That made Anna smile. "Well, for the next two days, we're back on the road together, just us."

"My beautiful wife, and our loyal dog," he said. "This is a perfect day."

5 A.M.

At this abnormally early hour, it was just plain cold. And soon, David got quiet again, which was his normal morning behavior. No talking, and no music. He always saved that for later in the day. David had his routines all set. He said it helped him deal with all the years full of miles.

It's amazing we've talked this much already this morning. Anna wondered at this additional change in his behavior, however long it lasted, and then willed herself to become quiet now too and pulled her knees to her chest, wrapping her arms around her legs. She scrunched her fingers into fists inside her black mittens. The knitted beanie hat and new parka helped retain some warmth until they stopped to get some food in their bellies. But that would be a while yet.

The trailer David picked up to attach to the Pete was his dry van. It had no refrigeration, just a big, empty box ready to be loaded at the warehouse. The trailer was fifty-three feet long and all white, like the Pete tractor, though the years had added scratches to the finish on both. But back when he'd bought the rig, the price had been right, and while it limited the types of cargo he could haul, he made a good living.

He swung the Pete in front of his trailer and pulled forward to line up the edge of the wheels with the edges of the trailer. He'd told her the steps so many times, when he was in coaching mode, which he enjoyed.

First, he backed up, exactly centered, so the kingpin on the trailer would engage with the lockjaw latch of the fifth wheel coupling. She loved hearing the confident snap it made when it connected into a set.

Since it was so cold, she wanted to stay in the Pete, but she loved to see him connect with the trailer, so she told Casey to Wait and clambered down and watched in the mostly darkness from her side of the catwalk. "How can you even see where to go when it's so dark?"

"Well, we have the yard lights…"

"You're amazing."

"That's why you married me, I know," he said. "Because I could connect a trailer set with my eyes closed."

They both laughed. "When I married you, you'd only had your driver's license for two years, and you worked in a hardware store."

He climbed back up to pull the air valve to lock the pin

brake, then back out to make the connections from the rear of the cab to the trailer. He took the blue air service line from the stowaway and secured it into place on the front of the trailer. Then the green pigtail, connecting the electricity for lights and trailer brakes. Finally, the red emergency air line snapped in place.

Grabbing a flashlight out of his parka pocket, David bent to look at the fifth wheel and make sure it was locked together. Anna got back in the cab as he walked behind it to crank the landing gear handle counterclockwise to lift it off the ground. Because this time they'd be hauling their trailer back to the storage yard empty, he wouldn't need to lower those jack stands again until they returned Thursday night and dropped off the empty trailer in this same yard.

She buckled in and scratched Casey's ears. Meanwhile, David climbed in, buckled up, and released the trailer and tractor brakes by pushing the red and yellow buttons, resulting in a big hiss of air. He brought back the Johnson bar to lock the brakes, put the Pete in gear to make sure of the trailer connection, and moved the Johnson bar to its original position. He eased the big rig out of the lot and onto the collector street heading south toward the nearby food warehouse.

"It's nice having company again," he said softly, eyes focused on the road, vapor lights rolling by.

She closed her eyes and thanked God for getting her on the road with David again. That one comment had made it worth it already.

4

—————

5:30 A.M.

"Geez. Will you look at that?" he muttered as he maneuvered the truck toward the food warehouse loading dock and prepared to back up. "Some idiot parked illegally, right where I need to go."

"Can you back around him?" Anna asked.

"I'll have to," he said. After some artful backwards dodging, David got lined up with the loading door. Anna was always amazed at how he could wiggle the long truck and trailer around the offending car and still end up square with the loading dock. This time, however, he made it around the car, but he'd gotten too close to the dock. She knew it the minute she heard him yell, "Oh, man!" from the back of the trailer.

"Can't get the back doors open," he said when he rejoined her in the cab. "A few inches too close that time." He released the brakes with a hiss, put it in gear, pulled the set forward a foot, and hopped back to the ground to get the back doors wide open so he could back up to the dock and get the van loaded.

"I'll be right back, babe," he said, grabbing a plastic

sleeve full of paperwork from the console and sliding his long legs down the steps to the ground. "They're expecting us."

"I'll take Casey for a walk," she said to the back of his head as he shut the door.

At the sound of those magic words, the dog popped his soft head around the back of her seat. Anna stood and opened the small storage cupboard where she always stashed Casey's bag of supplies with his leash and food when she and Casey joined David. It wasn't there. She tried several more cabinets and finally found the bag. "Oh, here it is," she said. Like a camping trailer, the cab had limited storage, and David had a system for everything. Usually. Maybe he'd come up with a new system?

The truck was so close to the warehouse wall, she couldn't open the passenger door, so Anna clambered down the steps on the driver's side, each one a storage box in disguise. She avoided touching the hot exhaust pipe that stretched up next to the steps. Casey jumped after her down to the ground. She reached up to shut the door, and they walked out to the parkway along the street to do his business.

A forklift beeped somewhere inside the warehouse, ferrying pallets of canned vegetables into the dry van.

When they returned, she told Casey to Wait, climbed up to open the door for him, and released him with the magic word, "Okay!" He leapt in one enthusiastic bound from the ground to the floor of the cab.

She poured some of his food in a bowl from the bag she'd packed and watched him gobble it up. She reached for the valve on the five-gallon water jug strapped in on the shelf next to the mini fridge to give Casey water in the same bowl, but the jug was empty. That was another job David always did the night before a trip, but he hadn't done it last night in all his confusion.

When David finished securing the last load bars inside the trailer and climbed back in the cab, she waited 'til he'd maneuvered the long vehicle out of the loading dock area to say, "David, when we stop for breakfast, we need to fill up the water jug too."

"I've been meaning to do that," he said, "but I can't fire myself since I'm self-employed. Too bad. Ha!" He tapped his hands on the steering wheel in a syncopated rhythm. "But, yeah, breakfast, I'm starving! Maybe that'll warm me up." David had the heater blasting, so the cab was toasty warm. He still had his gloves and earmuffs on, too.

They rolled south on the interstate. On their left, dawn still hadn't bloomed into daylight. To their right, the Rocky Mountains, known as the Shining Mountains by the Ute people, reflected just a hint of blue light. They sped, passing a dead deer at the side of the road, reminding Anna how fast they were going and how much momentum a loaded truck had.

Anna located her cell phone. This section of the interstate, between Pioneersburg and Pueblo, had good cell phone service, so she sent a text to Jessie. *Good morning, dear girl.*

Jessie must have had her phone right next to her. Her response came immediately. *I can't believe you went, but have fun with Dad.*

Will do. Nice to be OTR (on the road) again. But this truck needs a cleaning. :)

Jessie replied with a frowning emoji, :(

Anna texted back, *See you tomorrow night.*

"Oh, honey, what's that behind us?" she said. The side mirrors allowed David to see both of them from the driver's seat, and if Anna moved her head to the left, she could see back to the right rear corner. She had turned in the seat to scratch Casey's ears again, when a glimpse of... what? Popped up in the mirror and disappeared again.

"What an idiot!" He growled a little. "Some dude in a toy car is drafting me."

Anna peered in her side-view mirror. "He's right on your bumper. I can't even see him."

"He's coasting behind us, trying to save five cents of gas. But if he slams into me, it'll sure cost him more than he's bothered to think about."

Not much David could do about a car right on his tail. They passed a blue metal sign, surrounded by plastic flowers and one white cross, at the side of the road. It read: *Please Drive Safely. In Memory of...* And then it was gone.

The guy in the little blue car appeared to pay no heed to the memorial sign, staying glued to David's bumper. Anna breathed easier when, after another few miles, David put on the turn signals, and they got off the interstate. The truck stop allowed plenty of room for 18-wheelers to move around so they could fill up with hundreds of gallons of diesel. A tank full now would last them the whole trip from Pueblo to Durango.

David pulled the red knob, and the yellow one came up by itself. That set the brakes for the tractor and the trailer with a big *shhhhhhhh*, Anna hopped into the space between the seats and the sleeper cab to check out the food situation, but when she opened the little fridge between the seats and the sleeping area, she found nothing inside it. That must have been why he'd planned to stop at the store last night. But where was the food she'd handed up to him before leaving this morning? Glancing up at him, she said, "David? Where did you put the kale?"

"In the trash?" he joked.

"No," she laughed as she opened more cabinet doors. "It was in the cloth bag with the pie and the other food." But now, opening the lowest cabinet, she saw it. "Here it is!" The bag was wedged in there, and behind it she found an old loaf of bread, gone green with mold, and a mostly empty peanut butter jar. "David, you've got moldy food in here, did you know?" She got an empty trash bag, threw the gross stuff in it, and twisted the top closed. Then she put the fresh items in the mini fridge.

"Looks like it'll be a microwaved egg biscuit for us today, my dear bride," said David with a tired smile. She noticed more fine wrinkles around his eyes than he used to have. *We're getting older, but when did that happen?*

"The quick mart will have some hot drinks and lunch supplies too, since you didn't get groceries yesterday," said Anna. "I'll go while you're filling up." She took her purse from the cubbyhole above her head and opened the passenger door. She loosened the water jug and set it on the floor with the trash bag so she could haul them down when she got to the ground.

Anna bought two microwaved breakfast burritos, some roast beef sandwich meat, two apples, a loaf of whole wheat bread, and a can of soup. She had to make a few trips from the mart back to the truck with the groceries, the water jug, the cup of coffee for David and English breakfast tea with milk for herself. *I hate these foam cups, but I didn't see the travel mugs anywhere in the cupboards.*

David released the brakes, put it in gear, they were off. Dawn bloomed a cold orange glow from the plains to the east. They headed south on the interstate again and munched on lukewarm burritos. The tea, though it was just lukewarm, revived her.

A truck approaching them in the northbound lane had one headlight out. As they passed each other, the moving company emblem on the side was easy to identify. David picked up the CB microphone and said, "Roach Coach, this is Dutch Boy. Did you know you've got a black eye?"

A call came back, "Dutch Boy, this is Fire Chief. What's your 20?"

"Mile Marker 119, Fire Chief. Just thought you should know." He un-keyed the mic.

"Appreciate it, Dutch Boy. I'll get that checked out."

"10-4," said David.

After a while, Anna broke their silence. "It's getting pretty warm in here now. Want to turn the heat down?"

He shook his head. "It's just feeling comfortable now."

They had an agreement that whoever was driving got to adjust the thermostat and the sunshades. It was the same for the radio, too, so she asked if she could switch it on. "Let's get a weather report."

David said, "Go for it, babe. But this trip isn't optional today, you know, whatever the forecast is."

"Well, I'm glad the rain stopped," she said, deflecting the little tension. What she wanted to ask him, what she wished she knew how to ask him, was why this trip felt so off. He was a laid-back guy in many ways, but the dirty cab, the missing supplies, the flaky stories …none of it was like him at all.

But she didn't ask. She pushed the questions back down into herself and tried to enjoy the ride.

Wednesday, November 27, 2019, 5 - 6:30 a.m.
Pioneersburg, Colorado

Jessie was one of the few people in the office on this Wednesday before Thanksgiving. That was no surprise. She wouldn't have come in either if not for the short commute from her apartment to where she worked for a government contractor. She'd only zipped over in the morning quiet to install some computer updates and do other quick maintenance, just a few hours of easy work, more easily done when the office was empty.

Jessie had gotten here about 5 a.m., which was much earlier than she had even planned, since all the racket from her mom and dad and Casey "sneaking out" had awakened her long before dawn. They'd probably imagined they were being so quiet. It almost made her laugh, thinking of it. And that note Mom had left on the counter about Jessie having the place to herself while they were gone for two whole days. That was another joke. Sometimes their attempts to be cool were so funny.

Her co-worker Kim was the only other person on the floor. She had the same idea as Jessie — do a bit of focused work and head out again soon for vacation.

Jessie looked out the office window as she waited for the screen prompts on the four computers around her, thinking how last night, when Dad had surprised them with the news of the extra work trip, it hadn't sounded like Mom would join him at the last minute—but this morning had dawned with two fewer people, and no dog, in her apartment. Solitude! She was glad they'd get a chance to talk. And... whatever. She smiled. Her cell phone chimed. It was a text from her mom.

Good morning, dear girl.

I can't believe you went, but have fun with Dad, Jessie wrote back.

Anna replied with a smiley emoji. *Back on Thanksgiving night.*

Jessie keyed in the thumbs up emoji. There wasn't much more to say. She finished with the computer updates and shut down all the machines. The office would be closed until Monday, and clearing off her desk, she thought how glad she was for the holiday.

Kim was ready to leave, too, and together they walked to the elevator.

"What is a 'bomb cyclone'? They're saying it might hit High Plains County," Kim asked as she scrolled on her phone.

"A what? Let me see that." The two paused while Kim handed it to Jessie.

"It says if this thing hits, it's unlikely any of us will see a storm this strong again in our lifetime." Kim spoke and made a sweeping gesture for emphasis as Jessie read the story's prediction.

"It might hit all of Colorado, and a bunch of other states, according to this," Jessie murmured. She looked at Kim. "Sometimes these things just fizzle out." Even as she spoke the reassurance, though, her stomach felt tight.

They reached the main entrance. "Let's hope it doesn't get here while everyone's traveling for the holidays," Kim said, pushing open the door.

"My mom and dad are on the road. I hope it waits until they're back from Durango." Jessie followed her colleague outside and the two headed toward their cars, parked near each other in the lot.

"If you're signed up for the local emergency alerts for High Plains County, they'll send out an alert if it's really coming, I bet. Right now, it looks clear and calm," said Kim. "Drive safely."

There was more to say to her mom. When Jessie got into her car and locked the door, she sent another text: *Check the weather report.*

WEDNESDAY, NOVEMBER 27, 2019, 6:30 A.M.

Colorado City, Colorado

Anna had just turned on the radio when Jessie's text came in. The meteorologist was in the middle of issuing a new weather warning. "Soon the developing storm will pull in cold air and hit the moist air," he said. "It'd be better for people who can change their travel plans to stay home and safe instead of driving anywhere over Thanksgiving. No kidding, folks," he added.

"Oh, get a load of this." David made light of the warning.

The reporter said, "A phenomenon called a 'bomb cyclone' storm will bring strong winds, and heavy snow on Thanksgiving Day to the central United States — from Montana all the way to Texas. The National Weather Service says it expects severe blizzard conditions in some areas, as well as isolated flooding in warmer areas."

"Ah, it's a blizzard! In the winter!" David said, ever the joker.

Anna shushed him.

The reporter went on. "What's unusual about this winter storm is its very intense winds, which are expected to reach up to eighty miles per hour in some places. The winds will rival what's seen in a Category I hurricane."

The hairs on Anna's neck stood up at the reporter's use of the words "cyclone" and "hurricane." She'd never heard those words used before in a Colorado weather report, not even when the report was about a blizzard. David, Anna,

Jessie, and Tiger Grandma had chosen Colorado as their destination after Hurricane Katrina, specifically because hurricanes did not occur in Colorado. They'd been through too much already to risk it happening again.

The news continued. "The 'bomb cyclone' will have a massive wind field across the Rocky Mountain region and into the Midwest. Here in eastern and southern Colorado, we can expect sixty to eighty mile-per-hour sustained winds, and gusts more damaging than that. Snow accumulation predictions range from ten to thirty inches," he said.

"But even a few inches of snow can cause problems with the wind intensities they're forecasting. Drifts can block roads out in the prairies. And in the high country, snow accumulations will be higher and give the wind more snow to work with. Watch for road closures and stay home instead of chancing it on those mountain highways and byways."

"Big deal." David talked over the weatherman. "We've already been through a hurricane on the Gulf Coast."

Anna's back muscles tightened. "You weren't there for Katrina, David."

"Oh, that's right. You ladies handled it without me. But I got back as quick as I could and swept you out of that mess." He glanced at her, then quickly back at the road. Switching off the radio, he said, "It's just a lot of hype. What are the chances of a hurricane coming to Colorado?"

Anna said, "How can you joke? They just said there's one in the forecast right now."

"Yeah, I heard that."

"Well, it sounds like it could hit tomorrow sometime. Maybe we should change our plans. Just stop in Durango tonight?"

"Yeah, we are stopping in Durango tonight. And then we'll drive back tomorrow and have Thanksgiving dinner."

"Don't you think we should just stay longer there and wait for the storm to blow over?"

He took a breath and kept his voice calm. "Anna, we should stick to the plan."

She said, "Maybe the plan needs to change. We didn't know about this weather forecast before."

"Why are you second-guessing me? This is my job. This is what I do for a living."

She said, "I'm not trying to..."

He interrupted in a falsetto, imitating her voice. "'Do you have an ice scraper? Did you pack any food? Aren't you scared of some snow?' I'm not sure what your problem is with me." He leveled a brief glance at her.

"Honey..." But she trailed off, not knowing how to finish the sentence. She had a feeling she wanted to ignore, but it just wasn't like him to be so irritable or scattered. She didn't know how to begin this discussion. "Lately," she began tentatively, "you've seemed kind of, I don't know, less focused?" How could she ask him if there was someone else out there distracting him? Maybe someone he was trying to impress? She couldn't.

He huffed in surprise. "Me?" he said. "I'm the one who's less focused?" He paused. "Anna, you always make the best of things. From the beginning, when we were living with my mom and dad, and little Jessie cried at night, you'd cuddle with her and tell her she would grow up strong and smart, with those strong lungs of hers...." He trailed off. "But lately, I can't seem to get my name on your dance card at all."

She tipped her head to try to process what he said. "That's not true, David. That's the opposite of true."

"Well, why haven't you been coming along with me as much as you used to?"

She expelled air from her lungs. "It's been a crazy year.

And honestly, honey, you've been kind of aloof with me, too."

"Well, I'm just your David. The guy you've been married to since... what year did we get married? 2002?"

"No, it was 1992," she whispered.

5

WEDNESDAY, NOVEMBER 27, 2019, 6:45 A.M., APACHE CITY, COLORADO

As a diversion from his gaffe, she pulled the truck logbook out of the console. The Pete was a 1997 Peterbilt 379, so it didn't have the electronic logbook that the newer trucks had. The driver had to fill in data: the hours on duty, hours not driving, hours on duty/driving, and daily mileages and show the book to weigh station officials along the route. Blank spots in a logbook could lead to a violation that resulted in fines that could negate the profits of the whole day's work. The department of transportation could even issue a speeding ticket at the end of the day, based solely on the times and miles traveled. The logbook was key.

When Anna rode along with David, she'd taken on the record keeping as her way to help and have something to do, but when David drove alone, of course, it was up to him. Flipping through the logbook now, she started to enter the necessary data, especially since she didn't have a knitting project to work on. Scanning the entries for earlier in November, though, she was concerned. "David?" She glanced at him. "I can't read your entry here from yesterday."

"Ah, nuts," he said. He'd calmed down, but now he sounded hurt. "Are you looking for trouble?"

"David, I'm just trying to help. I'm not the one who makes the rules. You know as well as I do that you have to get the logbook filled in right."

He changed his attitude and said, "Man, I've been trying to do better on that," he acknowledged. "Okay, so, hit me. Whaddaya got?"

As she told him what was missing, he thought out loud with her to come up with the answers. She did some calculations and wrote the numbers in again, more legibly. As the truck ate the miles, she gently questioned him, referred to her phone's GPS map for some point-to-point mileages, and finally the logbook was ready to pass government inspection.

Tucking the record book back in the console, a slip of paper fell out. Scribbled in David's writing, it read like a to-do list: *water jug. Anna b-day Nov. 3. Call dispatch Ohio. Shirts. Doc appt.* It also listed Jessie's apartment address in Pioneersburg. *What an odd list.* Not knowing what to make of it, Anna stuck it back in the console and closed the door. But her mind wouldn't quiet. Why had he written down her birthday on such a random list?

With the offending logbook out of sight and her accusing pen put away, she phrased her question with gentleness. "Honey, have you had any logbook violations lately? Since I haven't been coming along with you, I mean?"

David maintained his focus on the road. However, his hands, which had been steady, began to dance on the big brown steering wheel.

"Have you had some fines?" she repeated in a soft voice.

"Yeah, a few." He pressed his lips into a tight line.

"That's not like you," she said softly.

"Nope."

She thought for a while. No sense rushing into this conversation either when they had two days of total togetherness ahead of them. And some quality alone time to look forward to at the motel tonight.

"So, um, I didn't see the bill for the fines. You must have paid them yourself?"

"Yeah, that worked out better."

Why, so it would be a secret from me? She was on thin ice. "But when I've been paying the bills … I don't know. It doesn't seem as if the numbers add up. We've still got the mortgage on the house in Garnet. At least there are no utilities to pay, since those are shut off." She paused again. "And Jessie's letting us live rent-free while we repair all the damage." She hesitated, "But it's been hard to come up with enough for the insurance, health insurance, the mortgage payment, and our share of the food." She looked at David. His movie star profile, the short beard on his face. Her gorgeous husband of all these years. "You've been working so hard," she said, shifting her glance, looking without seeing at the passing landscape. "You're gone so much, and working harder, but our bank balance is lower than ever."

"I told you," David said, after a long silence, "that's why I'm taking this extra run."

Casey snored on top of the bed. Sweaty sheets and blankets made him a Contented Dog. Sometimes he even slept on his back with his belly facing up. Zonked.

Anna shifted in the seat, trying to loosen the muscle behind her right shoulder blade. In a quiet voice, she said, "I'm just glad I understand better what's happening." If he'd been paying multiple logbook violations, that explained why the outgo was more than the income. But why? He never used to make so many mistakes. What was going on? Was he losing his mind? Covering up a secret relationship? Driving himself too hard? She didn't know what to do or where to go with any of it.

David didn't say anything. The telephone poles streamed by in the pre-dawn darkness. She tried to distract herself, wondering why they were called telephone poles when they didn't even carry telegraph or phone lines anymore. Just electricity.

But idle speculation was no use against the storm of worry inside her, and the building snowdrift between them that just wouldn't melt when they needed to talk about serious things. Both of them just froze up instead.

"David?" She spoke his name but kept her eyes on the highway as the truck gobbled the pavement.

He said nothing.

Just ask him! The voice in her head would not be still, and finally she obeyed it. "Are you mad at me?"

No response. He just tightened his jaw and drove.

Winter, 1980, Anna's kindergarten memory, Chinatown, San Francisco, California

Part 2

Even after the sun set, the tourists and merchants still swarmed up and down the street, and bright neon lights blinked on and glowed in the mist. Anna fell asleep on her cot, and later, she felt Mama tuck a blanket over her. Baa never came in until after midnight. Mama had told Anna once that he had another job at night, after the noodle shop closed.

After that first day, Anna walked to school by herself, all eight blocks, past the greengrocers, the smelly gas station, and the store filled only with items made of brightly colored plastic. She made it home by herself, too, walking past the same buildings.

She decided when she was done going to school forever, she could help Mama all the time in the shop and learn to make noodles. *Maybe that would make Mama happy.*

One day at school, in the middle of a lesson about The Letter M, a girl raised her hand and asked, "Teacher, what is the big orange road going across the water?"

Teacher stopped. "Above the ocean?" She always encouraged the children to ask questions as long as they did it with respect. "Do you mean the Golden Gate Bridge?"

The girl shook her head. She didn't know.

"Raise your hand if you've been to the waterfront to see the Bay," the teacher instructed, looking face to face. Only about half the children raised their hands. Teacher looked surprised. With pride and delight mixed together, she told the children how their school, high on this hill, was just a few blocks from the beautiful San Francisco Bay. She said the famous Bay Bridge was the gateway to the Pacific Ocean, and all the excitement of San Francisco. Right outside their windows! The children asked a hundred questions, but none of them were about The Letter M.

The next morning before school, Anna screwed up all her courage to say, "Mama, I want go to Fisherman's Wharf."

At first, Mama didn't even look at her. "Why you want to go spend all money we work so hard to get?" She put down the knife on the cutting board and turned toward Anna. "I never go close to ocean anymore. Never. Sea snake, poison octopus when we swim to Hong Kong. We find boat. They take all our money and always want more, and we almost die." She turned to Anna with tears in her eyes. "Go to school. Learn English. Be smart girl." She handed the blue backpack to Anna and began chopping again.

Life was predictable. On weekdays, go to school, help Mama. On weekends, help Mama, go to Chinese Presbyterian church on Sunday. Start again with school on Monday. No sea snakes in Chinatown. Safe.

But one morning after Christmas, Anna's class was out on the playground when the ground—the earth itself—began to shake.

And shake.

And shake.

In a few seconds, every child on the playground was flat on the ground, looking at each other. *What is wrong with the ground? The ground is moving!* Students and teachers streamed out of the school.

Anna wanted to hold onto something to make it stop. But everything was moving. She curled up in a ball and held her head by her chest for such a long time. And the ground shook like almond jello under them, wobbling and moving.

And then it stopped.

And the earth pretended to go back to the way it was, hard and dependable.

For months afterwards, Anna worried that the ground wouldn't stay solid, and if it didn't, how could she trust it to keep them out of the water? It could not wobble like almond jello. It was not safe. She wondered about the big water and the poison octopus her mama talked about. Would she fall into the sea if the ground shook like that again?

She clutched her doll close to her at night and in the

morning snuck her into the blue plastic backpack so they would not be separated.

WEDNESDAY, NOVEMBER 27, 2019, 6:55 A.M.

North of Walsenburg, Colorado

"David, are you sorry you married me?"

His silence continued.

Her eyes felt tighter as they drove, and she hoped no tears would start. Many more long minutes elapsed before she asked, "When I showed up at your mom and dad's farm, you got me, and the baby, and even my mama after that, in just one wedding—"

"Stop" he said. "No," he told her. "No," and reaching over, he turned on the radio again.

Her heart eased when he turned on the music.

Classic rock was the reason they'd met and what brought them together, and the soaring sounds of their favorite songs had always had the power to take them out of a serious moment, even out of an argument, and back into the past, when nothing had mattered but the intricate drumbeats and inspiring lyrics. The words they remembered from high school.

No dreamy ballads or hip hop for them, but instead songs like the one playing now: Rush's "Chain Lighting," about how a journey of a thousand miles begins with one step. "My mama quoted that proverb to me all the time," Anna said, grateful to change gears, "It was 'a journey of a thousand miles', but what it meant to her was that nobody gets a free ride, and you should just start slogging along as soon as you could to get the job done." She glanced at David and the knot in her shoulders eased a little when he smiled.

He said, "She grew up in a different universe. China in the '60s and '70s. The Great Leap Forward and all that chaos..."

"I know. But that wasn't the way the song meant it. Rush means it in a much more hopeful way. A brief moment being so right and bright." She sang along, "Hope is epidemic. Optimism spreads..."

David sang along softly, and it was as if all the previous troubled moments hadn't happened. "When the moment dies, the spark still flies, reflected in another pair of eyes." He met Anna's glance for a second as they both sang the lyrics that seemed to roll along with the miles.

When the last note died, Anna said, "You know, that song that was playing when we... the night we... After you'd been in San Francisco a few days and we kept meeting up and..." She blushed in the half-light of dawn.

"I know," said David. "Then we *really* met up!" He smiled. "I've always wondered if that 'other pair of eyes' turned out to be our baby." He smiled and peered at Anna again for a microsecond, then back at the road. "In the winter, when you had the baby, and I saw those eyes of hers, and they looked just like yours, it took my breath away."

"A journey of a thousand miles." She smiled. "It says in Isaiah, you who carry the vessels of the Lord... You will not leave in haste or go in flight, for the Lord will go before you. I didn't mean for that to be my plan, running away from San Francisco right after graduation!"

He laughed. "Pretty crazy timing, yep. I graduated, and the same week you called asking if you could come see me at the farm."

"I'm glad we wrote some letters back and forth after spring break. I was feeling so vulnerable, and I didn't know if I'd ever see you again, as fantastic as our spring break week was..."

"That is for sure. I never expected to meet someone like you..." David smiled. "My dad let me borrow his car to pick you up at the bus station. But I had no idea... about the baby. I'm glad you told me, and we could talk before we got to mom and dad's house."

"We must have walked five miles in that park in town," said Anna. "But if you'd said you couldn't handle it, I would have left." She paused. "I had absolutely no other plan, though. I couldn't go back home. My mama wanted to kill me," said Anna. "That last semester of high school ... our little apartment in Chinatown felt even smaller than it already was. After Mama found out, she wouldn't even talk to me."

"She did go to your high school graduation, though."

"Well, yes. She'd been working so hard for years in the noodle shop to make sure I got a good education in America. She would not miss that. That wasn't supposed to be the end of my school career, though."

"Nope."

Anna pondered the change in her mama over the years. By the time Jessie was in grade school, Mama sold the noodle shop and left San Francisco to live with David, Anna, and Jessie in Mississippi. She was only middle-aged then, but Anna and her family were Jiexen's only family, though she pushed them away in so many ways.

They didn't talk for a few miles, but the silence was comfortable. Anna watched the tufts of dry grass along the side of the highway.

The cab of the truck had heated enough that Anna had taken her mittens off, and twining her fingers together, she straightened her arms in front of her to stretch her back in the confined quarters. She had relatively more room since she was just over five feet tall, while David was a foot taller. The knot in the muscle persisted.

She asked, "Don't you want to take off your gloves yet?"

"Nope. Can't seem to get warm enough today," said David.

Casey decided to wake up and hopped down from the sleeping area to stand between the seats, with his head resting heavily on Anna's leg. She scratched his ears for a while. He yawned and climbed back into his nest. *It probably smells better to him back there than it does to me,* she thought.

The scenery along the interstate stayed the same: high mountain desert, dry brown earth with very little snow, sage brush, scrubby bushes. High Plains County was behind them. To the south lay Pueblo County and Huerfano County.

On the east side of the interstate, the land was totally flat. Long, early morning shadows reached toward them from low sagebrush and yucca plants.

But the Rockies were to the west, sometimes closer, sometimes veering farther west, away from the interstate, changing from gold sunlit walls, to green trees, and back to dry rocky humps.

"David, thank you for sticking with me and Jessie."

"What else was I gonna do, put you out in the cold?"

"You could have."

He shook his head. "I would never abandon you, Anna. I love you."

Wednesday, November 27, 2019, 7 a.m.

Heading west from Walsenburg into the mountains, Colorado

The sun had been up for half an hour by the time they hit the weigh station at Walsenburg. The port of entry officer verified the logbook entries about the number of hours driving and made sure the truck did not average over 42 miles per hour, based on the mileage between destinations throughout the month. No blanks or problems this time, but that was because Anna filled them in. Suppose she hadn't pressed David for the necessary information earlier this morning?

He left the weigh station and got back onto the interstate. A few miles down the road, he exited the interstate, followed the US highway for a block, and pulled the rig into a truck stop. "No more interstate on this trip." He switched the CB radio from Channel 17 to Channel 10. "Time to head west," said David.

Anna got some tea for herself and coffee for David and let Casey run around and do his jobs. Then David pointed the Pete west, up the two-lane highway toward La Veta Pass.

US Highway 160 took them from Huerfano County into Costilla County and on into the Sangre de Cristo mountains. The road hugged the contour lines following the Cucharas River canyon for a ways, but this was the first of many river valleys they would follow on their route. Miles of mountains went by. The town of La Veta hid itself south of US-160, and all Anna could just see was the sign pointing to the turnoff for CO-12.

"All the trees are dead here," she said. "This was a fire area."

"Yep, this was the, ah—the—I can't think of the name of the fire a few years ago." David looked puzzled.

"Was it the Spring Fire? Hm. No, I remember thinking at

the time, it wasn't in the spring, but it has the word spring in it. It was last summer."

He grunted his affirmation of her statement.

"Oh, I know, it was the Spring Creek Fire," she said. "Last year was a bad fire season for Colorado."

David said, "Was it?" and kept driving.

"Sometimes they'll let a fire burn, when there's no town in the way, Prentice says," she said. "But Spring Creek Fire was another one that burned over 100,000 acres. They had more than a thousand firefighters trying to contain it. It took months." Anna had learned so much from Prentice.

David said, "They couldn't let the Garnet fire burn for miles. The houses are built right in the middle of the forest, or close to it."

Anna nodded. "Yes. The houses are being built in the fire-prone areas. Hard to separate the two anymore."

"It's amazing our house didn't get totally burned down. But all the smoke and water damage..." said David.

"Water damage," echoed Anna, thinking about their house in Garnet. "Prentice said the houses don't necessarily have to catch fire when there's a wildfire. It's a matter of making sure there's no fuel for the burning embers blowing everywhere. If they don't find fuel to eat, your house doesn't catch fire, and it won't burn down, he said." She smiled. "He has a good way of explaining things."

David said, "Who said that?"

"Prentice."

Anna thought David was about to ask another question, but then he stopped himself.

With a funny feeling in her belly, she added, "Jessie's boyfriend Prentice."

"Oh yeah, right. Prentice," said David. "I know."

She wasn't sure if she could believe him.

The miles went past.

A tiny faded sign read, "Muleshoe, CO — Pop. 2."

Then a reflective green sign, "La Veta Pass — 9,413 feet."

Soon after those, there was another sign about the Uptop Ghost town on Old La Veta Pass. Over a century ago, the Denver & Rio Grande narrow gauge rail line went over the top, the highest railroad in the world. Then it was a logging camp. And Highway 160 curled up along it with two very tight curves. Later, they built the new section of US Highway 160 to divert traffic along a higher route that had fewer sharp curves.

"Remember when we stopped there, David?" she asked, jerking her thumb back at the sign which was already behind them. They had spent a great weekend up there one summer, with the truck parked in the meadow parking lot full of other cars, and using the cab's sleeping area as their RV.

"Huh?"

"Remember when we camped at Uptop? The weekend music festival?"

"Hm. Sounds fun," he said vaguely.

She couldn't see how he wouldn't have a comment about it. It had been an idyllic, relaxing weekend on Old La Veta Pass. They danced, drank beer, gazed at the stars from a blanket in the meadow, and had so much fun.

Never mind. If that didn't make a good impression on him, what can I say?

A car in the eastbound lane moved into their westbound lane to pass another car. It didn't go back into its lane, though. It came straight toward the truck! *What's wrong? It's in our lane!*

"Watch out!" she yelled. David had already touched the brakes, but on this narrow road full of curves, he had nowhere to go without putting the truck into the canyon. When it came to physics, the car would lose the battle if the fully loaded truck had to hit it head-on. All of this awareness flashed through her brain in one horrified millisecond.

Miraculously, the little sedan swerved back into its lane just before the truck would have smashed it.

"But it's a no passing zone." The words flowed out of Anna in a long breath of relief.

"There's no difference between being right and being dead," David said, putting an abrupt end to another topic.

Anna thought about that for a long time. David could be so wise sometimes. So why was it lately that those wise moments sometimes lurched into him, not making any sense at all? What did he have on his mind that was diverting his concentration?

In the past, she'd gotten used to the companionable silence of "shoulder time" on all the runs she had joined him on before. Though he did like to tell stories sometimes, overall David didn't talk as much as Anna did, and over their quarter century of marriage, she usually could navigate his mood and get the timing right for a new conversation.

However, she realized the other, more uncomfortable silences had been happening for months. Some unknown distraction was causing unexplained lapses, missing answers.

And pushing him is not going to help one single bit.

David's primary focus was on the ballet that his feet and hands had to perform to keep the truck engine within the right number of revolutions per minute to manage the ever-changing elevations. As long as he kept the RPMs between 1700 and 2100, the ride wasn't any louder than before, and he had to focus.

They were now really in the mountains. The pass they navigated was 9,400 feet high, and the two-lane highway wound around through curve after curve, climbing the slopes following the contour lines, trying to find a way up the steep grade and back down the other side.

A road sign warned: *Falling rock - next seven miles.*

Whizzing along at up to fifty miles per hour, Anna appreciated the occasional stretches of guardrail made of ribbed steel attached to wood posts dug deep in the ground. On some curves without guard rails, only green metal poles with three orange reflectors stood between them and the canyon. Warnings everywhere about the precarious road configuration through the mountains.

"It's shaded down in the canyon," she commented. She remembered on other trips when the black water had moved imperceptibly between the river's banks and around snow topped rocks glistening in the sun. Today, the water flowed mostly white, except for the occasional open patch where the light combined with the current to make different hues.

Along the road's edge, yellow reflective signs helpfully reminded them of the big curves approaching and the corresponding drop in speed limit. David slowed the truck and adjusted it down even more when the going got trickier.

Truckers - curves tighten next seven miles, the sign read.

Motorcycles - use extra caution, another one said.

Sometimes Anna had a bird's-eye view right down into the canyon, especially outside the elbow of one sharp bend where the pavement almost doubled back on itself. She held her breath and closed her eyes at the sharpest point of the hairpin turn and even on some of the straight sections of road, too, where the hill sloped away quickly from the guardrail.

But she couldn't look away for long, and scanning the scenery, her gaze might drop straight down the slope to the river valley, or across an expanse of decomposed granite scree that made up one whole hillside. Here and there, a scraggly conifer held on for dear life.

They navigated a turn that had no guardrail, just a curved row of square yellow signs with black chevrons pointing left, reminding drivers there of steep turns. *Don't go down here, either. Keep your eyes on the curve,* they seemed to say.

On the north side of the river, the gray and black boulders threatened to burst into bits—maybe next week, maybe in a hundred years—because of the freeze-thaw cracks slanting from top to bottom. The bits would then join the scree pile at a forty-five-degree angle of repose. Time worked differently in the mountains. Geologic time. *God is good all the time. But I'd like to ask him a few questions,* she thought as the scenery flew by.

Where conifers could grow on the steep slope below her, sometimes all she could see was their tops peeking up next to the road. On the other side stood the rock cut for the road, red boulders hacked off in the middle. Brown mountains, but the shades varied. Tan, beige, white, gray, maroon. She saw a jagged scar going up a hillside on the far side of the river, back and forth, north of them. It must be an old mining road, carved out of the topography for wagons pulled by horses to haul men and their gear to the isolated mining towns before the railroads got through.

She considered how Sangre de Cristo meant Blood of Christ, because the mountains appeared so red sometimes, and started to say this to David, but swallowed the thought. He didn't seem interested in those kinds of observations these days, not like he used to.

She wondered if he were getting tired of the sound of her voice and then stopped the thought in its tracks as she realized she was blaming herself for something that might have nothing to do with her at all. But she felt like she'd already confronted him, asking if he'd noticed he wasn't himself lately and if he were mad at her.

Oh, stop it, Anna. I'm tired of the sound of my own stupid voice.

David took it slow. Both the downgrades and the uphill grades. *You go down a hill too fast only one time.* David had said that back when she'd ridden with him more often, after her mama had come to live with them in Mississippi. Jessie had been in grade school by then, and Anna had acquiesced to leaving her with her Tiger Grandma.

He was concentrating on driving, shifting the gears, pressing the accelerator, and spinning the steering wheel around the curves that came one after another. She watched through the windshield as the big white truck and trailer descended the pass, and the scenery flattened out. Someone had planted a mile-long line of junipers along a fence line as a snow break. The next property had lined up rolls of narrow red wood slats to guide the snow. Both landowners were clearly ready for any blizzard that came along and attempting to keep the highway from filling with snow.

There wasn't a sign of so much as a snowflake so far, but from the forecast, Anna knew the worst wasn't anticipated to hit until tomorrow. She turned to David. "Want to listen to the weather again?"

"Whatever," he shrugged. "Doesn't matter what they say. We're still going to Durango today."

"I'll take that as a 'yes,'" she tried to joke, as she turned the knob.

6

WEDNESDAY, NOVEMBER 27, 2019, 7:20 A.M., WEST OF LA VETA, COLORADO

"See Morris, the movie star alligator!" cried a man's voice on the radio commercial. "Feed free roaming tortoises, fish for carp to feed to the alligators, and go boating on ponds heated with geothermal energy!" She recognized it was a commercial for Colorado Gators Reptile Park in Mosca. A wonky jingle reminded listeners of the address and begged them to come visit soon.

"That's some place we haven't stopped before," said Anna. "It's just north of Alamosa."

David grunted but sounded slightly amused. "You can fish for carp to feed the alligators, huh?" he chuckled. "Isn't that barbaric?"

The weather report started up, and they both fell quiet as the newscaster, a woman with a pleasant but grave voice, launched into the forecast. "Well, folks, let's begin with some record-setting weather history because we may be dealing with a whole new set of records after this week. A decade ago, it was a low-pressure system that produced the lowest pressure ever recorded, 970 millibars, which met the criteria for a 'bomb cyclone.' The barometric pressure readings then dropped over twenty-four millibars in a twenty-four-hour time frame."

"I've never studied weather forecasting," Anna commented. "How do they ever get it right?"

The reporter went on. "That storm, which occurred in 2009, created widespread blizzard conditions across Colorado, including High Plains, Pueblo, and Huerfano Counties. Some wind gusts were as high as one hundred miles per hour. One to three feet of snow fell across the mountains with up to fifty-two inches at Wolf Creek Pass."

Anna turned to David. "Aren't we going over Wolf Creek Pass? Isn't that the super high one with all the switchbacks?"

"Yeah," he said. "But she's talking about a different storm."

"... combination of weather events shut down Colorado's Denver International Airport..." the meteorologist was saying... "canceling 1,400 flights and stranding over 5,000 passengers who slept on the floor of the terminal and concourses. They had nothing to eat after two days, when the airport restaurants all ran out of food. The snow blocked all access roads to the airport. All the major highways and interstates across the state were closed, from the Wyoming border to the New Mexico border, and from Kansas to Utah."

Her heart pulsed in her throat. Anna tucked her hands under her armpits and pulled her knees to her chest again.

"People tried to drive in the storm, and multiple multi-car accidents occurred. It stranded uncountable numbers of travelers in cars and at rest stops all over Colorado. Hazardous weather and road conditions throughout the storm area severely curtailed rescue operations for accidents and stranded motorists. The governor activated the

Colorado National Guard to aid over a hundred search and rescue operations."

Anna turned to David. "I remember that storm. Don't you? Jessie was a senior in high school. We were all tucked in at home for that one. You, me, Jessie, and my mama." Anna shifted her glance. "Oh, she hated the cold. We played a Monopoly game all the way to the end, and Jessie won."

"I was home?" David's brief glance was perplexed.

"Yes, I know you were because if you'd been out driving in that, I would have worried the whole time. I could never have concentrated on a game at all, much less a Monopoly marathon."

He didn't respond.

Anna filled his silence. "Also, you had more fun making funny voices for the metal game pieces than acting as a money-grubbing hotel owner," she said with a chuckle.

"The new storm is still developing and is expected to dump up to a foot of snow in a broad region by Thursday." The meteorologist's somber voice filled the cab. "Heavy snow could affect travelers at airports from Salt Lake City to Minneapolis-St. Paul just as it did in 2009," she said. "Likewise, what could be a record-setting storm system has the potential to turn into a bomb cyclone, meaning the storm will intensify at an unusually rapid rate."

"This is the part I don't get," Anna murmured.

The lady continued, "This low pressure system will probably undergo 'bombogenesis' just as the 2009 storm did, which will mean the same numbers with regard to the air pressure and subsequent conditions, a drop of at least twenty-four millibars in twenty-four-hours, by Thursday afternoon, with hurricane-force winds."

Anna sucked in air between her teeth.

"We expect blizzard conditions in the mountains of

southern Oregon and Northern California, with high waves and strong winds battering coastal areas as the storm comes in from the Pacific Ocean. We forecast wind gusts to exceed seventy miles per hour near the coast, and by late Thursday, the Sierra Nevada range could see from two to four feet of snow."

Anna looked at David. *This is crazy. Why are we driving?* The gnarled muscle in her back twinged again.

"See, they're talking about California and Oregon, babe," David said, passing off the threat as if it had no potential for touching them.

The radio announcer's voice in Anna's ears was relentless. "Oregon Public Broadcasting reports that Portland's branch of the National Weather Service is recommending drivers take chains if they're moving through areas that might see snow."

A local announcer took over. "For south-central Colorado, we expect from one to three feet of snow by Thursday night, with steady winds of fifty miles per hour with gusts that could exceed that by a good bit. What this means for Colorado is you should be where you need to be by Thursday morning, or else wait until Saturday to travel."

Anna kept her eyes on her husband, but he looked straight ahead, refusing to glance her way.

He tipped his gaze to the rearview mirror on his left, then back to the road. "So it won't hit until Thursday night. We'll be home by then."

"They said morning. David. We should be off the road Thursday morning—" She broke off to listen, but the station cut to a commercial about a tire shop with locations all over southern Colorado.

David switched it off. "There must not be much else

happening in the world today to spend so much time talking about a snowstorm."

"Why do you act like you're not at risk here?" Anna protested. "Do you have some special magic powers that make it so blizzards don't bother you?"

"I grew up in Nebraska, remember? Went through tons of heavy weather and survived it." He flashed a grin at her. "We'll be back to Garnet by dinner time tomorrow, and if it snows, we'll watch it out the window."

"You mean Pioneersburg."

"Huh?"

"You meant to say we'll be back in Pioneersburg, not Garnet, by tomorrow night, didn't you?"

"Huh? Yeah. Isn't that what I said? Why are you questioning everything I say lately, Anna?"

WEDNESDAY, NOVEMBER 27, 2019, 8 A.M.

Pioneersburg, Colorado

Jessie made a cup of hot green tea and reminded herself she was on vacation now, for the rest of today and for three more days after that. Getting up early and already being back from work had messed with her internal clock that separated work time from play time. Laughing out loud at herself, she remembered summer days kayaking with Prentice at the lake and hiking some great trails when she'd have to convince him repeatedly to stop and have fun. She needed to listen to her own advice about taking better care of her inner child.

She stood at the sliding door that overlooked her apartment deck. To her civilian eye, there was nothing to hint at the snowstorm the weather forecasters seemed convinced about. No cloudy sky, no fierce winds the meteorologists had warned about, beating the scrawny tree branches. While she hoped they were wrong in their predictions, she knew a false alarm this time would make people less likely to listen next time. Turning from the view, she puttered around, doing some wash and cleaning the bathroom.

When her cell phone beeped, she was sitting on the sofa, reviewing the list of food she planned to begin preparing later. Glancing at it, Jessie straightened when she saw an emergency alert Winter Storm Warning which read:

Issued: 2019-11-28 08:00

Expiring: 2019-11-30 00:00

New Alert

NORTHERN HIGH PLAINS COUNTY BELOW 7500 FEET-

...WINTER STORM WARNING AND LOW-PRESSURE SYSTEM HAS BEEN ISSUED FROM 8 AM THURSDAY TO MIDNIGHT FRIDAY...

* WHAT...HEAVY SNOW EXPECTED. TOTAL SNOW ACCUMULATIONS OF OVER 1 FOOT. WINDS GUSTING AS HIGH AS 100 MPH.

* IMPACTS...TRAVEL COULD BE HAZARDOUS.

PRECAUTIONARY/PREPAREDNESS ACTIONS...

IF YOU MUST TRAVEL, KEEP AN EXTRA FLASH-LIGHT, FOOD, AND WATER IN YOUR VEHICLE IN CASE OF AN EMERGENCY.

She said to the empty living room, "This alert is for tomorrow through midnight Friday. Oh, Mom and Dad, what are you getting into?"

Feeling abruptly chilled, Jessie pulled the blue and pink afghan over her. Maybe the forecast had changed. Maybe they were making a big deal out of nothing. She turned on her TV with its digital HD antenna and listened as the local news station picked up where the digital alert on her phone had left off. Prentice told her she was a rarity in her peer group to have access to live local television like this, since many people now only had digital streaming services. She opted to be prepared.

"How do you prepare for that kind of weather, you may ask?" the weather forecaster was asking. "Ladies and gentlemen, first responders are pleading with news outlets to be blunt with you. Please do not travel during this storm. Stay home. If you're already on the road, stay in a hotel, stay on the floor in your office. Do not drive on closed roads; they are closed because they are impassable. Do not bypass those closed roads by driving on smaller roads that have not technically been closed, because conditions there will be worse, not better."

Jessie pulled the afghan up closer to her chin.

The announcer remained stern. "There's no reason for you to drive anywhere during this storm. The airplane flight you're trying to catch has been canceled. The party you're trying to make has been postponed, or should be. The meeting you think is vital for you to attend needs to wait until everyone can attend safely. There are not enough first responders and volunteer rescue responders to help everyone whose cars get stuck in snowbanks during this storm." As he spoke, a series of past weather-related photos of stranded cars flashed across the screen to accentuate his point.

"Unless you're prepared to live, sleep, eat, and go to the bathroom in your vehicle, which is as cold as the outside air temperature, for twenty-four hours, or longer, then don't drive. Just stay indoors."

Pushing the afghan down to her lap, Jessie got her phone and texted her mom. *How far R U now? Did U C*

Thursday's blizzard forecast is getting worse? B safe. C U soon. She waited, phone in her hand, but no text came back. She knew cell service got patchy the farther they traveled into rural Colorado. Restless, a bit worried, she texted Prentice, who was coming over later, but she thought he might know something more than she'd already heard about the storm. Or maybe she just wanted him to calm her nerves.

Did U C weather this morning? She wrote to Prentice.

After a brief delay, he replied, *ZZZZZ will go look.*

Sorry I woke you up.

OK. And then another delay before he wrote, *It will be bad tomorrow,* he replied. *C U soon.*

Thanks Prentice. C U soon.

There was nothing to do but wait. One thing she'd taken to heart as she learned about life was knowing she could not control her parents' actions, just her own behavior. *They're adults. But sometimes they're just fifth graders in grown-up bodies.*

So her next step was to remind herself to step aside from worrying about what was happening to them. It was really out of her control. She made the deliberate decision to unplug and got out an whimsical young adult paperback she'd saved for a rainy day.

WEDNESDAY, NOVEMBER 27, 2019, 9 A.M.

Fort Garland, Colorado

The road sloped down out of La Veta Pass and leveled out in the San Luis Valley, the big agricultural area between the Sangre de Cristos and the San Juans. A little town called Fort Garland barely showed up next to the road in real life, much less on a road map. The green sign read: Elev. 7,936 feet but gave no indication of the population.

"What a relief," Anna murmured, grateful for the break from the twisty roads.

"We're taking our time today, aren't we?" David smiled at her. "But it's a short day, and we'll be to Durango by mid-afternoon at this rate, no problem."

Anna could have snorted, but she stopped herself from saying what she thought. *Taking our time? We got up hours before dawn.* A moment later, she asked, "Isn't there an Internet café along here, David?" She pulled her phone from her purse and looked at the screen. "I've got no bars now."

"Let the girl have a vacation like we're getting," David teased.

Anna said, "I know, but I told her I'd check in."

"Like I've said before, she'll miss the dog long before she misses us hanging around, babe." He pulled the truck into a parking lot near the Cactus Flower Café. "But I guess we could use a bathroom break anyway after all this coffee."

The dog sensed the truck's change in speed and hopped to the floor. Turning to him, Anna said, "I didn't bring your treats, Casey, but how about I put some of your food in my coat pocket for you? I did bring plenty of that." Casey didn't argue, and they both climbed down to stretch their legs. Casey chose a convenient shrub to do his job, then he and Anna went into the building, which definitely did allow dogs. She logged into the café Wi-fi and replied to Jessie's text while she waited for their hot drinks.

Quick stop in Fort Garland, she wrote.

Did U C more about blizzard coming?

Yes, texted Anna. *Dad not worried.*

Anna tried to stretch out the tight muscle in her back

with no success, and soon they were on the move again. She amused herself by trying to remember the silly lyrics to "Wolf Creek Pass" by C. W. McCall, the truck-driving country singer. She loved the part about telephone poles "goin' by at the rate of four to the seventh power. Well, I put two and two together, added twelve and carried five. Come up with twenty-two thousand telephone poles an hour." She chuckled.

They passed a sign for Blanca, CO - Pop. 406. Anna dozed off.

David hit the brakes. She jerked upright just as he swore under his breath. The truck made a huge noise, a shuddering thump that rattled Anna's teeth. The wheels had barreled directly over something, a hard lump right in the road. She barely glimpsed a gray animal flying into the air and rolling along the shoulder. "Oh!" she cried. "What is it?"

"Coyote." David said. "Was," he added.

"You must have hit it straight on."

"Yep, or we wouldn't be here," he said. "If we swerve, we die."

Anna couldn't fall asleep again, thinking of what David had said. It was true. The laws of physics would not allow a truck weighing 80,000 pounds to make either sudden turns or sudden stops. David had explained to her back when she'd first started riding with him that it could come to a stop in the length of about two football fields when the road was dry, but not if it was slick. And if an animal crossed the road in front of him, he'd said, that was all she wrote, at least for the coyote or deer. On a bad day, it could also be the end for the driver.

The foggy, icy air was drawing in, but the highway was still dry.

She wondered about the ruins of a cabin at the side of

the road. It had four walls, but no roof, and tall yellow grass grew up in the middle. *I wonder how long ago that was somebody's home. Did they make sourdough bread in the wood stove?* She could almost taste a bite of sourdough bread on her tongue, just thinking about it. Aloud, she said, "My mama spent so many years in San Francisco, but she was always in Chinatown. Do you think she ever ate sourdough bread?"

"What?" David peered briefly at her, blinking. "What about Chinatown?"

"She lived so long in Chinatown, so do you think she ever ate sourdough bread?"

"What does Chinatown have to do with sourdough bread?"

Anna sighed. "Nothing, really. Even though there must have been American bakeries a few blocks from mama's apartment."

"I don't follow you."

She stopped. What was the point? David was next to her, but he wasn't with her. He was far away, some place where she couldn't reach him. "Never mind." The words slipped into the silence between them. Anna stared from the passenger window. Willows and cottonwoods filled in along the low spots that would contain some water in the summer. But right now, the trees were naked branches.

By mid-morning, they got to Alamosa, in the middle of the valley. It was flat enough for a railroad to cut right through the middle of it, north to south. This was a central place market town, with stores, restaurants, a few motels, and schools, providing goods and services to the people living in the surrounding productive agricultural valley where the first water rights in Colorado had been claimed. They got most of their water from winter runoff, not rain. In the summer, the residents grew potatoes, and wheat, carrots, alfalfa, lettuce, broccoli, canola, and cauliflower. And barley to sell to the big beer companies. Plus, there were sheep and cattle ranches.

David used the foot brake combined with the noisy Jake brake to slow the rig as they drove through town. Anna felt Casey nuzzle her shoulder as he peeked out from the sleeping area to see what excitement might come his way. *Oh boy, a new parking lot to sniff! Maybe someone will scratch my ears. Let's go!* His doggie thoughts played through Anna's mind, especially when they didn't stop at all but rolled on past town. Eventually she said, "Casey, go lie down."

They drove into the west side of the valley and crossed out of Alamosa County, past a faded billboard that read, "Welcome to Beautiful Rio Grande County, Gateway to the San Juan Mountains." Another smaller sign advertised the annual Monte Vista Crane Festival.

They passed a reflective green sign that informed them that Durango was 130 miles ahead. Lots of winding miles and another doozy of a mountain pass.

She focused on the landscape that in its own way was beautiful even in late fall or early winter. Dry yellow grass stretched for miles behind barbed wire fences until it reached the mountain ranges. As an artist, Anna appreciated the unique differences among the styles of barbed wire fences. Some were three lines of wire, horizontal to the ground, strung tightly between metal T-posts pounded in the ground. Others were still three horizontal strands of wire, but the rancher had added two more vertical lines of barbed wire between the posts to stiffen it, and those sections looked like nine-squared checkerboards.

A herd of bison clumped together near a cluster of aspen trees dusted with last night's light snow. On the far mountain slopes, the green pine trees appeared black. A sign proclaimed the next town was Del Norte, which used to be a stage-coach stop but was now a rock-climbing destination.

"There's not much to this side of the county, is there?" she said to the window, and David had been quiet for so long, she was almost surprised when he answered.

"You missed one of those historic markers you like so much a while ago. Point of interest. You were asleep."

"Oh, did it say what it was?"

"Something about a mining town that's not there anymore. Ghost town. Snakebite City? Something like that."

"Huh. Whatever it was, it doesn't sound like it would be much fun in the cold, does it?"

He didn't answer, and she dozed again with her eyes open.

South Fork, the burg at the far edge of the valley, came into view. Pine forests pushed closer to the highway here. Anna pointed to an unlikely-placed restaurant, a dark log cabin with an adjacent empty parking lot nestled up against a seeming wall of trees. "Hey, David! That place says it'll be open tomorrow, on Thanksgiving. How about that? The Cozy Conifer Lodge."

"Nah," he said, with no further explanation.

"But I bet they're dying for customers. If the weather's bad, we could stay..."

He plowed on. "Let's save the money and just get home to all that food you and Jessie have planned."

She felt a tightness in her chest, painfully aware of how her pitiful art income had dried up to almost nothing after she lost her studio in August. *I think I've sold all the pieces I had out in galleries when the fire hit. And I can't make new ones yet.*

7

WEDNESDAY, NOVEMBER 27, 2019, 11:59 A.M., WOLF CREEK PASS, COLORADO

Now the road began the slow, tortuous route up and over Wolf Creek Pass, which was thirty-seven miles of Hell, as C.W. McCall called it. Anna pictured spreading dark green paint over the canvas as she captured this scene in her mind. She would paint it, she decided, as soon as she could. With her brushes she would bring to life the dark trees, the white and gray snow, the cold. It was breathtaking.

They'd made this climb before. The key was to keep the truck in the gear that matched the engine speed and not push the truck too hard up the steep, winding grade, which would risk overheating the engine or the brakes. He couldn't slip into the wrong gear, either.

In short, David couldn't make a mistake.

For him, it was all part of the routine. He'd explained the dangers and requirements to Anna over the years as she accompanied him on so many runs. She couldn't drive the truck, but she enjoyed watching him and understood the key ingredients.

"I'm glad we still have good weather." Anna waited, but David didn't answer. "I hope they're wrong about the storm."

He drove.

She watched as a herd of elk climbed the slopes across the river gorge.

Climbing higher, more and deeper snowdrifts loomed above the road on the north side of the slopes in the shade of the conifers. Where the trees thinned out, a shell of old ice from last March and April's heavy snowfall still covered the mountainous terrain. It was growing foggier, but the road was dry, yet.

David kept the truck in low gear, and the engine did its job, crawling up the steep grades at a speed so slow that Casey got up periodically to check things out. Anna imagined he was thinking they might be rolling into another rest stop. Knowing David didn't need the distraction, she said in a low voice, "Go lie down," and after a moment, the dog hopped back on the bed.

Every time David shifted gears, the truck hesitated a bit, and the turbo whined as it adjusted its speed and load. It was like a lullaby to Anna. The scenery had been spectacular, but it was also exhausting to take in every tree, rock slope, and vista and try to remember it for a future painting. With the fog now cloaking the view, she let herself close her eyes and lean her head against the tall seat back.

The engine continued its comforting sounds and her eyes opened a half-hour later. On and off, the midday sun found a way through the fog. Scattered crusty snow existed in the tree shadows. Otherwise, it was ethereal in the misty light.

In some stretches, the two-lane road had an extra uphill lane so cars could pass slow-going vehicles like the Pete. An accumulated line of cars and SUVs zoomed past them on the left, many of them loaded with skis and snowboards, heading to Wolf Creek Pass Ski Area, which was famous for getting an average of over 400 inches of snow a year. Legendary powder. The psychedelic bumper stickers of several cars that passed them said, "Wolf Creek: The Most Snow in Colorado."

Their ascent continued as they passed the ski area. The passing lane ended, and the road kept going up and around. Curve to the right, wind to the left.

"Have you ever wanted to try skiing, David?"

The only sign he might have heard her was the tightening of his grip on the wheel. His focus appeared to be nailed to the upcoming turn.

She tried to make a joke. "It would be the opposite of driving a truck downhill, right? You could enjoy the speed instead of having to control it."

Her heart eased a bit when he chuckled.

BANG!

It was the sharp, loud noise of something breaking. The truck shrieked to a stop, and she and David flew forward in their seat belts. She felt Casey thump against the bulkhead. David had not even touched the brakes this time.

"You've gotta be kiddin' me!" David's yell broke the ringing silence.

"What was that?" Anna shouted at the same time.

David put the truck in park and messed with the brake knobs, but no hissing sound resulted. This was a bad sign. She watched, wordless, as he unbuckled his seatbelt and opened his door to get out of the truck.

We're stopped in the middle of the road, and he's climbing out?

"Where are you going?" she asked.

"Gotta check the trailer controls."

David had been trucking since 1998, when he was twenty-four. A quarter-century later, he was a veteran over-the-road driver who could fix anything. She'd seen him pull off all kinds of miraculous repairs on the Pete in all kinds of weather and lighting conditions. Anna always had just one job: to stay safely out of the way in the cab so he could focus on the work at hand, and she was fine with that.

But this time they were blocking a whole lane of the two-lane road.

At the top of a two-mile high mountain pass. At the end of November.

With a major snowstorm predicted.

God, please help me be helpful in the right way. She popped over to the driver's seat and looked in the rearview mirror to see if there were cars coming behind them, not that she could do anything about them.

So, Anna reminded herself, instead of questioning him again, to think *I love my dear husband, and I thank you for him every day, God. I'm so glad I'm with him again on this trip. It's been too long.*

She opened his window to listen, and the air was icy out there at this altitude, even in the middle of the day.

A tiny electric car appeared next to them with no sound at all. She saw David start with surprise as it whizzed around them in the other lane, completely silent. He stared after it for a few seconds, shook his head, and turned back to the truck.

Will we get moving soon? Will we get to Durango before the warehouse closes? She thought. *Are we going to be okay?*

WEDNESDAY, NOVEMBER 27, 2019, 12 P.M.

Wolf Creek Pass summit, Colorado

Outside, she heard David muttering at the back of the cab at the catwalk. It surprised her to hear him swearing as he made metal-wrench-hitting-something sounds. *Did he just yell at the Pete, the truck he loves?*

The trailer controls were coupled to the tractor using two gladhand connectors for the air lines, which provided air pressure to activate the brakes, and an electrical cable, which provided power to the trailer's lights. He would have just checked them this morning when he connected the trailer in the parking lot illuminated with vapor lights.

She moved back to her seat and settled Casey next to her, rubbing his ears and looking into his deep brown eyes. David climbed back in the cab and stared through the windshield with a grim face. She waited for him to release the brakes, put it in gear, and head up the road. But he didn't move.

He said, "The red air line broke. All the brakes froze. Emergency brake is locked. It's a fail-safe thing."

"Okaaay...." Anna drew out the syllables. "You can fix that, right?"

He sighed. "I know what's broken, but I can't fix it." He looked at her, and his shrug was a gesture of helplessness.

"You don't have the parts?" she ventured.

"I should have 'em in the cargo box, but, for some reason, I don't. And I can't get the truck out of this lane with the brake engaged."

"So... we're stuck?" She felt her pulse beat in her ears.

He nodded. "For now." He got out, and she caught glimpses of him through her own rearview mirror as he got out to set up several reflective triangles downhill of the stranded truck. Climbing back into the cab, he wiped his hands down his face and took a breath. She saw his jaw muscles relax a little.

"I'll see if I can raise some help on the regional channel."

Anna said, "That's Channel 10, right? That's the local one, and if that doesn't work, we'll switch to Channel 9 for emergencies."

David's eyes twinkled. "You remember!" He liked teaching her about the CB radio. Anna felt that coaching mode was one of his skill sets he didn't get to use as often as he would've liked.

David keyed the CB mic. "Breaker 1-0. Anybody got their ears on? This is Dutch Boy. We got a 10-34 up on Wolf Creek Pass. Anybody copy?"

No response. They sat in silence, waiting.

Anna watched as he repeated the message requesting assistance, his voice getting tenser each time.

In the ensuing silence, she averted her glance, knowing it was killing him to have to ask for help, because the parts he needed were commonly used and replaced, and he should have had extras. A rookie mistake. He had told her about air lines so many times.

The minutes ticked by. Anna closed her eyes and prayed for someone to answer. For help. For patience.

She and David both flinched at the sound when a voice, a man's voice, cracked the awful quiet. "Come back, Driver. This is Four Eyes. Do you copy?"

David gripped the mic, hard. "Affirmative, Four Eyes, this is Dutch Boy. What's your 20?"

"Just stopped at the ski area for some lunch, heading west over the pass. How about you, Dutch Boy? You got some trouble?"

David explained the situation, and the guy said he'd give David a ride into the next town on his way west.

"How long will it be, do you think, before he gets here?"

"Not long. The ski area's not too far behind us."

"Are you hungry? I'll make sandwiches while we wait." Early this morning, before they'd heard about the bad weather coming, she'd hoped they'd share a picnic in Pagosa Springs, and possibly take a dip in the hot springs if they were on schedule to reach the warehouse in Durango before it closed. But all those ideas were blown to bits if the truck needed repair.

David said he could eat, and she opened the mini-fridge and cupboards to get the sandwich fixins. She had one sandwich made and set on the paper plate when she heard a pickup truck pass them and park on the shoulder in front of the Pete.

David hopped out and hailed the driver, a man with a peppy voice. "Hi! My name's Doug. Like the past tense of 'dig'!" He and David both laughed, already fast friends. "I'm in the construction equipment business," Anna heard him say through the open window. The two headed behind the Pete, and a moment later she heard sounds of metal latching and unlatching. She shot a glance upward, along with another prayer. *Please God, maybe this guy will have the parts to fix the Pete.*

David's scruffy blond head popped back up into the cab, and he sat in his seat. "Anna? We're gonna move the truck a little. You should sit down."

"What? I thought it was stuck," she said as she buckled into the front seat again. "Who's we?"

"Me and Four Eyes. His name's Doug. He reminded me about using the service brake air line for a stopgap repair so we can move the rig at least a few feet off the road." Rubbing his eyes, David shook his head, mumbling something about the blue air line being hooked up where the red air line goes. Anna had the sense he was talking more to himself than to her.

He eased the truck into gear and pulled it forward, closer to the edge of the drop-off on Anna's side, and the emergency brake made a loud noise before the tractor slammed to a stop again. Now it was halfway out of the traffic lane. And half in it.

"What's up, David? We can't keep going?"

"Nah. That was an emergency fix. This guy, Doug, he had a great idea. But now I gotta get some parts."

"So, we're still parking on the edge?"

David was animated. "Yeah, but not for long. Doug's heading down to Pagosa Springs. He said he'd drop me off so I can get a replacement red line. He says to get the rubber kind, since the plastic ones break a lot."

Anna nodded. "I've heard you mention that before. Red and blue plastic air lines....That's why you always have spares."

"No. I don't know. Have I said that before?" David was unfazed.

She nodded slowly. "Yes, you actually talk about air lines every time we hook up the trailer. It's one of your favorite topics, honey." *This doesn't make any sense.*

"How about that. Well, I don't know why I don't have any today," he said without much emotion. "So, Doug's waiting for me. Do you want to come along?"

"What?" She knew what he meant, but she was getting flustered by his lack of attention to detail. She saw Four Eyes pacing behind his pickup. "How long will you be gone?"

David just said, "Doug said you'd fit in his truck, too. Come with us?"

She shook her head. This didn't feel right. "No, I'll stay here with Casey and take a nap or something." *How can I need a nap? I've been sleeping half the morning already.* But she was exhausted.

"Don't miss me too much, okay?"

Doug had walked back and now asked through David's open window, "Hey, are you comin' with me or not, Dutch Boy?"

David nodded and said, "Yep, be right there."

"I always miss you when you're gone," Anna smiled. "But I'm used to it, honey. It's just not usually at the top of a mountain when you leave me alone."

He smiled. "Nope, I guess sometimes it's when there's a hurricane coming."

She sighed. "I'll be fine," she said. "Will he give you a ride back?"

David shook his head. "Nah, but I'll ask at the auto parts store to see if someone's heading back east."

She nodded. She did appreciate how truckers helped each other out of pickles. She'd seen this before, too. "Here," she got up and handed him the sandwich on the plate. "Take this to eat on the way."

"Great!" He folded the plate around the sandwich, stuffed it in his old red parka's pocket, and started to get out of the truck.

"Wait!" She handed him the whole can of what they jokingly called 'stacked, potato-based crisps' and asked, "Do you have your wallet?" He usually tucked it into one of the cubbyholes above his seat, and she was already reaching for it. Sure enough, he'd almost left without it.

Why is he forgetting everything he used to do automatically? She was sorry that she was finding so many valid reasons to keep an eye on her husband.

"Ah, nope, I guess not. Thanks, babe," he said, tucking the wallet into his other parka pocket. He opened the can of crisps as soon as he stepped to the ground. He called up to her, "Back soon. Enjoy the view from up here."

Anna rolled up the window as another thick bank of fog rolled around them and David got into Four Eyes' truck and they disappeared.

~

12:30 P.M.

In the silence, she took a breath and closed her eyes, trying to believe what she'd just done. Sent David away with a stranger while she stayed here with just the dog, a CB, and a whole lot of not much else. This didn't feel like a first date. It felt like a bad dream, and she wanted to wake up, but she couldn't. David was her farm boy, her knight in shining armor, but he was also just a man. A flawed man who needed help, and it hurt in her belly that she didn't know how to help him.

She made herself a roast beef sandwich, Casey drooling all the time, attentive as he could ever be. She sat on the bed where Casey waited and scooted over to the driver's side of the mattress, where there was a small window. Casey moved with her, watching. She took a bite of the sandwich and watched the skiers' cars zooming by over the hill on the way to, or from, a day of fun.

Enjoy the view, she thought. *I could walk down to the ski area, but I don't know when he'll be back.*

The sun struggled to make it through the clouds and fog blowing down the mountain. She cuddled under the blankets and watched the world go by. *With all the fog, this looks like the view from the upstairs window in mama's place in Chinatown. The clouds, the busy world going by on the street, and me up there with my dolly trying to stay out of the way. Stay out of trouble.*

She ate a piece of raw kale, chewing and chewing. *Mama was always mad when I couldn't do things she thought I should be able to do.* Anna shook her head. "No, that's not it. She was just mad all the time. I don't think I had a chance of pleasing her. And that's the truth." She ate some more kale, nodding at her own adult observation.

But here I am now. David and I make a great team. We always have. "At least we were a team, right, Casey?" She chewed. "I'm still on his team, but I'm not sure about him."

The dog lifted his left eyebrow as he looked into her black eyes, then his right eyebrow lifted as he looked back to the food in her hand, hoping for a snack.

"He's got something on his mind, Casey. How can I find out what it is? Or who it is?" She shook her head with that thought. The minutes ticked by, and she munched on the sandwich, but she wasn't hungry. Her stomach felt like it was full of lead.

She fed the rest of the sandwich to Casey, who gobbled it down in a few big dog chomps and looked back at her for more. She fed him the last two slices of roast beef, emptying the package, and rubbed his soft ears. "You are a Good Dog!" She zipped up her green parka, added her black mittens and orange hat, and grabbed the rest of the loaf of bread and the bunch of kale. She climbed down to the road on the driver's side, away from the edge of the mountainside and the valley full of pine trees below. Casey jumped down after her, hoping for more roast beef, but instead getting clipped to his leash to keep him away from any cars and from the mountain edge.

The air looked thicker, darker now. More moisture in it, maybe a snowflake or bit of precipitation. She stuck close to the truck on her way up the hill and sat on a flat rock on the inside shoulder, just ahead of the Pete. In the cold, flat light, she threw chunks of bread and green leafy kale tidbits to the deep blue Steller's jays that clamored for more. One black Abert's squirrel investigated for morsels on the ground, and when Casey showed interest in the squirrel, Anna told him to Wait, and he did. He was a Good Dog.

She couldn't text Jessie. No chance of service here.

With room to move, she stretched out her back and legs, using the yoga poses she could do standing up and squatting. Mountain Pose, Forward Fold, Lightning Bolt, Warrior I and II, and Garland. That helped. Her hip popped during Triangle, a big relief, but her back muscles would not loosen up in the cold, damp air. *There's a reason people do hot yoga but not cold yoga. Most days I can warm up doing yoga, but not today, even in my parka.*

Back in the cab, she cuddled up with the dog for a nap. No sleep, but she closed her eyes and monitored the CB for a while. She heard random bursts of static as people many miles away had conversations she could not make out.

She turned on the regular radio to listen to some reassuring classic rock, but instead she heard more warnings about the incoming storm tomorrow. The sense of unease in her stomach grew the longer they had to delay their progress.

She scooted off the bed and picked up the CB mic off the rack on the ceiling. "Four Eyes and Dutch Boy, this is Art Mama. Got your ears on?" She listened for a while, tried again, and then put the mic back. Nothing.

In a rebellious mood, she got out the beautiful homemade pumpkin pie she'd meant to save for tomorrow, Thanksgiving. With a plastic fork, she scooped a forkful straight out of the middle of the pie plate. Then another.

And she could not stop. The pie looked so forlorn with a third of it hacked out, but that's how it was. She covered it up with the foil and stuck it back in the cupboard where Casey couldn't get it. He loved pumpkin.

So much quiet time to think. And worry. And pray.

David came back several hours after he left. She was fast asleep. She heard a truck pull up from the west and stop on the eastbound shoulder, farther downhill. He rattled around with somebody at the back of the cab, replacing the broken air line, and he hollered a thank you. He put the box of triangles away and climbed back up. "Anna? I'm back." She was back in the bed curled up with Casey.

"Want to come up here?" he said, gesturing to her passenger seat with a grin.

Anna wanted to say no thanks. She wanted to stay curled up. But she couldn't ride down a mountain back there on the bed, so she dragged herself to her seat and buckled in.

When they broke down, the truck was almost at the top of the pass, so it was all downhill from here to Pagosa Springs, literally.

In a semi, descending a long, steep grade was as tricky as climbing one. Multiple sharp bends in the road like the one that led through Wolf Creek Pass required every ounce of David's concentration, more ballet footwork on the pedals, and massaging the gears into place at the exact right range of RPMs for the engine. Every step of the coordinated process was vital to keep the asbestos brakes from overheating. This highway had a few runaway truck ramps, but the consistent message from the Colorado Department of Transportation was, "If you over brake it, you can't make it."

She looked over the edge into the river canyon as David handled each new hairpin turn, one at a time, down the west side of the pass. She couldn't see too far because of the clouds. Just like in C. W. McCall's song, the road went down and around and around and down, to Pagosa Springs on the other side of the pass. Anna's nose wrinkled as the cab filled with the distinctive smell of sulfur from the geothermal hot springs. It was late afternoon now, and the air was foggy white. Not with snow yet, just an eerie whiteness that limited the sight distance. And made it look cold outside.

"It's too bad about the hot springs," she said.

David gripped the wheel and tightened his shoulders. He had to slow the truck going through the downtown Pagosa Springs, and Anna read the names of businesses through town: RiverWalk Inn, Treasures of the Rockies gift shop, a whiskey bar called The Iron Dram. She could see people soaking in the steaming pools just off the highway. Today's foggy weather didn't matter to them, though when the blowing snow came tomorrow, it would stop them from going outside.

"I know it's late and we can't stop today." Anna went on as if her chatter might thaw the chill, inside and out. "It would have felt good on this knot in my back."

"Sorry, babe." David's apology sounded automated.

"Tomorrow, the snow's supposed to come in for sure, so there's not a chance we can stop on our way back, either."

"Nope," he said between his clenched teeth. "Too bad, though. It would be nice to warm up."

Warm up? He'd had the heat cranked high in the cab all day.

He drove west. The road slipped off the mountains and leveled out, but it still wound along the river, and the tiny guardrail on Anna's right side was a minor consolation to her from her perch so high above the road's surface, although she knew if they were ever to hit one, it would only help tip them over the edge. "This storm they're talking about..."

He interrupted her. "Relax, will ya?"

She straightened. "I don't think it's hype this time, though—"

He briefly met her glance. "Haven't I been supporting our family doing this job? Haven't I, Anna?"

"I'm not..." but she closed her mouth and turned from him, the rigid set of his shoulders, the clench of his hands on the wheel. She couldn't remember him snapping at her like that before, but today it had happened several times. All the possible reasons why bounced around in her head, and though she'd tried to ask him directly, she was getting nowhere, leaving her imagination to run wild.

The fog got thicker, the winter sun hiding somewhere above it, as they traced back and forth, following the topography. The farther west they went in Colorado, the drier it got, as the mountain sides spilled down and eroded into the river canyons, on the other side of the San Juans and the Continental Divide now. Near Chimney Rock, the road followed another curve of another river.

She waited until they passed Bayfield before speaking again. "Maybe we could come back here for fun, in the car, some other time. Just ourselves. No dog, even. Jessie could keep him. And go to the hot springs for a vacation." If he said no, she thought her heart might break.

But he didn't say no. He didn't say anything.

8

WEDNESDAY, NOVEMBER 27, 2019, MID-AFTERNOON, PIONEERSBURG, COLORADO

Mid-afternoon, Jessie was excited to hear the knock on the door of her apartment. Even though she knew who it was, she asked in a silly, flowery voice, "Who is it?"

"Me, Prentice!"

Jessie welcomed her blond-haired boyfriend with a warm hug. He smooched her on the lips and she shrieked. "Oh, you're so cold! Come in here and warm up, and I'll fill you in on everything."

"You're not very warm either, Jessie, I gotta say. Let's put the priority on warming up," he smiled, kicking off his boots and following her to the sofa. "Have you heard from your mom?"

Jessie shook her head and pulled him by the hand over to the sofa, drawing the colorful knitted afghan over them both from feet to their chin as they snuggled together. Her Nebraska grandma had knitted it in bright shades of 1980s blue and pink nylon yarn, and she was glad it had been at her place and not at her parents' house, so it didn't get smoke damaged this summer. "That's what I've got to tell you about."

"So, this means, when your dad dropped that bomb about going on a run over Thanksgiving, and then inviting her along... she actually went," he summarized what he knew as she nodded and smiled. "Unexpected!" They held hands under the afghan.

"Yes. I think she's trying to treat this like a surprise vacation, even though Dad's working. They took the dog like they always do, and she also took my snow boots!"

"Well, that's good, with the weather forecast what it is. Maybe Casey will keep their toes warm in the truck. And we can keep each other warm right here!"

She hugged him. "But we also have work to do."

"So, we're on our own cooking Thanksgiving dinner?"

Jessie smiled. "Yes. If they somehow stay ahead of the storm, by the time they get back tomorrow night, we'll have everything ready."

Prentice shook his head. "The forecast is terrible now. It's taken everyone by surprise. Maybe they will do the smart thing and just stay in Durango until the danger's past. We can eat all the food ourselves!" He was a notoriously hearty eater, being a firefighter who worked out in the gym all the time.

"Except no pumpkin pie. Mom took that with her."

"Maybe she'll make another one for me when she gets back."

Jessie swatted him on the arm. "It's not that hard. I'll teach you," she said. "But meanwhile, I'm just glad you have your time off at the same time I do."

"Me too. Time to chill out and not think about fires or anything serious. And time to learn how to cook an entire

Thanksgiving dinner on our own…" He chuckled. "Hope that doesn't turn out to be ironic!"

"My brave firefighter boyfriend sounds worried about setting my kitchen on fire." But now, the moment she'd said it, her hand flew to her mouth. Prentice actually had survived a kitchen fire, but it was the same fire that killed his brother when they were little boys, and his whole life was altered because of it. "I'm sorry, Prentice, I can't believe I said that."

He smiled and was quick to reassure her. "It's okay. That's all past." He paused. "Well, no, but I'm working on being okay." That was more true. "But making actual food in an oven is new for me, remember? Dad and I always got Swanson's TV dinners and heated them in the microwave." He added under his breath, "I would like to learn how to make a pumpkin pie sometime, yes."

They laughed and snuggled under the afghan on the sofa, watching *Toy Story* 2, a movie they both remembered from grade school.

At one point, Prentice grabbed her knee, announcing, "This is my favorite line," then quoting along with Buzz Lightyear, the toy astronaut action figure. He said in Tim Allen's silly cartoon space ranger voice, "'Woody once risked his life to save me. I couldn't call myself his friend if I weren't willing to do the same.'"

Jessie laughed, marveling that he could also mimic Buzz's facial expressions. "Buzz said that even though he already realized he was just a toy and not really an invincible space ranger," Jessie joked. "Just like you, Prentice."

"Huh?"

She explained. "When I met you this summer, you always took everything so seriously. And now you've learned how to leave the responsibility to other people sometimes. You realize you're not invincible."

"Yeah, well, that's okay." He smiled, snuggling closer to her under the blanket and looked around the room with a proud grin. "Jessie says I'm a space ranger," he crowed, and she giggled.

By early evening Wednesday, while she was chopping some vegetables and Prentice was working slowly to chop pecans, Jessie heard one of Anna's texts get through. She could tell it was from her mom by the distinctive whistling song Jessie'd set for her mom's number. She put down her knife, and picking up her phone, she quickly read the text. "Oh no, Dad had a problem with the truck's air brakes, and it's delayed them getting into Durango to drop off the load."

"Where were they?"

Jessie frowned. "Near the top of Wolf Creek Pass."

He shook his head. "That is rough."

"Dad can fix anything. But that must have been nuts."

"How's the weather there? Does she say?" he asked.

"No. Maybe it hasn't hit there yet either. They're just dropping the load in Durango."

Prentice shook his head again and resumed chopping pecans.

"I guess we should keep getting ready for tomorrow, but I don't see how they're going to be back here by then, even if they get on the road early tomorrow like Dad said they would."

"I wish they would just stay put there," said Prentice. "There's no rush. We can eat dinner together any time."

WEDNESDAY, NOVEMBER 27, 2019, 4:30 P.M.

Durango, Colorado

Late afternoon, and Durango approached. It was sunnier here, and the glare made it hard to see the road. As the road veered northwest before Carbon Junction, Anna watched as David glanced down at his cell phone that he'd set on his lap. He had the volume turned down and kept glancing down from the road to see the screen. Now he pulled off one of his gloves with his teeth so he could punch the screen.

"What are you doing?" Anna asked. David never looked at his phone while he was driving, for any reason. Never. "I can hold the phone, David. That's not safe."

He grumbled something about using his phone GPS.

"Where's your truck GPS?" The little unit should have been mounted on the dashboard, but she just realized it wasn't there. "Doesn't it tell you the truck routes for getting around in town?"

He growled again and messed with the phone.

"Can I hold your phone at least so you can keep your eyes on the road?" None of this was safe, and alarm made her push him more than she meant to. "I mean, doesn't the truck GPS also help with bridge weight limits? And heights?" She'd been paying attention through the years, and all of a sudden this was more critical than it had been all day on the easy highways. Now they had to navigate in a city of 20,000 people wedged in a narrow river valley. "Remember when we came through here last time?" She paused, waiting for his answer that never came. "Where's the truck GPS, David?"

"I have no idea, Anna." He didn't look at her.

"But..."

"Could you drop it, babe? Don't you think I know how to do this?"

"But usually…"

"I drive a truck for a living, Anna." Daring her to challenge him again.

She took a breath, telling herself to let it go. That it wasn't worth ruining their whole day over. But it was harder now to ignore the mistakes, lapses, mental blanks—whatever they were. What could she do about them, anyway? And this was becoming a safety issue in several ways. The knotted muscle twinged in her back. Every single imagined explanation for his inconsistent, irritable behavior scared her.

They rumbled down the main highway, entering the south end of Durango, nestled alongside the scenic Animas River. In town, the river and topography resulted in one-way streets, low bridges, and narrow frontage roads.

When David exited the highway to enter the city collector streets, she prayed he remembered where he was going but saw a look of confusion on his face. A couple of sharper turns, one to the right followed by another to their immediate left, brought them onto a frontage road. The next second, the phone GPS thunked at him that it had to recalculate his route since he'd taken a wrong turn maneuvering the long truck along the frontage road. Noting the hard set of his jaw, she dared not break his concentration. They had come to a particularly gnarly left turn, where oncoming afternoon traffic had the right of way. The wait for a clearing seemed endless.

David drummed the steering wheel, and Anna couldn't have said why it annoyed her other than her nerves were shot, other than she had no clue what was going on. What experienced trucker forgets his GPS? Had it fallen out of the cab? Had he thrown it in the trash by accident?

She heard Casey stir and a moment later, he hopped

down to sit between them. Anna barely had time to stroke his neck before David barked, "Get ahold of him, will ya?"

She grabbed Casey's collar but didn't reply.

Finally, traffic cleared and David pulled onto the road, heading south again. He'd only gone a few hundred feet on this neighborhood street before he groaned.

Looking the same direction David was, Anna saw it. The pedestrian bridge crossed over the road a few blocks ahead. "Did you not know it was here?" she risked asking.

"It must be new since the last time I drove this way."

For a moment, there was only the low growl of the truck engine, the hammer of Anna's heart.

"I can't fit under there, can I." David wasn't asking.

Anna stayed quiet.

"Ah, nuts." He swung the wheel hard to the right so he could take a different loop and avoid the bridge. "This would'a been easier if I'd taken the next exit."

Anna bit her bottom lip and looked out the window. He'd have known about the obstacle if he had his truck GPS, since it would have rerouted the tall truck around the low bridge. David executed a series of turns in an attempt to get where he needed to go to deliver the load. As Casey struggled to keep his balance, Anna rested her hand on his neck, bracing him, absently scratching him. *What did you do with the truck GPS, David?* The question crawled through her mind.

"Here we go, Durango Regional Food Bank," he announced, with the pride of a tour guide, and the weariness of a servant.

The dull gray, one-story building didn't seem glad to see them. Neither did the entry drive. It was narrow and lined with scraggly trees and trash dumpsters. The loading bay was perpendicular to the road, as if it had been built to accommodate shorter box trucks, instead of fifty-three-foot tractor-trailer sets, and while Anna had seen David back the truck straight into a dead-end strewn with other trucks and cars before, she knew it took time and strategy.

"Maybe there's a loading dock on the other side?" Although she meant it as a suggestion, she waited for him to snap at her. But he didn't.

Parking the semi right in the middle of the street, he said, "I'll go look for the manager. It's almost 4:30 now. Hope he's still here."

Understatement.

And the sun would set in less than half an hour.

He grabbed the plastic sleeve of paperwork out of the console and left the cab. Anna watched him walk toward the desolate building. His blond hair was a little long and maybe needed a trim. Or not. She loved his unkempt hair and scruffy short beard, but it was bordering on slovenly now... Despite how tired he must be, he still walked with the strength of a farmer and the grace of a music lover.

He wore the red parka that had been his dad's on the farm. When David took his family to Mississippi, his dad gave him the parka as a parting gag gift. Nobody needs a parka in Mississippi, after all. His dad had been another jokester.

It occurred to her that the reason that parka survived the fire in August was because David still had it in his truck, even though it was summer. She wondered if he always kept it in the cab, since his truck travels took him all over North America, including cold temperatures even in the summer months.

Or was it that he just never got around to cleaning the cab at all this summer? Over the years, he'd always been so proud of the tractor and kept it in pristine condition. What was different this year? The missing truck GPS system, the absence of spare parts in the cargo box, the unwashed bedding, the lack of food in the mini-fridge... But she was so tired of her mind, grinding over worries she had no answers for, could do nothing about. To distract herself yet again, she took the logbook from the console and filled out the necessary data. Returning it to storage, she turned to Casey. "Do you want some food?"

He perked up. He knew those words. *Finally!*

Anna could almost hear him. His eagerness made her smile, eased her heart. She scooped kibble out of the bag and into his bowl and set it down for him. In about thirty seconds, it vanished. There was still no sign of David, so she attached Casey's leash to his collar and took him for a walk along the river, which was not too far away. The sight of more black, cold water made her shiver.

They were a half a block away when she heard the cursing and yelling, and her stomach tightened. Had to be coming from the warehouse. There was nothing else around. Casey stuck with her as she retraced her steps.

"I've been here for hours, waiting for your sorry butt to show up. What gives?" said a red-faced, frowning man Anna took to be the warehouse manager.

While David answered, his voice was so low, Anna couldn't hear his words.

She heard the man's reply, though, "No, I'm the only one here now. We didn't hear a word from you, so everyone else clocked out."

The manager grabbed the paperwork David gave him and made a series of sharp gestures before disappearing back into the warehouse. Standing on the sidewalk with Casey, Anna watched David climb into the truck. He got the truck aligned with the side of the building where it needed to be. But while the Pete was in perfect position, she saw that David had forgotten to open the back doors and now he was too close to the dock. He figured it out and took care of it, but he hated wasting his energy, and Anna shook her head. It was another rookie mistake, like the one with the air lines today.

It was almost dark by the time the manager finished unloading all the pallets with the forklift. The temperature dropped as soon as the sun hid behind the hills, and by this time Anna had climbed back in the cab with the dog. David still had the heat blasting, and she held her hands against the vents putting out warm air. She heard the huge warehouse door slide down. David got in, pulled forward a little, got out, and swung the Pete's rear doors closed to lock them.

"I'm glad we got here in time, before they all went home," she commented when he was back in the cab. "It sounded like he didn't know we were running late," she ventured.

"Yeah, I guess not. I didn't think of calling him with all the distractions this afternoon," he said. If getting chewed out by the warehouse manager had bothered him, he was over it now.

Anna started to say there hadn't been much cell service on top of the pass, but the truth was David could have called from Pagosa Springs. But she was getting tired of making excuses for him. *It's his job to remember things like that*, she thought. *Not mine.* At this point, she tried to convince herself it didn't matter.

Now that they were in town, she checked her phone, which she had left in the cab when she took Casey out. "Look here, David. Jessie texted me this afternoon."

"Oh good. How's she doing?" David said. "Does she miss us after twelve whole hours of us being gone?"

Anna said, "She's worried about the weather, too, honey." And she wrote back, *We just got unloaded. Running late.*

Rock out, Mom, Jessie answered. *Be careful.*

Dad's tired, Anna wrote. *But it's music time.*

Now driving again, part of the afternoon ritual was for David to turn the radio back on. Music was always a pick-me-up, but this evening, especially as they were running so late, it seemed even more important than that.

It was an emotional ballad by the Scorpions. David sang along, and as he did so, his fun self resurfaced in a way it hadn't all day. His deep voice was an octave deeper than Klaus Meine's, but he mimicked the slight German accent perfectly as he sang the plaintive words right into Anna's heart, "Here I am! Will you send... me an angel?"

She smiled and watched him sing as he drove the side streets into the center of town. It was amusing to see him as a rock star who sang wearing earmuffs. "I've always loved that song," she said. "Ever since high school. And it has so many meanings, as I get older." The hauntingly beautiful melody always echoed in her ears for hours after it played. "Here I am..."

The atmosphere in the cab was happy again, even relaxed. It wasn't just the music. Despite all his unpredictable behavior, Anna felt optimistic again about their marriage. Or at least about the evening together, which she was looking forward to. She caught herself doing it and allowed herself to hope. She told herself, *just go with it. Maybe this is how we can survive, living moment to moment.*

He kept singing and driving, but after a few moments, breaking off, he said, "Tonight, let's go with the high school meanings of the song, okay?" His voice was hoarse again, maybe with longing. "I'm glad you decided to come along with me again, Anna."

5:30 P.M.

Durango on Thanksgiving Eve was cold and dusted white in places with old snow. They headed back to the main road. One tiny home they passed had bedraggled Christmas lights turned on already. Maybe they were left over from last year. The building that used to house their favorite Mexican restaurants was now a recreational marijuana shop lit up with green and white lights. She saw the "grow" operation in the back building, complete with heavy duty aluminum fans and air filtration system to keep the worst of the rotten smell away from the neighbors.

"Gives me a headache to think about that," she commented. "Are we stopping for go-juice next?"

"Yeah. It's right up here." He began a wide right turn at the light, but despite the yellow warning label on the back of the truck declaring, "Caution: Wide Right Turns," a car snuck in on his right side where it didn't belong. David hit the brakes to not smash the guy.

He took a deep breath as the car zipped in front of them. "I hate it when they do that," he grumbled.

The guy in the sedan flashed an indelicate hand signal in his rear-view mirror. David didn't comment but pulled ahead into his turn.

After filling up with go-juice, normally he would move the truck to the rest area section of the truck stop to sleep in the cab for the night and leave the truck running to keep the diesel and sleeping area warm. But not today.

"Okay, almost home for the night," he said, smiling over

at Anna while heading straight down the main street a little farther.

She smiled back at him, and soon the Motel Durango came into view on the right. The Animas River flowed behind the motel, and she remembered stopping there in the summer, a few years ago, or maybe a decade ago, and spending delightful quality time with her husband behind the chokecherry bushes and willows one warm, starry evening. Durango had been a much smaller town then, and they had more privacy.

Another '90s song played now, "Enjoy the Silence," by Depeche Mode, shifting from major to minor key every other measure. "Words are ve—ry... unneces—sary..." sang Anna. "Remember the video for this one? With the guy walking through the mountains wearing a red robe and a crown?"

David nodded. "I heard their lead singer was very unhappy about that video concept at first. Can't imagine why." He smiled as he watched the road.

I'm so glad he feels like talking again. Words may be unnecessary, unless you really need to be communicating with each other.

She sighed as he positioned the truck in the back corner of the motel parking lot. He parked straight across about ten empty parking spaces. This was not the place most people chose to spend Thanksgiving, so there was room for the long tractor-trailer set. From her high viewpoint in the cab, she took a twilight photo of the mountain stream tumbling through town, behind the parking lot, almost invisible in the dark except for diffuse city lights highlighting the dusting of snow. She sent it in a quick text to Jessie that said, *G'night, Animas River.*

David pulled out the red knob, and the yellow one came

up by itself. Then came the very loud hissing noise of all the air brake pressure being relieved. "Good to go. Or, to stop, I should say," he laughed.

"Things you should never take for granted," Anna smiled at his lame joke, unbuckled and reached for her purse and overnight backpack. She attached Casey's leash, though he would have followed her and David anywhere, even without it, and climbed down the steps to let Casey do his business.

Before she got out, she asked, "Do you have to run the engine all night?"

"Nah, it won't be too cold for the Pete."

As for himself, it was another story. He wore his jeans, black t-shirt, old red parka with no hood, and boots. He had his earmuffs and gloves on still, too. She saw that instead of coming with her, he stood next to the Pete, looking back up as if trying to remember something.

And as they headed into the motel, she noticed David didn't bring an overnight bag inside with him. He was empty-handed.

9

6 P.M.

"**W**elcome in," said the tall, thin teenage boy working at the front desk. He wore a Durango Demons Wrestling sweatshirt and a proud expression.

"Hello," said Anna, holding Casey's leash. "We'd like a room for one night."

"Just you and your dog?" The boy was so serious, Anna wasn't sure if he were joking or not, and she was too tired to care either way. She laughed. "No, we have two adults and a dog. My husband was right behind me." She turned to look for him. "Oh, here he is. And Casey's a Good Dog. He knows how to behave."

The TV behind the teenager was scrolling through images of cars stuck in snowbanks. *Why did they say a bomb cyclone was different from a blizzard? I wasn't paying attention. Something about the air pressure, or the wind speed.* This was not something she could solve right now.

I'm glad the hotel doesn't smell like an old refrigerator. Or a locker room. She thought ahead to when they got back to Jessie's apartment tomorrow night when she would haul all the bedding inside and wash sheets while they ate turkey in their late Thanksgiving celebration. David's job or not, it needed to be done.

She waited again in the hallway for David to catch up with her and Casey. In the room, she put her purse and backpack on the nearest of the double beds. The first thing David did was turn up the heater near the window, full blast.

"Thanks, honey," she said, standing in front of her husband. "Hey, I've still got this knot in my back. Could you work on it for me a little?"

"Yeah, sure." After all these years, they had a good system for things like sore muscles. She stood in front of him and leaned her head on his chest, and he had no trouble finding the aggravated spot on her back and massaging it. She blew out some air and let her arms hang down to relax. She leaned in more and appreciated his warmth and the strong touch on her back. She breathed in his familiar smell, though his shirt did need a washing. She stood back and looked into his eyes with a smile. "I love you so much," she said.

"I love you too...." He continued to rub the muscle next to her shoulder blade.

She put her arms around him, hugged him closer, and nuzzled into his chest, more purposefully this time. She hummed the same haunting classic rock tune they'd heard at the food bank. *Send you an angel, for sure,* she thought.

"Well, let's go eat, huh?" he said, stepping back.

All of a sudden, she was nuzzling the air instead of his chest. He had backed away. "Right this minute? Really, honey?"

He smiled. "Let's take our time, babe. I don't want to hurry this night."

What can I say to that? "That's... nice."

Anna put Casey's leash back on him and the three of them went out through the lobby, David walking a few steps in front.

"Casey, now that we're outside again, could you do your other job, too? You only peed last time." He cooperated by leading her over to the grass at the back of the parking lot, and Anna picked up the evidence in a plastic bag she pulled from her parka pocket.

She felt a surge of smug revenge in handing David the bag of dog poop to drop in the outside trash can. Even though she felt guilty at the same time. "I'll be right back." She took Casey back to the room, gave him a treat, and watched him turn three circles before lying down on the carpet between the two beds. "Wait, Casey," and she went back outside.

In a minute, David and Anna had crossed the expansive parking lot behind the motel and entered a takeout barbecue restaurant. The manager must have the same taste in classic rock music they did, because the band U2 played loud on the tinny sound system. It was a song much more at home booming off a rooftop in downtown Los Angeles. Maybe the music was a treat for the staff working on the day before Thanksgiving. Almost no one else was in the restaurant. So they played "Where the Streets Have No Name" at so many decibels the glass vibrated in the windows. *Good choice instead of demeaning it by playing at unobtrusive elevator music levels.*

"What'll you have?" asked the blond teenage girl behind the counter, speaking up to be heard over the music.

The aroma of sweet, barbecued ribs warmed up the little restaurant. Anna looked at David. "The usual?" she smiled.

He looked back at her but didn't smile. "I'm trying to

remember what we usually get. Get what you want. I'm sure it'll be great."

Seriously? "Okay, honey. You must be so tired." She turned to the cashier. "How about a beef brisket, macaroni and cheese, pickles, and stewed apples?"

Only one other customer waited at the counter for her order. She was young, had spiky black short hair, dark makeup in a full circle around her eyes, and she was no taller than petite Anna. Her clothes and boots were all black, and she looked harsh at first glance, but she smiled at Anna and David as they came in, and her eyes were friendly.

While they waited, Anna thought, *Goth? Punk? Grunge? I'm out of date on the right terms.* To make up for staring at her, she struck up a conversation. "You must have ordered something fancy to still be waiting."

The young woman laughed. "It was supposed to be a quick stop, but maybe they're recharging the bubbles in the pop machine." She yawned, then stretched her arms up high above her head and then scooped them low as her feet in a graceful motion, which she repeated three times. "I've been on the road all day," she said as she straightened up. "But I delivered my shipment in time, and now I'm completely off duty!"

Out of the blue, the young woman did a little dance of joy, swinging her hips back and forth and moving her fists in front of her, in a horizontal circle, the same one professional football players do when they score a touchdown. Anna joined in right away. Celebrations with other truckers made them into friends right away. "How far did you drive?"

"From Flagstaff today. This run started in Shaky City on Tuesday." She began to stretch each arm in front of her, pulling on one wrist and then the other. "My muscles get so stiff when it's cold like this."

"Oh, I know," said Anna. "I've got a kink in my back too. We came from Pioneersburg with a load of canned goods for the food bank." She nodded toward David. "But I wasn't driving. David's the owner-operator. I'm tagging along. I'm Anna." She reached out her hand.

The lady shook her hand and replied, "Hi! I'm Lily. Nice to meet you." She appraised both of them with curiosity, but it wasn't rude, just intense. Her eyes didn't miss anything, like the bright eyes of a cat.

"Do you drive as part of a team or solo?" asked Anna.

"It's me, myself, and I," said Lily, who then stretched her arms up high and down low again. "Glad I got my load dropped before this storm."

"Where are you headed tomorrow?" asked Anna.

Lily's face crinkled in a frown. "Tomorrow? I'm not going anywhere tomorrow. I told my dispatch there was no way I could drive my trailer empty in the kinds of winds that are supposed to hit. I want to make it back to Tennessee in one piece, thank you." She looked at the ceiling. "And if I wait another day or two, the freight broker will help find a load to take with me, so I don't waste those miles dead-heading. Something almost always comes up."

"That's right, it does. They'll take their share, but that's what they get paid for." Anna looked at David and back at Lily. "And the blizzard... We're heading back to Pioneers-burg in the morning." She gave David a questioning look, wishing again he would change his mind. Trucking took more brains than brawn, but on this trip, they were getting things the wrong way around.

Lily's eyes rounded. "Are you insane? You've heard, right? Listened to the weather reports? This is not just a bliz-zard." Lily searched Anna's face. She moved her cat-like gaze to David's face. "Why don't you wait it out? What's your hurry? You're your own boss."

Anna wondered how David would respond to this direct question from this little lady. It could have come across as impertinent, but he took it as she intended it, just showing concern. He said, "It's not that far. I'm sure we'll be over the pass before the worst of it, and it'll be fine after that. Anyway, I've got another run on Friday from Pioneersburg, heading to Pittsburgh. Got to get back."

"What?" said Anna. "Oh, I should've known," she added in a disappointed tone. David's work never followed a regular schedule. "David, I didn't know about that Friday run, either. Did you tell me about it? Pittsburgh?"

"I meant to, babe. I'm sure I did." He added, then addressing both of them, "A man's gotta do what a man's gotta do."

Anna stared at her husband with a combination of discontentment mixed with gratitude that he had such an amazing work ethic. His parents had raised him right. She gave a half-smile to Lily, who had this helpful look of understanding on her face. Anna felt like she had a sister in Lily, though they'd just met.

They both picked up their bags of food from the counter at the same time. Anna asked, "What'll you do tomorrow while you're here, Lily?"

"I splurged and got a nice hotel room tonight, since I'll be here so long. I'm taking classes online to get my bookkeeping certificate. Tomorrow, maybe I can find a Nepali restaurant that's open on Thanksgiving Day. Or else I'll get something from the deli at the grocery store." She glided toward the door on graceful feet despite the big black boots, but turned back to say more to them. "It's going to be horrible tomorrow. They said the winds will be hurricane force."

Anna kept the smile on her face, but inside, her stomach churned again. "Thanks, but we promised our daughter we'd be back Thursday for Thanksgiving. And I guess David's got this other load I didn't know about." She shook her head and felt her throat get tight.

"I bet she'd understand the delay," said Lily. "I'm serious. You're nuts to go anywhere tomorrow with an empty trailer, or even a loaded one. And those winds and snow."

David said, "It's not supposed to come in until later in the day. We'll be fine. And, like I said... duty calls." He turned and headed toward the door.

"Be careful out there, Lily," said Anna, stopping to shake her hand again. She thought Lily couldn't be more than thirty years old, but she had so much confidence. *I wish I knew how to be that blunt with David. This trip is pushing me toward it, for sure.*

Lily shook her head. "I don't want to hear about you two on the news. Keep the shiny side up. No kidding." She kept smiling and shaking her head as she headed out in front of David, who held the door open for both of them.

They waved at each other as Lily headed to the upscale hotel on the other side of the parking lot. Lily's stride was as light and elegant as a cat's, but she was a skilled driver who could control a "grossed out" big truck, including keeping it off the road altogether, just to be safe.

Just to be safe, that's David's regular motto. So, what's changed, then?

6:30 P.M.

They sat on the bed closer to the window to eat their dinner. The sky outside still didn't look that threatening for November, despite the repeated forecasts. Anna wanted to bring up Lily's trucker warning, but David had heard it too. So she stuffed it. Tonight was supposed to be their vacation time, their together time, their quality time.

As they spread out the meal on the bed between them, David noticed there were no plastic forks in the bag. "Oh man, we didn't get any cut-ler-y," drawing out the fancy word to be funny. They both laughed. That felt so much better than the silences.

"I'm sure you have some plastic forks in the truck," she said. "But I don't want to go outside again. I'm feeling chilled to the bone." She rotated her arm and shoulder, trying to loosen the muscle spasm that had not gone away despite the back rub and the heater going strong.

"Let's just eat with our fingers," he said with a grin, the one she remembered from high school. She giggled and felt lighter inside. The brisket, macaroni and sticky juice from the buttered apples stuck to their fingers and their faces. They tried to get it off each other with a few kisses. Casey got to try licking their fingers, but not their faces, though he was quite willing. It was slobbery all around, without being effective.

Finally, Anna pulled her workout top over her head, dropped it next to the bed, and challenged him, "Race you to the shower." She tossed the rest of her clothes on the floor by the door, and David's ended up by the TV. A good, warm shower is an excellent cure for so many concerns, whether it's sticky fingers, or tight muscles, or too much time apart. Anna's fears about him not wanting to pay attention to her melted away as they scrubbed each other all over with lots of bubbles until they were more than clean. The bathroom mirror hid behind the cloud of steam.

They got dried off, and Anna wrapped a towel around her wet head to try to stay warm and scooted under the covers. David towel-dried his longish hair. "It's been a long time since we were all alone," he said, as he cuddled with her in the warm bed, skin to skin, promising more, but in no hurry, again.

She said, "That was one good thing about you becoming an over-the-road driver, David. When I went with you for those trips, we'd be away from my mama and our little girl, as lovely a girl as Jessie was." She nestled her head, still wrapped in the towel, under his chin and pulled up the sheet and blanket above her shoulders.

"Away from your mama," joked David. "She was a lovely lady... NOT!"

Anna agreed. They nicknamed her mama the Tiger Grandma for lots of reasons and talked and strategized about how best to cohabitate with such a fierce lady. Then, Jiexen had died just before Jessie graduated from high school. Another new chapter.

Back to their evening alone together, Anna gazed closely at David's face more than she had in months, since at Jessie's, they were only really alone in their dark bedroom. Now, she noticed his face was a little puffy along his strong jawline. *I'm no spring chicken anymore either, I guess.*

He said, "And now we're letting Jessie have her own space back, at least for a few days." He tried to get comfortable by adjusting his shoulder under her head.

Sighing, she said, "I'm so glad we got to go on our honeymoon eventually, so it could be just the two of us without the baby. It was awesome of your parents to take care of Jessie and send us on our trip after she was born."

David looked around the room at nothing. "Yep," he said, sounding distracted despite their closeness.

It felt to Anna as if he were disappearing on her again. She went on, determined to keep him with her. She reminded him of the Netherlands, where they'd honeymooned. "I thought the windmills and the way they reclaimed the land from the sea were amazing. Didn't you?" Anna's eyes were distant with the long-ago memories of themselves as a young couple. "I'd never seen anything like that growing up in San Francisco. And the long bike rides. Remember Kinderdijk?"

"Oh, yeah. Nebraska did still have a lot of historic windmills when we got married. There was one kinda near the farm, so you'd seen that one already," said David. "But we didn't go bike riding. And Nebraska's nowhere near the sea."

Anna picked up her head, undid the towel, and looked at him. "No, I meant the windmills and... what was the word? Oh, the polders, they called them."

"Who did? Polders?"

"No, polders are the land reclaimed from the sea," she said. "I learned that from your mom and dad." She went on, "The people in the Netherlands are Dutch." She threw the towel toward the bathroom door.

"I know," he said. "And Holland is one of the provinces. People get that mixed up all the time. There's North Holland and South Holland." He seemed more comfortable as he got into coaching mode again, and he squeezed Anna's shoulder. She settled back down, leaning her head on his chest with his arm behind her, and he shivered when her long, damp hair covered his chest. He massaged the sore muscle on her back. "My parents weren't from Holland, though, they were from Friesland."

Anna sat up again and turned so she could see David's

beautiful blue eyes, really see them. "Yes, honey. We lived with them for six years. I know their story." She reached out to stroke the short blond beard on his chin and pull at a strand of his damp hair that curled into his eyes.

David tried to move things along, back to the cuddly version of his wife. "Right. I got sidetracked by the Dutch thing." David seemed confused about a topic that he and his family knew more about than Anna did.

"Sidetracked? But that's what I'm talking about. Our honeymoon." She snuggled back into the covers to keep warm. "It was so kind of your parents to send us there, so I'd understand more about your whole family's history. Well, so we both would learn about it, since you'd never been there either. It was a lovely adventure." She smiled, eyes wandering up to the left as she thought about it. "Those food stands in the Alkmaar village market square, where they sold those tiny Dutch pancakes. Weren't they called poffertjes?"

"What're you talking about?"

"Poffertjes? They made them in those cast-iron pans with rows of round wells for the batter. And remember, after they flipped them out, they covered them with strawberries or powdered sugar? You ate them by the dozen." She smacked her lips. "You're making me hungry for food, instead of hungry for you, David DeGroot!"

"I'm hungry for you, too, my delicious bride." But he shook his head. "No, I mean what are you talking about, going to the Netherlands?"

She sat up, reached for her top, and pulled it on. Her stomach churned more than it had all day. "David. That was our best trip together, ever. Our honeymoon." She wanted to cry, but before she lost it, she had to tell him, "It was in 1994, two years after we got married."

"Anna, I don't know what you mean. I've never been to the Netherlands," he said, looking her right in the eyes and shaking his head. "Maybe you're talking about stuff you saw on one of those travel shows."

She tried to swallow, but her throat was tight with panic. Did he truly not remember? Was he joking with her like he did so often? She looked back into his eyes, searching. There was a flicker there that might have been panic in him, too. "David, don't you remember?"

He shook his head and kept his eyes locked with hers. She'd never seen him this serious. "Remember what, Anna?"

She reached up to trace the side of his jaw, the blond stubble. Tears sprang to her eyes, but she couldn't answer his question again when he was being so dense. *What do you mean, don't you remember going to the Netherlands with me?*

She climbed out of bed and rummaged in her backpack for her pajama pants. She sat on the edge of the bed closer to the door, where she had piled her bag and their coats. She picked up the carryout cup from dinner and sipped the last slurps of the pop.

It was mostly ice water now.

Like the feeling in her stomach.

Her eyes felt so heavy.

"Hey, where'd you go?" he asked.

Right, where did you go, David? She said nothing.

Casey noticed there was a vacancy in the bed, so he jumped up to the warm spot next to David, who scratched his ears but kept watching his wife, who stayed seated on the other bed, stared at nothing, and then switched to stare right at David, for an uncomfortably long time.

Nobody talked.

~

8 P.M.

Anna thought, *I don't know how to react to this. I'm stuck.*

David was still in the bed, with nothing on but the sheets and blanket pulled up to his neck, still looking a little chilled despite the warm shower. He picked up the remote and switched on the TV to fill up the silence in the room. Anna still sat on the edge of the other bed.

Good idea, thought Anna. *At least he's as uncomfortable as I am now.*

The TV showed the national weather channel. "A powerful storm will produce widespread heavy snow in parts of the western and central U.S., the National Weather Service says," said the announcer, who was reporting from some sunny environment that had no risk of a snowstorm.

"Hurricane-force winds, blizzard conditions, heavy snowfall — and a bomb cyclone are the dire predictions of weather forecasters who are warning Thanksgiving travelers to be cautious and prepare for delays," he said.

"The National Weather Service's U.S. forecast map is draped in alarming shades of pink, purple and red, reflecting winter storm warnings in effect from California to the Midwest. The winter storm warning posted by the NWS office in Las Vegas will remain in effect through 4 a.m. Pacific time on Saturday."

Anna glanced at David during the report to see how he took it. She didn't comment on the announcer's stern words, but inside her, the reality of their situation made her stomach hurt. She still didn't have a way to change David's mind about the travel plans, though denying it would be dangerous. Watching his face during the weather report told her it hadn't impacted him either.

Attempting to push it out of her mind, in hopes she could actually fall asleep tonight instead of staying awake worrying, she got up to brush her teeth and towel dry her hair some more. But the concern inside her wouldn't go away. David's unpredictable reactions, bad choices, memory lapses... it just didn't add up to anything good.

On top of that, the forecaster's voice carried to her, announcing ever more dire warnings of heavy snowfall west of them, moving east. The Utah Department of Transportation was implementing road safety closures due to adverse weather and treacherous road conditions for Thursday and Friday. Forecasts for additional heavy accumulations of snow, high winds, blowing snow, and low visibility warned of upcoming hazardous travel conditions.

She felt so torn inside. Wanting to lean on David and trust his judgment, but the evidence of the last few days weighed heavily on her. Normally, he was strict about safety, however, he'd failed to be with her during her most disastrous times. Not that it was his fault he was gone during the hurricane and the wildfire. It wasn't his idea to bring her domineering mama to live with them.

But why couldn't he remember personal things about their life together? That was more of an abandonment than the other ones, in her heart, because it put their whole relationship in doubt. They'd promised their lives to each other, through good and bad, sickness and health. *I have to keep trying.*

She returned to the edge of the bed where he was, with Casey between them. David changed the channel to an old western, the kind where the cowboys were all good guys who could do no wrong. Anna felt like it was ridiculous to watch shows like this in Colorado, a state where the "other" side of history was in evidence in every town, park, or river with a Ute or other native American name. The cowboys and settlers had taken over their land. At least Utah commemorated the "Ute" people, but even that name came from an Apache name for the Navajo people. *The winners get to write the history books.*

A quote from the princess movie surfaced in her mind. "Life is pain, highness." It sure was, right now. She had so many conflicting emotions inside her battling it out, and the result was a tightness in her belly and the muscle in her back. She prayed for peace in whatever form it might take.

Meanwhile, he channel-surfed in search of something worth watching, pausing for longer than he normally would have on the home and garden channel, where they were doing something about making a garage look spiffier.

She saw frustration in his face as he gave up and turned it off.

She spoke, "Aren't you going to get cleaned up and some PJs on?" *Oh my gosh, why am I nagging him? Stop it, Anna.*

But maybe watching some TV had helped him, since he shook his head and then grinned at her, which was a welcome surprise. "Nah, I didn't bring my bag inside. I'll sleep like this." He made a goofy expression as he lifted the blankets and gestured up and down at his tall, good-looking, unclothed self. He was in pretty good shape for a middle-aged trucker, despite the lack of attention to his appearance lately.

Did he even have a bag with him? She doubted it. Was he okay, or was he falling apart? Forgetting to fill out the logbook. Losing the truck GPS. What if we break down tomorrow and he doesn't have the right parts again? What if he forgets how to drive the truck, or steers us right over the edge? He forgot our honeymoon. What if he forgets he has a wife at all? So much for peace. A stubborn block of stress filled her chest.

She could not control his actions, only her own. *He's a big boy. Whatever is going on, I can't solve this for him. But I can't give up, either.*

So, she didn't go sleep in the other bed, as she could have. Instead, Anna nudged Casey out of the bed and scooted under the covers next to her husband. They fell asleep holding each other, but not like they'd meant to. Sleeping together without sleeping together.

It hit her like a ton of bricks. One day, they would be permanently separated. She'd never thought about it literally, but the wedding vows said, "In sickness and in health, 'til death do us part."

10

THURSDAY, NOVEMBER 28, 2019, 6 A.M., DURANGO, COLORADO

They should have left hours ago, but they were still fast asleep. Lucky for them, whoever had stayed in this motel room last had set the clock radio, and it turned itself on at high volume at six a.m. David groaned from under the covers, and Anna snuggled closer to him, forgetting where they were.

No talk about Thanksgiving or festivities on this local radio station. Reality bombarded them as soon as the field reporter's crystal clear alto voice said, "This time, the strong differences in temperature between a warm subtropical air mass and a cold Arctic one to the north will cause a bomb cyclone."

Anna kept her eyes closed but turned toward the radio so she could listen. She wished the alarm hadn't sounded at all, so they might've accidentally slept for hours and would have had no choice but to hang out here another day.

"The mid-Mississippi Valley could get tornadoes, while Kansas and Nebraska could see severe hail, the National Weather Service's Storm Prediction Center said. Between one and two feet of snow could fall in some areas of

Colorado, Wyoming, Montana, Nebraska, and the Dakotas," the lady said.

David fumbled around in the dark, trying to turn the radio off.

Anna said in a sleepy voice, "That's a big area!"

The announcer continued. "It's extremely rare for the Plains region to experience a bomb cyclone. It takes an unusually large air temperature difference over land for such a disturbance to take place, but this one has such low pressure, it's already breaking records in Colorado, according to the NWS."

David growled, hitting the buttons blindly with his whole hand, but it didn't shut off the radio. "Oh-you've-gotta-be-kidding-me."

It was an extended special report, and the no-nonsense announcer kept talking. "It's important to stress: Winter weather is very dangerous. Cold temperatures and high winds are a recipe for frostbite and hypothermia. Hospitals routinely see an up-tick in admissions for cold-related symptoms and heart problems in the days after a snow-storm. And then there's traffic: About 800 people die in cold weather-related traffic accidents every year."

David's arm reached past the alarm clock now, following the cord behind it toward the outlet. "Almost there!" he triumphed.

"The National Weather Service is advising residents of Utah, Colorado, Nebraska, and Kansas to cancel all travel plans today. Blizzard conditions are expected from the central mountains across the central and northern Plains. Travel will be dangerous, if not impossible. So, as we wrap up these last days of autumn with this winter-like storm, stay warm, stay off the roads–"

David finally had a good enough hold on the clock

radio's cord to rip it right out of the outlet, silencing the woman's voice. He'd had to scoot out of the covers to mess with the cord, so his whole naked backside stuck out into the cold air of the room. He scrunched himself back down next to Anna under the sheet and blanket.

"Brr! It's cold out there!" he complained, sliding closer to her. "I just can't seem to get warmed up lately."

"Good morning, honey," she said. *Cancel all travel plans?* "How are you feeling this morning?"

"Hey Anna, really good sleep," he said warmly. "How'd you sleep?"

"Really hard. That was a long day yesterday." *That was one of the longest days of my life,* she thought. *Except for the hurricane.* It still wasn't funny that he didn't remember going to the Netherlands. Going there had been his idea, and his parents had been so pleased about him showing interest in their family heritage after all the years of dairy farming in Nebraska. She asked, "Are you sure we should still try this today?"

"Well, yes, if by 'this' you mean 'this!'" He lifted the covers on her side and looked her up and down in an affirming way with his blue eyes. "You're still all dressed? Can we do something about that before we go?" He lowered the blanket and tugged gently at the hem of her top while giving her a delicious smile.

She scrunched the messy blond hair on top of his head and rubbed the blondish gray stubble along his jaw. He nuzzled her nose with his own and made warm noises.

Maybe I need to keep my priorities in order. She wrapped her arms around his neck, and they helped each other wake up in a much better mood than they'd been in when they fell asleep last night. *Let's just hide here all day.*

Casey was the one who got them into gear. After his

masters had ignored him for too long, he stood up and rested his head on the edge of the bed, staring at them with deep brown, laser-focused eyes until they laughed and paid attention to him. Anna got up, put her pajamas back on and took a scoop of food from the zip lock. She snagged the thin plastic bag from last night's restaurant meal to keep for doggie duty later on.

Casey ate his breakfast while his masters took a quick shower. David put on the same jeans and long-sleeved cotton shirt he'd worn yesterday, and he put on his earmuffs and gloves, though he was still inside.

She packed up the few things she'd brought into the room and tried again to get him to stay in Durango today, like Lily planned to do.

"David, we could call Jessie and tell her we'll see her Friday?"

"Babe, I've got the Pensacola run on Friday."

She shooshed out a breath of air. "Can't someone else take it?" Wait a minute. "Didn't you say Pittsburgh before? Not Pensacola?"

He stood his ground. "Babe, if I start bailing on people, word will get around and they'll stop giving me work. No. I told them I'll be there Friday for that load, and I will."

"But this storm... We could just spend the whole day together." She and Casey followed him from the room.

"I said no, and that's final," he told her, and turning his back, he took off toward the lobby.

Anna's mouth dropped open as she watched him stride off. *I know he doesn't hate me. He loves me. But...he's not making sense.* What did it mean? Attempting a smaller win next, she called after him. "David? Maybe the front desk could give you a toothbrush?"

He surprised her by turning and agreeing. "Yeah. Okay.

Sorry about that morning breath, babe. I'll do that and meet you in the truck, okay?"

It was an insignificant victory, but at least he listened to her about one small thing. The smell of breakfast cooking coming from the motel kitchen made her feel slightly better, but she still felt uneasy about the day. "Great, I'll take Casey out." Then she specified, not quite trusting him, "Will you get us some breakfast, maybe some hard-boiled eggs and pastries? And sausage?"

"Hot drinks for the road? Tea for you, coffee for me."

She nodded. "Sure, that sounds perfect," she said, but he was already asking the desk clerk about the toothbrush.

The TV in the breakfast area blabbed on about this snowstorm. Anna cocked her head to listen for a second. *There's nothing we can do about it. David says we just need to get over Wolf Creek Pass, and that will make all the difference.*

How do I question him without it sounding like a criticism?

6:30 A.M.

Out in the parking lot, the sky didn't appear threatening. The same light snow from yesterday had hardened to a glittery dust on the hoods of the cars, the air was still humid and as white as the sky. But she wasn't comforted.

Watching Casey poke his nose here and there, she said, "Casey, you're a Good Dog!" she told him, collecting the results in a baggie and throwing it in the trash can. He followed her to the Pete and flew up into the cab, going straight to his wonderfully aromatic bed. Casey was the only one that could appreciate it. Anna wrinkled her nose against the smell. A blast of chilly air from the driver's side whooshed in at her as David climbed into the cab, handing her the foam breakfast box and coffee cups. She stowed them on the console as he started the truck's diesel engine to warm it up and get the air pressure to at least 60 PSI so the brakes could unlock.

"Honey," she said, hazarding a glance at him, "didn't you say you had some clean clothes stored in here?"

"Oh, maybe so," he answered congenially enough, but he didn't make a move to find his bag or get changed, though, as they sat waiting for the truck to be ready to go. *He just totally blew me off,* she thought. *Doesn't he care that he smells like a... I don't know.* She wondered if he needed a visit to the doctor to check on his sense of smell... and the memory problems.

The brakes hissed as David released them, pressed the clutch, and put the Pete into first gear. He headed back the way they came yesterday. The city streets were empty due to the Thanksgiving holiday and the storm warnings, but Anna felt his impatience to get to the open highway and crunch some miles. She was anxious for that too, resigned to it. The quicker they got over the passes and up the inter-state, the better, since she couldn't get him to hole up today.

The sky was low with clouds, but the air was clear as they reached the highway and headed east. David turned the heat up high. Anna felt it blast her face, dry and too warm. She looked out the passenger window, biting into a pastry. It wasn't worth arguing over. She just wanted to beat the storm home, then she'd deal with whatever this was, the bad thing that seemed to be happening—to her husband, to her marriage.

Picking up what she thought was her hot tea, she took a sip and wrinkled her nose. It was black coffee, David's drink.

Setting it down, she got the other cup, and took a bigger sip, but it was bitter coffee, too. She looked at David.

"Did you know you got me coffee instead of tea?"

He frowned. "Don't you like it? I guess motel coffee is not the best."

"But you know I only drink coffee when there's nothing else." She took another dubious sip and made a face. Too late now. "Is there still powdered milk in the cupboard?"

"How should I know? Anyway, I come from a long line of dairy farmers. Why would I have powdered milk?" he joked.

Unbuckling her seat belt as they drove, Anna shifted around and began opening cupboards, hunting for sugar in addition to the dry milk, anything she could use to doctor the disgusting liquid. She found the soup, chocolate bar, the remains of the pumpkin pie she'd hacked a chunk out of, but not much else. A plastic zip bag contained a bit of milk powder and a few old sugar packets, enough to make the coffee palatable. At least it was warming her up. She knew she had stocked tea bags in the cab this spring. Who knew, though, what he'd done with them? Maybe Jessie drank tea when she met up with him in Maryland. Or maybe not. Hot tea, in the summer, in Maryland?

Or maybe while I was in Colorado trying to get our house rebuilt, he was with some other lady who preferred tea to coffee, just like I do.

The knot behind her shoulder blade tightened. Was he cheating on her? She glanced at him, his hair sticking up every which way, the rumpled smelly clothes. Did he only clean himself up now for someone else? She wanted to say the words, demand the answers, but she closed her teeth against them. They couldn't have that discussion now. They had to get over Wolf Creek Pass and La Veta Pass. They had to get home. Then...then she would have it out with him. It was for sure she couldn't go on like this.

To distract herself, she... she just realized how much she needed to distract herself on this trip, and it made her stomach hurt again. Everything she had learned about self-care started with acknowledging what was happening. So, noticing that she was doing this was a step, at least, and she thanked God for the grace to let her figure this out.

Consequently, it was with purpose that she got her purse from the cubby above her and pulled out her cell phone. She tapped out a text to Jessie, thanking her for the loan of her snow boots and wishing her a Happy Thanksgiving, but hitting send, she realized they had already driven out of cell range and wouldn't have it again until Pagosa Springs. She put her phone into airplane mode so it wouldn't run down the battery looking for service in the meantime.

"The mountains aren't brown this morning," she said against the chill in her heart. "Not like they were yesterday." She tried one more sip of the bitter coffee. "They've had some snow overnight."

"We'll be on the other side of the storm before you know it," he said.

"You can't know that," she said, wondering if it would aggravate him. But maybe she wanted that. "It hasn't even started yet," she went on. "They said it would hit like a ton of bricks when it comes."

"Babe, stick with me." He grinned at her as if everything was normal, ordinary when every cell, every pore of her was screaming how wrong his thinking was, how off he was. Along the roadside, she spotted a sign, bordered in flashing yellow lights: *Icy conditions may exist.* Anna read it as they whizzed past. And worse, she thought. Worse things might exist.

~

Spring, 1980, Anna's kindergarten memory, Chinatown, San Francisco, California

Part 3

She worked hard to learn English. She wanted to talk the way Teacher did. Every day, she tried so hard to do what Teacher said so she could be done with school. But when Teacher read her papers, she shook her head and wrote on them with red ink.

And when Anna said, "I smart girl," Teacher smiled with her mouth, but her eyes were sad.

Teacher said, "No, you *are* a smart girl."

Anna brightened, repeating, "Yes, I smart girl."

Teacher shook her head and said, "No, I *am* a smart girl."

It didn't make sense. Isn't that what she'd said? Or maybe Teacher was bragging about how smart she was and how stupid Anna was? Teacher was really a nice lady, but why would she make a little girl feel bad?

All day she learned English letters and words, and Teacher read stories about Dick and Jane, and snowmen, and maple syrup. Anna didn't understand all the words. Neither did a lot of her classmates. They glanced at each other sometimes when Teacher and the other kids laughed at a joke made of words that they didn't get. What's a Pilgrim?

Another day in January, Teacher was all excited about last night's hockey game. She called it the "1980 miracle on ice." Anna wished she could ask more questions, but it all went by too fast. Hockey? Ice? Olympics? Then Teacher moved on to a new subject. George Washington. And then how to write more letters in uppercase and lowercase.

Maybe it didn't matter. It was hard to know what she heard about at school that she must remember for Teacher and what was just for talking about for no reason.

At recess, Anna ran fast to be first on the swings so she could sail above the playground and get glimpses of the blue water she could not touch. Sometimes the water was covered with white fog, but she knew it was still there. Her pigtails flew behind her head on the upswing and then into her face on the downswing.

And if the ground shook again, she would be safe, up high on her swing.

One day, after many months, Teacher sent home a paper about the School Open House. "We invite all your parents to come. We'll show them all you've been learning this year, and your artwork, and how you're learning your letters. All the information is there on the paper. See you then!" Teacher was so excited about School Open House. Anna was too.

But at home, when Anna pulled her paper out of the backpack, Mama studied it, pointing at the words and reading them to herself. Then she said, "I no have time for this. You just learn and be smart girl. I stay here and work."

The day after School Open House, many of her classmates found notes and prizes that parents had tucked inside their desks when they had visited the classroom. Anna wondered what the notes said that the parents couldn't just say at home?

She worked so hard to learn, and Teacher smiled at her each day. Now she could sing the alphabet song with the other children. She lined up for recess. She raised her hand when she had to go to the bathroom. She learned words and numbers and math and Abraham Lincoln.

The path to and from school became familiar as the months went by. The very old lady with curly white hair would look up from her sewing machine and make eye contact through the window as Anna went by. The round-shaped young man who sold things under a white awning smiled at her. She could read the word "beer" now, but she didn't know what it was. She dipped her chin at them as Mama taught her, but no more interaction was needed.

A white cat lived near the school, and she saw it in the afternoons when she headed down the hill. Once she got close to it and could almost touch it. She spent a long minute looking into the deep green eyes of the cat. Maybe she could pet it? It turned and ran into the alley. She followed, but it disappeared. Anna realized this alley had no outlet, no road going out. The cat was gone.

She stuck out her lower lip, turned around, and went home to help Mama. Maybe the cat didn't think she was a smart girl, either.

One day at school, a wonderful thing happened. Teacher told a joke in English, and Anna understood it all and laughed with all the other children! It meant she was really learning. She wanted to tell Mama the joke, but she could not work up the courage.

In the spring, Teacher brought forth another mystery: Report Card Day. Every student got a white envelope. Anna tucked her Report Card into the blue backpack with pride. In it, Teacher would tell Mama and Baa how much she was learning at school!

Anna evaded the usual car and foot traffic on her way back home to the shop, tucked between the dragon fortune teller and a bakery.

... Oh, the bakery! Pineapple buns stuffed with sweet guava butter tantalized her senses. She tried not to look at the window filled with egg custard tarts or white lotus seed moon cakes. The bakery sold them all year long and other people bought them every day, but Mama said those treats were only for the Mid-Autumn Festival, which was months away. She said Christ-followers could blend in with everyone celebrating and eating moon cakes, giving thanks for the harvest and worshiping the moon, "But we praise God and his creation."

No use trying to convince Mama to have a moon cake now, even though today was Report Card Day, a day to celebrate for sure. She walked the last block past the bakery to the yummy noodle shop, her small thumbs jammed behind the backpack straps on her tiny shoulders, thinking about how proud Mama would be that Anna got her Report Card from Teacher.

"Mama, look," she said as she got inside. She reached into her little backpack to get the prize to show Mama.

"Go wash hands, forgetful girl."

Anna did, then returned to Mama, who spent several minutes scrutinizing the card, holding it closer, then farther, from her eyes. Her face turned angry.

"Why this say you not know English?"

Anna was confused and shook her head. She did know English and so many other things now. That wasn't right. What did the Report Card say?

Mama jabbed the card with her finger. "Why this say 'English Language need improvement'? Why you no work hard for Teacher? You not smart girl!"

Anna's breath caught in her throat. Her eyes burned with tears that fell out of her eyes and slid down her cheeks.

"No, Mama." *That could not be right.* Teacher loved her. Anna understood her jokes, her words.

"What you mean, 'No, Mama'?" she shouted. "This say 'need improvement.' You go to room. No dinner for you."

As she put one small foot on a stair step and lifted her little body to the next one, it seemed to her that someone had added more steps between the kitchen and their upstairs room. *Maybe I am not a smart girl.* Her dolly got all wet from Anna's tears.

11

THURSDAY, NOVEMBER 28, 2019, 7:45 A.M., WEST OF PAGOSA SPRINGS, COLORADO

A deep male voice crackled over the CB radio. "Hello Highway 160," the trucker said. "Treefrog here. Anybody got your ears on?" Pause. "Downstroke on west side of Wolf Creek Pass." That meant he was descending toward them. "Rockslide on the road about five miles east of Pagosa Springs," he announced. "Bears on scene. Get ready to back it down in both directions when you get east of Pagosa."

She unzipped her parka. Though for the last twenty years, David kept the cab chillier than she liked, today he had it toasty again. So many things to wonder about, but why should she question him about his new habit of now keeping the cab at a comfortable temperature?

When David didn't reach for the mic to respond, Anna did. "Treefrog, this is Art Mama. Do you copy?"

"Art Mama, come on. What's your 20?"

"Thanks for the 2-1-1 about the rockslide, Treefrog. We're in Archuleta County on 160, heading east. We just passed Haystack Mountain, so we're almost to Nutria."

"Copy that. Heading right toward you on 160. Happy Thanksgiving. By the way, any idea why they'd name a place after an invasive rodent?"

His question was so unexpected, and she laughed. "No idea, Treefrog. What're you talking about?"

"Nutria. It's an invasive rodent."

"Tree Frog, it's too early in the morning for this," she bantered.

"Sorry about that. How's your morning going, Art Mama?"

"Fine so far, but I have to ask you, did you climb Wolf Creek Pass in the dark? It's so early to be on the downhill side already."

"Yes ma'am, I slept in my berth in South Fork and got going super early this morning. Wanted to be over the pass and home to Gallup before the storm hit."

"You're not too far, then. Just a few more hours for you, Treefrog. Can you give me the 10-13 on the weather in your part of Archuleta County?"

"Art Mama, it was not bad a few hours ago, but if you're heading in there now, you're in for it."

"Thanks for the local info. There's a mountain in the way so we can't ask the guys on the other side yet, can we?" She knew the answer. She was joking.

"Negative, Art Mama. Are you driving that rig? Why don't you take the day off and let the storm blow over you instead of blowing you over?"

Anna grimaced, glanced at David, and replied. "Treefrog, it's my husband driving. We're in a 379 Pete, white dry box. See you soon, and thanks from Art Mama and Dutch Boy, good neighbor."

"I'm a black Come-a-part Engine," he said, referring to

his Cummins engine. "Hey, come again?" he questioned. "You said you're in a dry box on a windy day like this?"

"Affirmative, Tree Frog."

"This would be a good day to tell dispatch to go... ah, to reschedule your load."

"Pree-she-ate-it, Tree Frog, but Dutch Boy is the O-O, and he has a load for Friday scheduled." Anna looked at David as she answered, but Owner-Operator David didn't appear to be listening.

"Be safe, Driver. Catch you on the flip-flop, Art Mama."

Anna hung up the mic and hoped for some sign from her Dutch Boy that he'd heard anything. But he stayed quiet.

The miles peeled away, heading toward the Great Divide.

Soon, their old white Peterbilt passed Treefrog's black Cummins coming the other way, and when David honked the air horn at Treefrog, Anna was glad to know he'd been listening after all. So, was he worried? *You're in for it*, Treefrog had said. *Get dispatch to reschedule*, he'd said.

Anna remembered other trips in bad weather that had delayed David exactly because he did pull off the highway for safety, and he even scoffed at the idiots who continued to drive.

It wasn't just his wife that David was ignoring. He also wasn't paying attention to the warnings from the media, or fellow truckers. That made her feel more scared, on one hand. On the other hand, it was a relief that he ignored them as well as her. It confirmed the problem was not just with her.

But that meant the problem was with him, and she didn't have a way to help him figure it out. Until they could get home and see a doctor. Or a pastor.

The sky got grayer, and the wind picked up. Anna saw a flock of wild turkeys huddled in the trees along the side of the highway. Snowflakes in the air obscured them from clear view.

She wasn't aware of it when she fell into a doze. It was the sulfurous smell as they hurtled through Pagosa Springs that woke her up as it had yesterday. Immediately, she straightened, got her phone, and fired off the text to Jessie.

Mom, where R U? Jessie's reply came at once.

Pagosa Springs. I'll check in at Alamosa.

We've got the turkey in the sink.

Anna wrote, *Thanks. I saw some snow just now, but just flurries. Can't wait.*

Jessie might have responded, but Anna lost service. A bit later, they got to the rock slide that Tree Frog had warned them was blocking the westbound lane. State patrol was set up on both sides and signaled when they could proceed through the remaining lane. Rocks the size from grapes to grapefruits and watermelons were scattered across that eastbound lane, but it was, thankfully, passable.

Or, she wondered, maybe it would be better if they stopped us here and made them stay in Pagosa today.

Wolf Creek Pass loomed above them through the gathering gloom, and David focused all his attention on the curves in the road, the steep grade, and keeping the truck in the right gear. He turned off the CB radio, and she knew it was so he could hear the sounds of the engine and the Jake brake. No passenger cars zipped around them when they came to the passing lane. They must have been the only vehicle on the road.

They reached the Continental Divide and Anna recognized the spot where they'd broken down yesterday, and then the ski area, which she noticed was less crowded than it usually would have been on a holiday. Actually, the parking lot was almost deserted. While the silence in the cab was deafening to Anna, she didn't break it and neither did David.

A few snowflakes were definitely swirling when they reached the bottom of Wolf Creek, the first of today's two passes, just before 10 a.m. The parking lot of the remote Cozy Conifer Lodge was half full already. Odd, Anna thought. "Maybe they're doing a Thanksgiving brunch as well as dinner," she said, and the sound of her own voice was almost startling.

"Yeah, maybe," David readily answered, as if they'd been speaking to one another all these many miles.

Encouraged, Anna said, "I know the storm hasn't started yet, but I see some snow. Maybe we could stop and ask if we could stay here."

"Babe," he said. "We're over Wolf Creek now, and it's barely even snowing. See?"

A series of strong wind gusts, full of snowflakes, hit the truck.

She would not look at the swirling snow. She closed her eyes for a while and did not say anything. David was the most kind-hearted, careful, wise man she'd ever met, and yet sometimes his words still hurt, dismissing her ideas time after time. Maybe the problem wasn't him after all. Maybe it was her.

Maybe I'm just not a smart girl.

~

THURSDAY, NOVEMBER 28, 2019, 9:45 A.M.

South Fork, Colorado

South Fork was the town east of the little lodge. The truck shot straight past it into the wide, flat, windswept valley when she could stand the silence no longer. "So, what do you think of Prentice?" she asked as if it mattered, with all the rough ground between them and her suspicion. She needed a neutral topic of conversation.

"He's a good kid, seems to me," he answered. "I haven't spent too much time around him."

Before she could respond, another ferocious gust of wind slammed into the Pete, pushing the truck broadside. David's grip on the wheel was white-knuckled as he fought to control the fifty-three foot semi with just his two hands. Anna felt David reduce his road speed. Although her heart was pounding, she tried not to show her alarm, and taking up the thread of the conversation, she said, "No, I guess you haven't. He's over at Jessie's a lot, but you haven't been there too much either."

"Nope. The less I'm on the road, the less I make."

"It's always been like that," she said, trying to make it sound funny, but it came out wrong. "You, on the road, making money. You, staying home, not making money." And if he stopped driving altogether for some reason, he would make no money at all unless he listened to one of her ideas about a new career. What were the odds of that, at this rate?

He tried to lighten things up, though he was completely serious on this next point. "Staying on the road more, that reminds me, you know that's why you should never drink out of a Gatorade bottle that has been stored in my truck, right?"

"Oh, gross." She made a face, thinking about a bottle's alternative use as a urinal. "Yes, I bet that cuts down on the number of female truckers." She froze at that new realization. He might be having an affair with a lady *who was a trucker*. She hadn't thought of that before, and it made her shudder inside. What if that was the cause of the financial trouble, and all his spacey behavior? She forced herself to keep talking in a light tone. "I'm sure it cuts into the profit margin when the women have to pull over to stop for a bathroom when you guys can just... keep on going," she trailed off.

She watched out the window, not that she could see much as the air filled with fresh falling snow. New snow falling. The storm was upon them. Just like inside her, the storm of worry about him was taking over her whole body.

Another big wind gust rocked them sideways and filled the cab with the sound of buffeting turbulence.

"Oh, my gosh!" she said, reaching toward the chrome door handle but diverting her hand up to the door itself. "I wonder how strong that was. Woah!"

David pushed on but kept his speed down. His hands still gripped the wheel tight, and she wondered how he had the energy to do this day after day. Year after year. She said, "Honey, I probably don't tell you enough how proud of you I am. For all the miles you drive." He nodded, and she saw his body relax slightly, as if her words gave him energy. She continued, "It's not what you were raised to do. Trucking's a big change from dairy farming, like your dad taught you growing up..." Maybe if she could get him on a comfortable topic, it would help.

He did seem interested. "We could never leave home when those cows needed us to show up twice a day for milking, every day, no matter what. Sun, rain, or a Nebraska blizzard. We could hardly go anywhere."

"It's a miracle I ever met you in San Francisco, David.

Your parents must have had to arrange so much to be able to take all of you boys on that big vacation to California."

He agreed. "They didn't get to travel much in the U.S., but that was one place on their list." He nodded as he thought about it. "That spring, for our trip to California, they hired a neighbor to be a cow sitter so we could all leave for a week. And we got to go on the Grand DeGroot Family Vacation."

Anna smiled. "And that was the last one ever for just your family, because that summer I showed up and stole you away."

He was getting almost conversational. "Well, you didn't steal me. They got to keep me, or us, I guess, until I figured out the best way to get us out of there and on our own with the baby."

"You really led the way, David." She shook her head at his literal reply. "You know what I mean. Good thing your brothers liked cows more than you did. So someone would stay and run the farm with your dad."

"You can say that again. I hate cows."

She saw the opportunity to ask again about the idea that had been brewing in her imagination: quitting long-distance trucking. *When I brought it up the other night, it was a no-go, but I have to try again.* "But what about being home more? Would you consider changing to a dispatch job, or mechanic work, or a yard jockey? Instead of over-the-road? Or even day work? So we could be together more?"

He didn't answer for a while. "Being an O-O is hard work. You're right. But would sure be a big adjustment. I like the freedom of driving, Anna. Nobody checking on me..."

She joked, "except for the guy at the weigh station who checks your logbook... and me! I check on when you put the money in the bank, and I'm in charge of spending it." She forced a laugh.

"That's worked out great. I hate paying bills."

Me too, she sighed, "I still don't understand why the money's not coming out even lately. I'm keeping tabs on the bills." She wondered why the conversation always got back to money. "You're working so hard, but it feels like we're still short."

"Nah, we're doing fine."

How could he say that when he never looked at the checking account? "Really David, I think I've gotten our finances in a mess somehow. Especially this year. Maybe I've missed something—" She broke off when the wind came at them again. She felt the empty trailer lift, felt like it was trying to get into the lane beside them, which made her grip the door handle. She somehow found her voice and managed to keep her fear out of it. "Luckily, it's Thanksgiving, and only a few people are out on the road. Less traffic for us to blow into..." she trailed off. Her mouth was dry.

She looked at David, who was grim again, then back through the windshield where the snowfall had thickened into a white film that partially obscured her view. Soon the road changed color from gray to white. Peering through the icy fog, she hunted for the mountains that had been visible just moments ago but had now disappeared—like the road. She realized with a sharp intake of breath that the road was gone, too. There was no sign of the pavement at all. In such a short time. "It's the bomb cyclone." Had she spoken aloud? If she had, David didn't answer.

Within half an hour, the snowflakes morphed from wet cement into the whitest, most ferocious blowing blizzard conditions Anna had ever seen.

The truck barreled through Del Norte. It was like driving through a white tunnel now.

More long minutes ticked by, they approached Alamosa. There might be cell service here, so she sent another text to Jessie.

Any stops would slow them down, delaying their progress. Was David ever going to stop driving, trying to outrun the storm bearing down on them in the wide, windy valley? She wanted to stop making progress altogether. She wanted to just park the truck in a safe spot and wait out the storm.

No, no stopping. No lunch stop on the horizon. Anna's mouth watered, thinking about the rest of that pie. Her brain thought it would taste good, but her stomach, still tense with worry, did not agree with the idea. Too much chaos, too little order.

Today the valley was windier than she'd ever seen it on all their previous trips. "A bomb cyclone," she remembered the description from the radio, "occurs through the process known as bombogenesis, when a weather system drops pressure very, very quickly. That means storms intensify and spin counterclockwise and wind speeds can approach eighty miles per hour."

The snow today was getting crazier every minute.

And it's now on top of us. It's bigger than all of us. We're just puny humans in a world being swallowed up in a winter hurricane.

~

THURSDAY, NOVEMBER 28, 2019, 10:30 A.M.

Del Norte, Colorado

Anna turned the radio back on for a while, hoping for

music to soothe their raw nerves, but instead the weather warnings kept coming in between each set of songs.

"Travelers are urged to visit COtrip.org for road closure information..."

And, "A CDOT operator bulldozing through several feet of snow in western Colorado this morning triggered an avalanche. The plow was buried but not swept off the road. Rescue crews are on the scene...."

"Well, that's west of us," David said.

And, "The Colorado Avalanche Information Center has issued a High Avalanche Watch for the entire San Juan Mountain Range, Wet Mountains, and Sangre de Cristos."

"That's west of us," David repeated it as if it were law, as if they were invincible.

Not only that, he was wrong. The San Juans and Wolf Creek were west, but the other mountains and La Veta Pass were still east of them. Another hundred miles of danger before Walsenburg, but he wouldn't listen. She forced her mind to shut down, the way she used to close herself off from the world when her mama yelled at her and there was nothing she could do but endure the fear.

Gust after gust of wind hit the back and sides of the truck. Anna felt the world shift as the trailer tried to fly off the ground, sideways. They plowed on through Blanca. David gripped the wheel, not taking his eyes off the highway. *I don't think we've seen another car or truck in hours.*

They would reach Fort Garland soon, Anna thought, where they'd stopped yesterday to stretch their legs, get drinks, and use the wi-fi. The turnoff was only a few miles ahead. Surely, David would take it. She turned to him. "We should pull off here and park until the worst of this is over."

As they neared the town, Anna swiped her phone open, typed another text to Jessie as she had promised she'd keep doing. She turned off airplane mode to search for any kind of cell signal and stuck it back in her purse, setting it on the floor by her feet. Whether they stopped or not, at least she could ping Jessie.

David didn't respond. Neither did he show a sign of slowing down.

"David?" She said. "We could pull off here."

Strong wind gusts buffeted the truck sideways, and the snow got thicker. The windshield wipers pumped back and forth but now had trouble keeping up with the icy globs.

"We should stop here and rest. Have something to eat," she repeated. "There's the parking lot by the café."

"I'm fine." He barked the words. "If we keep ahead of this, we'll get out to the interstate and get on home."

"But David," she protested, "We're not ahead of this storm anymore. We're in the middle of it."

On the radio, the music changed to some 90s high-pitched synthesized mix of chaotic sound by The Police. The crazy keyboard instrumental bounced around the inside of the cab. Syncopated. Frantic. Unsettling. *I used to love "Synchronicity,"* she thought.

"Honey," Anna raised her voice, "we should stop. At least for a bathroom break."

"Yeah, okay," he answered.

And Anna went weak with relief.

"But let's make it quick. We've gotta keep going." He took the tiny exit. Nothing else in the village looked open, nothing going on like the Cozy Conifer Lodge here. He parked on the north side of the Cactus Flower Café, closed for the holiday. A wall of white snowflakes gusted into the front window of the cab, and it was so loud this time she rubbed her ears.

"What do you wanna do?" he asked. "A Gatorade bottle won't work for you, sorry my dear wife."

In frustration, Anna zipped her parka up as far as it would go, with the orange beanie scrunched down around her face, and braced her arm muscles to open the door. The wind almost ripped it from her grasp, but she was ready for it, and she held on, grunting with the effort. *He is being a complete idiot and I'm the one who has to suffer for it.*

She climbed down, called Casey to Come, and reached up to close the door. She didn't bother with Casey's leash, because in the ridiculous winds howling out of the north, the dog would go do the jobs he needed to do and run back to the truck.

Besides the wet snow, the air itself felt wet and heavy, not like normal Colorado air at all. And it slapped her in the face like a frozen towel, finding its way down her neck and right through her thin leggings.

What the heck is going on with David? She stormed toward the little café, hoping to find a door left open, but it was dark and all shut tight. Her bladder insisted she should not give up, and she tromped around to the leeward side of the building in Jessie's fleece-lined boots. Backed up to the wall, she pushed down her leggings, fumed at David for his stubbornness, and squatted. The wind and snow blew on parts of her anatomy that did not appreciate it. She did her business and pulled up her leggings.

Why is he being so obstinate about everything lately? she wondered. Why did he want to hurry this trip along? They could have stayed in Durango together all day, safe and warm, David and his delicious bride. But then there was his surprise announcement about needing to leave for Pittsburgh tomorrow on another run. Maybe the woman was in Pittsburgh? Or Pensacola?

She stormed back to the truck, wrenched the door open against the ferocious wind, and climbed in after Casey. *But then why did he invite me along on this trip at all?* The muscle twinge behind her shoulder blade knotted up again, making it hard for her to pull the door closed.

She'd been quick out there in the icy wind, and the same frantic song was still playing its discordant notes. "Syn-chro-ni-ci-ty!" Huffing and puffing with cold, she pulled off the orange hat and shook the snow on the floor. She kept her mittens on to brush the snow off the dog before he climbed back up on the bed. Besides unwashed sheets, the cab now smelled like Wet Dog, and David had the temperature way too high. She had an urge to retch at all the smells, but she couldn't afford that luxury. Instead, she tried to get settled and ready to cope with the next leg of the trip, conflicted, trying to justify what they were doing since she was stuck on this scary ride with her husband.

It's possible we could be home this afternoon like David says, if the roads will stay open. This could all be over soon. I don't want to wish away my life like I did when I was little, wishing I could hurry and grow up so I could move away from my mama.

Another ferocious wind blast hit the truck, but the gust didn't abate. It continued and became a sustained nightmare full of icy snow that wasn't in flakes. It felt like the air itself was made of snow now, instead of just blowing snow through it. A continuous wind tunnel.

Her shoulder twinged.

But if I could fast forward through this afternoon and just get home, I would cross my arms, blink my eyes, and make it happen, just like that. Like the cute genie on "I Dream of Jeannie."

∽

Thursday, November 28, 2019, 12:30 p.m.

Pioneersburg, Colorado

At Jessie's apartment, good food smells wafted through the air. She let go of Prentice's hand and picked up her phone when it beeped with the haunting trilled whistling notes from "The Good, The Bad, and The Ugly," that mimicked the howl of a coyote. To be funny, this was the ring tone she'd selected to signal messages coming from her easy-going, artsy mom. The irony usually made Jessie laugh, but today, with the worry about the weather, it got her attention in a second.

We're still on the way east, read the text from her mom. *At Fort Garland. Thank U again for the boots! Could U send me the photo from Alkmaar from our honeymoon album in the Netherlands?*

Prentice said, "Hey, I hope they're parked in a safe spot."

Jessie shook her head to answer that they had not, and she was already typing a response: *Mom, Y don't U stop and wait out the weather? The forecast keeps getting worse.* Jessie paused, then added another line. *No photos. Lost in hurricane.*

Right. Could you find me a generic tourist photo from Alkmaar? I want to show David to remind him. Cell service bad, wrote Anna.

"That's cute," Jessie remarked to Prentice, then wrote one more line back. *I'll find one. Stay safe. U can eat this food tomorrow! Let me know where you stop, OK?*

That was it.

"What's cute?" asked Prentice.

Jessie said, "Mom wants to show Dad a photo from their honeymoon. Isn't that romantic? And also kind of strange?"

"Who knows? Maybe they're having fun reminiscing."

"That must be it, but she said she wanted to 'remind' Dad. That's just weird." Jessie lost no time in using her phone to locate a quintessential image of tulips and wind-mills, which she resized to fewer pixels, so it would be easier for her mom to receive on her phone whenever she got back into cell coverage. Then she pressed Send.

"I wish she hadn't used the word 'remind' that way. Dad does seem to be having trouble remembering obvious things lately," she explained. "I wish they would just stop somewhere, Prentice. I'm really worried about them in this weather."

"Me too. Maybe they will. Those small towns all have a motel or two."

"I hope so. And I hope Dad's up for all this driving. He already seemed tired before they left," she said, and Prentice agreed again.

She said, "I was hoping you'd disagree with me and say I was being silly and that Dad seemed fine to you. But you aren't saying that, are you?" Being totally honest helped her deal with life, especially when it got scary.

Prentice shook his head. "No, when he asked me the other day what I do for a living, it really made me wonder what is going on with him."

They had no more cooking to do until it was time to baste the turkey, so Prentice got them both a snack. Ice cream for him, and a cup of hot cocoa for Jessie. She took two whiffs of the sweet chocolate smell before taking a tiny sip and smiling with satisfaction. She teased him, "How can you eat freezing cold ice cream when it's cold outside?" They snuggled under the afghan again, and they watched the fabricated outtakes for a 21st-century animated movie, dozing off when it ended.

Jessie enjoyed the movie, which she'd seen dozens of times, but in her heart, she had twinges of worry that did no one any good at all. She commented, "I'm having trouble relaxing, Prentice. I just wish they were home safe. Or somewhere safe. I keep picturing them slogging along in that big truck on a mountain road full of snowdrifts."

Prentice didn't argue. "We're supposed to just be vegging out, but it's work to relax when they're not home yet."

"Let's just leave it off for a while." She wished she had more cooking to do, just to keep her brain busy, though she was sure no one would be eating turkey today. Prentice went back to the sofa for a nap, and Jessie tried to read the paperback she'd started yesterday.

12

LAST DAY OF KINDERGARTEN, 1980, ANNA'S KINDERGARTEN MEMORY, CHINATOWN, SAN FRANCISCO, CALIFORNIA

PART 4

Every day, she still trudged up to Teacher's classroom and did her work and tried to be smart. The end of kindergarten approached. Teacher was excited about the Last Day. She told her class that the children would finish kindergarten, drink lemonade and cookies at The Party, and become First Graders.

Anna wondered what that meant. *First Graders? What does that mean?*

Is that why there are so many other children here? She had thought they were just slow and so they had to stay until they learned what Teacher taught them.

But now the truth came out. She had to go back to school again next year, even if she learned everything. *How long do I have to do school?*

Her eyes would not focus as she headed home that day and turned down the steps outside the school building. She didn't even peer at the sun-struck ocean, so tantalizingly close but still unfamiliar. She dragged her feet along the busy street, not paying attention to the vendors and carts and cars.

A commotion of cars honked behind her, and a man ran past her on the sidewalk, almost knocking her down. She felt his vacuum of air rush by her. He wore black dress pants and a white shirt like so many of the men in her neighborhood. Black hair, cut short.

But wait...

Was that man Baa? *Why is he running?*

She stopped walking.

A car zoomed past, heading down the steep hill. Was it chasing the man? He kept running and ducked into the side alley ahead of them. The car screeched to a stop.

Anna kept her eyes on the alley. It was the one where she had followed the white cat and found out the road ended. Why would the man run in where he couldn't get out? Maybe he didn't know.

Three men piled out of the car and raced into the alley. They all wore tight black jeans that tapered around bare ankles. White sneakers. They had spiky black hair with dyed blond highlights. One wore a black nylon jacket with a red dragon stitched on the back.

In seconds, they reappeared, dragging the man toward the car. He struggled but couldn't get free. She saw his long slender hands try to fight the three men, but he had only two hands and they had six, and they grabbed his arms and ankles. He yelled for help, but they pushed him hard into the back seat and jumped in after him. The car disappeared down the hill.

That can't be Baa. He in the shop working with Mama.

Anna stood still for a long time, watching where they had gone. *Who was he? And why were the other men so angry at him?*

She felt small. Grown-ups didn't make sense. Nothing did. Everything was worry and worry some more.

Why didn't they explain about school at the beginning?

She hooked her thumbs behind the backpack straps and looked at her feet planted on the sidewalk. *I hope the ground will not wobble again.* It was not supposed to shake like almond jello. It was not safe.

Her feet started moving again without her even telling them to, and she walked the eight blocks back home. Her feet knew what to do, but her mind could not stop thinking about what Teacher had said about more school. She thought hard about how she had to go to First Grade to do more school, whether she was smart or stupid.

Does Mama know this? She will be so mad.

~

THURSDAY, NOVEMBER 28, 2019, 12:45 P.M.

East of Fort Garland, Colorado

Back in the truck cab, Anna shivered and tried to regain the warmth she lost outside in the raging storm, and she brushed more snow off her parka and hat. Then she turned off the radio, stopping the unsettling noise. The music felt jarring right now instead of a comfort.

"What?!" He slammed the steering wheel. "I was listening to that." He pulled out of the empty parking lot and back toward the state highway.

"David, you can't keep turning up the music and pretending there's nothing wrong outside!"

"It helps me deal with the road conditions. You know that." They were picking up speed when he drove over a small snowdrift across the lane. Bump-bump-bump-bump. He reached for the radio knob again, but she put out her hand to stop him.

"But these road conditions are the problem. Why don't you just park and we can wait this out?"

The truck was on the way toward La Veta Pass now. "I told you, we have to get back tonight because I'm leaving again tomorrow. I've got a trip to Peoria," he said.

"What?" She shook her head in bewilderment. "Peoria?"

"Yeah, I told you that already."

"No, you said Pittsburgh. Yesterday, when we were talking to Lily, you said Pittsburgh. And later you said Pensacola." Her stomach did more somersaults. "Which is it?"

Meanwhile, he kept driving, somehow keeping the truck on the road, which was as white as the fields on either side now, but he shook his head as if to clear his thoughts. Finally, he said, "Pittsburgh. I'm pretty sure. I dunno. I gotta check my notes when we get home." He was obviously uncomfortable and acting like he realized that something was off in his memory, too.

She said, "It doesn't feel like you're paying attention to things like you usually do."

"We've got a lot of bills to pay. That's why we're pushing today and I'm heading out again so soon."

She could not figure out how any of this could be happening. She wanted to cling to the reasonable explanation. Or explanations... for all the bizarre behavior, not jump to conclusions. She didn't want to make him more tense in the middle of these awful driving conditions. What else could she say to him but, "Thank you, honey. I'm sorry." *He's trying so hard, and I just keep figuring things out wrong.*

But Anna's thoughts bounced around to no effect. How could she stop this runaway disaster that was her soulmate, her husband David? It felt like they were running down a hill way too fast. Or like they were driving a truck through an impenetrable snowstorm and no one could stop them. *Right.*

David broke Anna's trance by stating, in a helpful voice, "Babe, your phone pinged while you were outside." He seemed glad to stop talking about the weather. "I thought you might forget to check."

"What?" She clung to this beacon of hope from the outside world. "Oh, thanks. Thank you, honey." Sure enough, there were some replies from Jessie, and she had attached a tourist board photo of windmills and tulips in Holland. She had hoped if she showed him the photo, it would jar his memory about the honeymoon.

"David, this is great! Jessie sent the photo I asked for." She wanted to show him the image on her phone, but due to the treacherous road conditions she couldn't distract him that much, so she described it. "Remember the windmills, and how flat the land was, just like a pancake? And how straight the canals were? Just like they were drawn with a ruler." She paused while she was sure he was envisioning it all in his mind. "All the colorful tulip farms. Alkmaar is where we found the poffertjes cart. Those tiny pancakes were so yummy."

But he wasn't visualizing it. "Anna, maybe you have me confused with some other handsome devil," he said, with a gentle voice. "I've never been to Elk Mart or eaten puffer cheese or whatever you're saying."

She didn't know what to say. Her mouth opened and closed again. How could he really not remember something so important? Or maybe it was her own fault, somehow? Words from her mama forty years ago echoed in her head. *You not smart girl. You not smart girl.* She fought against the stinging memory. It felt like a mountainside full of snow piling on top of her. Or the earthquake from her childhood coming back to haunt her. Or the terrifying time during the hurricane. If she disappeared right now, would anyone be able to find her? *Would David even look for me if he lost me?*

She realized he was speaking to her again. "So, hey babe, if you're hungry, why don't ya' heat up some soup in the microwave, and we can have it while we're heading east."

Anna looked straight at her husband. Trying to summon all her strength. "How can you not remember that we went to the Netherlands for our honeymoon?"

"Our honeymoon was fantastic, babe. You know that." He harrumphed when she shook her head at him, waiting. "But you are upset. Let's figure this out. You have my full attention."

"No David, I don't think I have your attention, and I'm worried. It's not just the snow." His profile silhouetted by the white, whirling snow outside the cab made her want to reach for him and kiss him and pretend none of this uncomfortable stuff was happening. *I love you so much. But you are strange right now.*

"I am listening. So shoot."

She needed to ask the specific question she'd been avoiding. It was the one that would explain everything, all his odd behavior, all his memory lapses, the financial trouble, everything. She didn't want to bring it up while he was driving, but she felt like she had to risk it. She took a deep breath and made herself ask, "Are you stepping out on me, David?"

"Ha ha!" He laughed out loud and slapped his right hand on the steering wheel.

She blanched. *He's laughing at my question?*

"Who has time, woman?" He grinned, glancing at his wife sideways with his deep blue laughing eyes. "Who has time, really?" He paused. "Is that what you've been thinking? Seriously? I thought you were mad about driving in the storm."

"Yes, that's my most immediate worry. Getting killed in a snowstorm!" She cleared her throat. "But also, I just can't figure out why you're acting the way you're acting. I'm so worried about you. If you need a doctor. Or if you're unhappy with me, or...." She started to cry, and she found a tissue in her purse and blew her nose. It didn't stop the tears, though.

He nodded at her with his chin, but kept his eyes on the road, which got steeper and whiter with every passing minute. "No, babe, you're just worrying about things you don't need to," he reiterated. "I'm yours until the end of time, like they say in the songs." He paused. "I'm super curious about this puffer cheese thing you keep mentioning, though."

"Oh," she murmured. "You'll like them. I promise." *You loved it when we were in Holland.* She turned back to her phone before they got out of range. She sent a text to her daughter and shrugged her shoulders against the muscle spasm. *Thanks for the photo. Wanted to remind David of something. We're still on the road. Just left Fort Garland.*

She wished she could tell Jessie that David didn't remember anything about going to the Netherlands, because Jessie was so level-headed. Maybe she could come up with a reasonable, reassuring explanation for her dad's bizarre behavior. But it wasn't fair to bring this up to her in a text thread.

Jessie replied right away. *Mom, R U crazy? U didn't stop? Bomb cyclone coming!*

Anna wrote, *David's pushing to get home by late this afternoon.*

What time will U get here? Jessie wrote.

IDK, wrote her mom, and the phone slipped to her lap.

THURSDAY, NOVEMBER 28, 2019, 1 P.M.

Pioneersburg, Colorado

Jessie stood looking out the sliding door of her apartment.

"Wanna go for a walk?" Prentice asked.

She kept her focus out the window. "No snow yet. It's not even breezy," she said. The cloudy sky didn't seem troublesome yet in south central Colorado, just gray.

"The reports are saying it's already pretty fierce in southern and western Colorado and moving this way," he said. "But it's clear here for now."

"I'm worried sick about them, Prentice. Why won't Dad stop? It's not like him to take risks."

Prentice took her hand. "A short walk will do us good—"

Jessie was more agitated than she usually let herself be. "It's not just this—his driving in this weather. Remember when he asked you what you did for a living?" she asked. "It was like he was just meeting you—"

"He was probably trying to be funny—"

"No. And he kept telling us the same story. That happened this summer in Maryland, too, but I didn't think much of it." Jessie touched her temples and resumed pacing.

"We could just go out and get some fresh air before it really blows in," he said.

She saw his point. Closing her eyes and grinning his way, she said. "Prentice, thank you for helping me get a grip. You caught me going off the edge." It was a relief to have a friend like him who would listen. "You're right. Let's walk down to the park, and we can stop by for a fru-fru drink if they're open at that coffee shop near there."

Jessie wore sneakers, and Prentice put on his boots. They got their parkas and hats and set out. Not a big hike, just a breather, a mile out to the park, then the short loop around the frozen pond.

The sky remained indifferent, and so they agreed a stop for a hot drink would warm them up again. People filled the coffee shop too, even though it was Thanksgiving. *There is no such thing as a holiday for retail people,* thought Jessie, as she stood in line; it was her turn to buy. Meanwhile, Prentice went to scout out a place to sit, securing two spots on the sofa facing the gas fireplace, the other regulars and travelers chatted around Jessie in line. *I guess we aren't the only people delaying our Thanksgiving celebration.*

It took a while to get her order; the young cashier with multicolored hair said to the line of customers, "Sorry to be slow, but my coworker didn't show up for his shift because of the weather forecast." The people mumbled words of acknowledgment. She kept working, saying, "My boss said he'd get his pay docked because of it, but I can't afford to miss a day's pay." She added quietly, "and I'd just as soon be here, anyway."

Jessie heard that, wondered about it, and left a generous tip in the jar. She took the two cardboard cups and set them on the fireside table in front of Prentice before taking off her coat and sitting close to him.

He joked. "We came outside to get some air, but here we are sitting on our butts again." He sipped his hot chocolate, which had a dash of cinnamon, and held her hand on top of his knee. They gazed at the fire and didn't talk much. Jessie scooted down a little on the sofa to put her head on Prentice's shoulder. They finished their drinks while they were still warm, and no more than twenty minutes had gone by.

She sighed and said, "Well, we should get back."

They stood up to get their coats, and that's when they saw how the weather had transformed outside in that short time. *What?*

"Whoa!" said Prentice. "Look at the size of those snowflakes! They're like the size of the Batmobile!"

The coffee shop was emptier than when they had come in, but there were still a few patrons who had lost track of the outside world, too. When Prentice raised his voice, a few of them raised their eyes from their phones and tablets. They all stared at the swirling white snow globe outside that just a while ago was a boring, gray day with a leaden sky. Several got up to leave.

Jessie said, "The snow is sticking on the sidewalk already!" Indeed, at least an inch of fresh, wet snow covered the concrete, and the black asphalt parking lot was now pure white. A ridiculous blast of wind and snow chunks hit the window hard enough to rattle the glass. Everyone's attention was focused outside now. It felt colder in the coffee shop. Jessie wondered for the hundredth time what it was like on the road for her parents.

Jessie noticed the barista look outside and shake her head, and she asked her, "Can you close the shop and get home? How far do you have to drive?"

The barista shook her head and looked outside. "I live a half-hour from here." She didn't look at Jessie. "But if it's a choice between being stuck here tonight and going home, I'd just as soon be stuck here."

"On Thanksgiving? Oh, that's...." Jessie started to say, but Prentice zipped his parka up to his throat and then gently took Jessie's arm. *He's right, he knows me so well. I want to stop and talk with this girl, but we better get going.* "Okay, well, be safe. At least you have lots of good food to eat." The shelves were half full of cookies, muffins, brownies, and a few egg sandwiches. "Be safe," she repeated.

"I will," smiled the girl. "You too."

13

THURSDAY, NOVEMBER 28, 2019,
1 P.M., WEST OF LA VETA PASS,
COLORADO

East of Fort Garland, the road began its ascent up La Veta Pass. Yesterday, this winding, two-lane highway perched along the edge of the river canyon had been mostly sunny and the view of the surrounding hillsides was spectacular. Today, however, it felt like they traveled in a white tunnel snaking through the mountains.

All Lily's warnings from last night bounced around in Anna's head. That spitfire over-the-road driver had looked into their eyes and asked why they were dead-heading on a terribly windy day with a blizzard in the forecast, but David hadn't taken her seriously.

Or maybe he even took this as a challenge? That trucker probably weighed half of what David did. Was this bravado? *But that's not like him. What's eating him?* David's M.O. was to be safe. He was a free spirit, but he did abide by safety rules. He needed to drive the right speed down steep hills, watch for passenger cars misbehaving around trucks that could squash them, make sure the trailer was attached correctly, stop at a rest area if the road conditions were dangerous, and all the rest.

Except for today, when he just didn't.

Heavy, wet snow piled on the road and was turning to ice with the force of the wind. They could hardly see the road in front of them, although it was early afternoon. The frozen wipers couldn't keep up. The defroster could not keep up either, and David's field of vision shrank as the window got more coated with slush. Ice shrouded the swan hood ornament.

They couldn't get away without going through it.

Or just stopping and waiting it out! "We could just pull over here until it clears up," she said, again. *Why didn't they close the road?* Anna wondered. *Why doesn't someone stop us?*

He kept going.

The tires had trouble gripping the road, slipping as they went up the grade. They couldn't get much traction, especially with no weight in the trailer. It would be even crazier when they got to the downhill grade of La Veta Pass heading toward the interstate.

"Shouldn't we put on chains, David?"

His voice sounded kind of muffled as he growled, "Where would we stop?" It was like he was admitting, for the first time today, she might have a point. But it was too late for her to be right.

Anna turned on the CB and keyed the mic. "Who's got their ears on? Art Mama on the west side of La Veta Pass, heading east. Anyone know where we can throw iron on this stretch of road?"

Silence.

She was about to try again when someone answered, "Peyote Pete. Come back, Art Mama. You said you want to throw iron on La Veta Pass right *now*?"

She gripped the mic. "We're in a bind, Peyote Pete. I can't remember the CB code for that now. 10-something." *Come on Anna, you know this. Don't be such a flutter brain.* "But anyway, we have trouble. The snow hit so fast. Any ideas, Pete?"

"Art Mama, I'm east of you on your front door. Followed a salt shaker over the pass about half an hour ago. There's no chain-up area until you get to the east side of the pass."

"I copy that, Peyote Pete. What do you think?" she said. "The only way to go is forward."

"The snow's coming down so thick now, you'll never make it without chains."

"What if we pull off on the side of the road?"

"Negatory, Art Mama. That's a terrible idea."

Silence on both ends. Finally, Anna said, "10-4 Pete. Thanks for your help. I don't think we have a choice." She glanced at David, for all the good this had done already.

"Negatory. You're in a real pickle. I'll be 10-10 on the side as long as I can, but the mountain's gonna get in the way of the signal." He referred to the Sangre de Cristos. Anna could feel them looming out there on all sides, somewhere in the whiteness.

"Copy that. Threes and eights to you," said Anna, wishing him good luck. *At least I remembered that code. Big deal. Big help.* She said to David, "What do you think, honey? Like he said, we need to put chains on, but it's dangerous to stop now. Right?"

"Yep," he said. "Didn't think of it before," he stated the obvious. "So, I'm thinking of it now."

"So you're going to stop for chains? Now?"

"That's what I just said." He pushed through the storm, keeping his eyes open for the opportunity Anna had been praying for. Incredulously, David found a wider spot to stop the truck on the right shoulder; this close to the cliff that rose above them, the drifting pattern abated slightly, and there was less snow piled up. He parked the truck.

She offered again that they could just stop driving and stay parked right there.

"I don't know why you don't want to get home today, Anna," he said. It felt to her like he was twisting her words on purpose, but it wasn't like him to be manipulative. He just seemed to have his logic all messed up. "We have to keep moving or we can't get home."

He patted his earmuffs, already on his head, and lowered himself out of the cab into the raging, wet storm. Casey intended to follow him out until he got a nose full of cold snow in his face. Anna watched out the window as, for the next half hour, David fought with the chains.

Getting them out of the storage locker.

Hoisting them up and over the drive wheels of the truck. The tires that were hot rubber from driving, despite the cold temperature. The tires that wanted to crush the wet, packed snow into ice beneath them with their heat.

Trying to adjust them to be ready for when he backed up the truck a foot or so, went outside again to see if he could close the loop on the chains.

She bundled up to get out and try to help him, when he was on the passenger side, but he saw her open the door a crack. "Get back in the truck, Anna," he yelled over the wind. "I don't need help."

She wanted to let go and cry, but she was too mad. Her anger clamped down on the fear and confusion. She was stuck, and she scratched Casey's ears as if her life depended on it. Casey was willing to go along with the ear scratching. With fury at David, she took the chocolate bar and ate it in angry bites, leaving him just a few squares for later. She didn't care. This whole thing was so unfair.

Outside, David fumbled with the chain links in his gloves, finally getting them loosely connected. Then he hopped in the cab to back the truck down the hill another foot so he could tighten the chains properly. No way he could pull forward up the hill, only roll backward, because of the ice.

More adjustments to the chains. Have to be just right, not too loose, but not too tight.

He got back in the cab.

Anna couldn't help saying, "Your gloves are soaked! And your coat."

He grunted, "Let's get moving."

But they still couldn't get moving. He got out again, grabbed a shovel from the storage area on Anna's side of the cab, and walked sloppily over to the side of the road. With fatigue? No doubt. He shoveled piles of snow out of the way until he found gravel beneath it, tossed it on the ground where the tires needed that much more friction.

By the time he got back in the cab, he was shaking with cold. His wet blond hair was stiff and covered with icy crystals. He reached to turn up the heat, but it was already on high. He let it blow on his hands for several minutes.

She gave him the last few squares of the chocolate bar, and he wolfed them down.

Anna turned on the defroster when all the moisture he brought inside with him fogged up the windshield. The heat from the truck's engine helped clear the fog, but she wished it would clear her emotions, too. *I feel like I'm detaching from him, the way he's detaching from me. To protect ourselves, maybe. What's it going to take to get us listening to each other again, God?*

He got the rig moving, going backwards down the slope one more time to get free, then shifting forward and heading east, but the road itself was as full of snow as the shoulder had been.

∽

Thursday, November 28, 2019, 1:30 p.m.

Pioneersburg, Colorado

The storm had appeared, in full raging force, in only twenty minutes.

It took Prentice two tries to push the coffee shop door open. Each time the wind pushed back, stronger than he was. They got outside, and Jessie gasped when sheets of wet snow thwacked her in the face. The wind struck her like a cold, scratchy blanket. It took concentration to walk into the wind and not be blown over as it gusted from all directions at once, and she locked arms with Prentice for stability.

They couldn't talk because the wind was too loud. And it hurt when ice crystals blew right into her mouth and eyes.

It's just so terrible. How can it be this bad so fast?

The air temperature was significantly colder than when they'd left her apartment. And the wet winter air felt... heavy, besides the wetness of the snowflakes. If it had been sixty degrees warmer, it would have felt like Florida. Except for the snow. *Ha.*

It's not like they didn't warn us. A hundred times. The walk back to her apartment was like a different planet than the route they'd come an hour ago. The wind was now horizontal and drifts of snow made walls across the road and sidewalk. *When did this happen?*

A few cars tried to navigate the road and their wipers struggled to keep up with the wet flakes piling up. She just willed them to be safe. *Lord, please don't let them fish tail.* She worried about them even though she didn't know them.

She saw a car slow down at a curve and then bog down in the snowy cement on the road. Another one behind it followed too fast, tried to go around it, and lost control, sliding straight into a snowdrift in the other lane, blocking the road completely to cars going either direction.

This was a snowdrift crossing a road that had been clear, dry asphalt an hour ago.

It's totally stupid to be outside or try to go anywhere at all. She sniffled and wiped snow off her face with her mitten, but it was already covered with slushy snow and just made her face wetter. *This is unreal. How did the storm come in so fast?*

Oh. *This* is a bomb cyclone. They warned us. They warned us.

They took very small steps, post-holing through the deep snow on the sidewalk, and held onto each other in the buffeting wind. She watched more cars attempting to make headway. They might have been less than a mile from home, but they'd never make it. She'd tried to warn the first few that came their way toward the blocked road, but it was no use. They couldn't turn around. They'd go forward and find the way impassable. They would have to stay in their cars or walk to one of the homes or apartments nearby.

They'd been walking for almost an hour and were still not back to the apartment.

"Maybe we should have asked someone for a ride?"

"What?" he yelled back. "No way. Look at what trouble they're in."

Did it hit this fast where mom and dad were, too?

She tried to practice what she'd learned in her self-care groups, remembering she could not do anything for her parents right now, no matter where they were. The time would come to deal with whatever happened to them. She was so worried, but she needed to focus her energy on where she was right now, something positive to help her keep putting one foot in front of the other.

That's when she remembered a funny-yet-serious creative advice to inexperienced drivers confronted with slick roads. Despite the grim consequences if they failed, the image made her smile behind her zipped-up parka collar. It advised them, "Just pretend you're driving your grandma to church in your dad's new car. Grandma's wearing a brand-new dress and holding a crock pot full of gravy. In the back seat, there's a platter of biscuits and two gallons of sweet tea in glass jars." *That's the ticket,* thought Jessie. *Biscuits sound good, too. But not sweet tea today. It's too cold.*

As cars struggled by and got stuck, Jessie and Prentice kept slogging. The wind, full of ice crystals, blew up her nose and into her eyes. Her sneakers soaked up water. *I'm so glad Mom took my snow boots with her. I'm sure, wherever she is, she needs them more than I do.* And given Jessie's already miserable situation, that thought petrified her. She held on tighter to Prentice's arm, and they braced their legs to stay upright when the wind wanted to topple them.

Jessie's apartment parking lot was completely white with heavy, wet snow. No tire tracks. It was drifting already here, just like on the road. The cars and trash dumpsters all had drifts next to them, around them. The storm had walloped everything with thick precipitation so quickly.

A drift of snow blocked her sedan in its parking place. Looking at it as they trudged toward the building, she knew she wouldn't be able to get the car out again for a long time, the way the wind delivered buckets of fresh wet snow and dumped it everywhere all at once. The sheer volume of it, the sound of the strong wind battering everything.

By the time they got into the hallway outside her door, their faces were red with cold and wet with snow, and snowflakes coated their clothes. Her jeans were completely soaked through and crusted with ice. She slammed the door, dropped the bag and her coat, and tried to kick off her sneakers without untying them. That ended with her losing her balance and falling backwards, hard, onto the carpet, where she spent a long time trying to untie the soaking wet laces with her numb fingers.

As she pulled off her wet socks, air puffed out from between her lips. "Nobody should go anywhere right now. That was ridiculous." She wiped her hands up and down on her face to squeegee the water off.

Prentice had been ice-crusted from head to foot also and had peeled off some layers. "Hey, Jessie, do you have some spare clothes that would fit me?"

"Yes, for sure," she pondered. "I think my dad's pants will be about a foot too long for your legs. Maybe his sweatshirt will work, though." She went to David's living room closet and found a sweatshirt emblazoned with a Denver Broncos logo. "Want some of my sweatpants?"

"Yeah. I really do have a change of clothes in the blizzard bag in my truck, but I was hoping to skip going out there again for a while." They both laughed. That felt good.

"I wondered about that, Mr. Preparedness Guy," she said, rubbing his shoulder as they went to her bedroom to change into dry clothes, put their clothes in the dryer, and go back to the living room.

The window was caked white with snowflakes — big wet ones blocking the entire view. Jessie rubbed her hands together to get more warmth into them and texted her mom again. She sent one to her dad, too, though he had never been much of a texting guy. He hated typing on tiny keyboards, he always told her. Today was the day to make an exception.

Prentice, dressed in David's sweatshirt and Jessie's sweatpants, rummaged in the front closet. Jessie was delighted to see him unearth an old Hasbro cardboard box under his arm.

"Jessie," he said. "You've taught me that it's important to take care of your inner child when it's a stressful time," he smiled. "So how about showing me how to draw with a Spirograph?"

Thursday, November 28, 2019, 1:45 p.m.
Close to summit of La Veta Pass, Colorado
Wet slush and ice coated the Peterbilt's small, round headlights, and waves of gusting wet snow blew sideways, up, and down, filling the air and coating the road with precipitation that turned to icy quicksand. No way to tell from the sky what time it was, since the sun hid somewhere almost a hundred million miles away, but it wasn't even two o'clock yet.

She crossed her arms over her chest in the green parka. *Why are we still moving? Because now it's too late to stop. There's nowhere to stop without blocking the road. So what if we block the road? No one should be going anywhere now.*

We shouldn't be going anywhere now.

Some yokel on the CB took over Channel 10 with too much power and told his life story.

"I wish that ratchet jaw would shut his trap and not key down his mic constantly." David kept the truck crawling forward, navigating the curves in the road and the undulations in the grade. "Babe, why don't you try getting through with a radio check? Maybe he'll hear your sweet voice coming through the static."

Anna tried, but the guy was over-blasting the universe and not listening for anybody else on the channel. He must have been transmitting from his warm house and wearing bedroom slippers. She turned off the CB radio.

David focused on the blinding snow through the hole in the windshield ice as if it would help.

"I wish we'd stopped in Fort Garland," she said.

"Too late now." He shrugged his shoulders and shook his head.

She sighed in reply.

"Hey, I've been trucking since 1997, Anna. Don't you think I've done a good job?"

"Yes, of course! You've taken such good care of us. And you've had to be gone so much. You earned the money, and I spent it," she said, revisiting that tired, old family joke like a lifeline. And she'd always been frugal. She learned that from her mama, for sure.

But she'd also learned something else from her mama. It was ingrained in her to doubt herself first before doubting other people.

He said, "Just stick with me, babe." He really meant it. He was asking for her support, she could tell. He was still trying to win, but his strategy was for the wrong game. They were both pawns in a game they never intended to play.

"I'll stick with you," she said, "but David, I really don't have a choice."

He didn't acknowledge that, and his next words were the understatement of the hour. "It's getting dicey out there."

Every drifted pile of snow in the road caused the truck to lurch and stutter, and David adjusted the gears so they could go slower.

The Peterbilt's low chrome bumper allowed for almost no ground clearance, thanks to the previous owner who thought installing it was a cool idea. It was just fine on a clear road, like most highways and interstates were ninety-nine percent of the time. Today was the exception, and in the past, he would have called Anna from wherever he was and said he'd be a day late getting home, because he was off the road altogether.

The snow kept swirling. They'd come over this same pass yesterday and could see for miles, all the mountain ranges and trees and the river below. Today the snow obscured almost everything, but sometimes Anna could make out a familiar landmark near the edge of the road, or when the topography changed abruptly. The highway was following the Sangre de Cristo Creek canyon, so on and off, they had hills on both sides of them.

When the hills opened up, she remembered there was a meadow to the south, where the Old La Veta Pass road climbed up, up, up to the ghost town of Uptop. It was the older, trickier route over the old pass, the one that nowadays was only open in the summer for tourists.

To push down the anxiety in her gut, she focused on a good memory from up there, when she and David had attended a wild summer music festival in Uptop, maybe five years ago, a fund raiser for the La Veta Fire Department after the East Creek Fire. She tried to remember which bands had played. The music was Celtic ballads and Appalachian fiddle tunes, not their normal classic rock, but it didn't matter. Such a good weekend together. She'd worn flip-flops and a sun dress and the glowing Colorado sun warmed their bones.

Once upon a time, miners and tourists ventured that high in the late 1800s on the "Railroad Above the Clouds." It actually went over that steep pass. *Incredible*, thought Anna, deep in her escapist reverie, questioning the audacity of those puny people trying to conquer this vast landscape with picks, shovels, wagons, and railroads.

That's what they were, she and David, Anna thought now. Puny people, with an internal combustion engine, fighting their way through a blizzard.

Not quite at the top, she got a glimpse of the helpful blue sign that said the elevation of La Veta Pass. What a difference a day made. Today it was obscured by the blinding wind full of snow.

And then it happened. All in slow motion.

The laws of physics she dreaded finally won. The highway kept going straight, but the series of snowdrifts dragged the truck to the right despite David's best efforts. Even though he was going slowly, the truck angled slightly to the right instead of following the highway. The right side tires got caught in the softer snow on the shoulder, pulling the rig farther off the highway toward that shallow valley and the Old La Veta Pass Road, completely neglected and untraveled in the winter.

"David—?" She felt herself flung hard against her seat restraint.

The tons of momentum behind them pushed them through the first snow banks.

The highway slid out of sight on David's left side as the truck pulled to the right, heading into an old unplowed road, full of nothing but snow and whirling wind gusts, into the Old La Veta Pass turnoff.

David's eyes flared wide open, and he held onto the steering wheel. He fought to keep the wheel straight, even after steering was of absolutely no use, since the wheels had zero traction. Hitting the brakes would be of no help either. His years of building muscle memory kicked in, where logic could never win. Their only hope was to go straight now, into the drifts.

Anna's mind flashed to the first time she rode a roller coaster, in her early twenties. It was a weekend in Omaha, with David and little Jessie, his siblings, and his mother. David's mother held Jessie's hand while David took Anna on the scary ride. She remembered the moment where she couldn't see where the bottom was. What was so fun about a ride where they were all about to plunge to their deaths? But they screamed together at the same time, and by the time the ride was over, she was laughing and clamoring to do it again, but only with David. He made it worth the adrenaline.

This ride was not as steep, but she had no idea where they would stop. They flew off the highway and into wasteland. She cried out, but the horror in her throat trapped the sound. All she could do was stare straight ahead while they went off the roller coaster rails. The wind howled, blowing snow up at the windshield. Her hands reached out in front of her as if they could stop what was happening. She didn't know if she were screaming or not. In her mind, she was.

It must have just been a few seconds when the Peterbilt's fender and hood plowed into the deepest snow, arresting their forward momentum with an abrupt feeling of weightlessness.

Anna's head, hands, and feet flew forward, and the belts again held her in place, crushing her chest and hips against the straps. Casey yelped with pain as he must have hit the bulkhead in front of the sleeping area. Her head whipped back against the headrest at the same time as David's. Anna's lungs tried to breathe, tried to bring in a breath of air.

Nothing moved at all inside the cab.

It was quiet.

14

THURSDAY, NOVEMBER 28, 2019,
1:46 P.M., OLD LA VETA PASS
TURNOFF, COLORADO

Her own sob broke the awful silence, startling her. She tasted her tears and looked over at David. His cheeks were wet too, but he still held the wheel and looked straight ahead as if the truck were still moving. Behind them, the dog whimpered from the sleeping area.

But they were alive.

And shiny side up.

After skidding off Highway 160 in the middle of a bomb cyclone.

David found his voice first. "Anna! Are you okay?"

"Yes!"

"Can you move?"

"Oh, David!" she burst into fresh tears filled with relief, fumbled to unlatch her seat belt.

"If we swerve, we die. That's the rule. And we didn't swerve." David's voice shook.

Her neck ached. She patted her legs and arms with her hands, checking for injury. "What should we do!?" she asked, crying again. *Why am I asking him what to do? I've been telling him all day what to do, and he didn't pay the slightest attention. But I'm so scared. And he's my rock.*

The rock said, "Um. Let me think." He unbuckled too, and then, as if by agreement, they stood between the seats and held each other close. Anna wept into the chest of David's damp parka, and he rubbed her back.

Minutes later, without discussion, they crawled into the sleeping area with Casey, with their boots on, and leaning against the cupboard behind the driver's seat, they comforted him.

"I think he's okay," David said, gently palpating Casey's ribs, head, and legs. When the dog yelped, David apologized. "Oh, sorry, buddy. That leg doesn't feel good, huh? It seems like it's a muscle."

"Are you hurt?" she asked, peering at David.

He sighed. "Nothing specific. I kind of ache all over. Probably from the seat belt."

"They saved us."

He closed his eyes and leaned his head against the back of the bulkhead. "Yes. We're alive."

"And you saved us too, with your great driving."

He growled. "Go ahead, say the rest of it."

"What do you mean?"

"You know, how you've been saying all day. We should have stopped somewhere and just waited this out."

She sighed. "Well, yes. But not much good to say it now. We're going to have to wait here."

He chuckled weakly. "Instead of in a nice warm hotel room somewhere."

She burst into tears again and leaned against him. Then she said, "Honey, you know you don't have to prove anything to me. You've been such a good provider for us, and you don't have to show off for me. You're always going to be my strong, awesome husband. No matter what."

"That's a lot of pressure to put me under, Anna," he said, and that uncharacteristic edge was back in his voice. "You always say stuff like that, and then I feel like I have to make it come true."

"Oh no, I didn't mean it like that." She rubbed his knee. "I've always just been thankful for what you do."

"It feels like pressure," he admitted.

"I didn't know." They sat quietly on the bed of the truck. "I mean," she paused, "I'm not used to questioning you or disagreeing, you know. I'm always trying to encourage you. If I don't support you, who will? You're my rock."

Blowing wet snowflakes crusted most of the windows. The wind buffeted the cab, sounding as if it wanted to come in, but she noticed another sound, too. "Honey, the engine's still running. Should we turn it off?"

"No." He thought about it. "No, we should leave it running. We've got plenty of fuel. It's the only way to keep the cab warm." She could tell he'd decided something. "I'll go out and check on the exhaust. We don't want the pipe to get blocked by the snow."

What he'd said didn't sound right, and her deep black eyes looked right into his. "Don't the exhaust pipes point up into the air?" she ventured. "It's when you're in a car you have to make sure the tail pipe is clear of snow, right?"

"Er, yeah." He grunted an acknowledgment. "Right. I knew that."

"It was a good idea, though. We have to see where we've ended up, and think what to do." Then she said, with more alarm in her voice, "I think I smell diesel. Do you smell diesel? Won't it explode?"

"Oh, man," he said. "We must've damaged the tank,

plowing through those drifts. Or there might'a been a big rock. We could be leaking fuel, but it won't explode," he reassured her, rubbing her knee as he spoke.

She noticed how wet his jeans were from being outside to put on the chains a while ago. They both had their boots on, right on top of the sheet and blanket. She felt like she ought to take off her boots, but she just couldn't move except to lean closer to her husband.

Outside, the ferocious wind gusts hit the truck over and over. Casey licked at his front leg and whimpered. Anna looked out the window of the sleeping area into the world of whiteness. Blankets of wet snow hit the window and slid down as they hit the warmer glass.

How long would it stay warm in the cab? she wondered. She wanted to ask him, but she had absolutely no confidence in the answer her husband, her rock, might give her.

2 P.M.

"Okay, this is what we're gonna do." David separated from Anna, climbed out of the sleeping area, and around the bulkhead to the driver's seat, reaching for the CB. Anna heard the over-powered guy out there somewhere out there. He still blathered on. David keyed the mic. "Breaker 1-0, this is Dutch Boy. We have an emergency."

The guy kept talking, oblivious to the plea for help. It made Anna mad. Where was this guy? Why wasn't he paying attention to people who needed to use the channel?

"Break. Break. Breaker 1-0, this is Dutch Boy," David tried again, in a louder voice, though that was of no help on a radio channel full of blithering idiots. He said to Anna, "Anyone we can hear must be line-of-sight from where we are, which right now is pretty limited. He might be in La Veta."

A shriek of wind rocked the truck.

"Can't we try a different channel?"

"Yeah, let's try Channel 17." He paused and asked her a question that rocked her to the core. "Do you know where we are?"

She blinked hard at his doubt, his lack of awareness.

But she had an answer. "Yes." She'd been watching the landmarks through the snow. "I think we're at the turnoff for Old La Veta Pass. Near Uptop."

"Hm," he said. "You think so?"

Inside, she was shaking, realizing now that her previous concerns hadn't even scratched the surface of how David's brain was working. All she could say without crying was, "Yes." It was her first glimmer of feeling useful at all in the deteriorating situation.

"So, Old La Veta Pass. Then, the radio might be able to hit the interstate if we're on the other channel. But it's pretty far, and there's still the line-of-sight limitation on the transmission..."

With her eyes closed, she leaned back against the bulkhead, scratched Casey's ears, and prayed.

David cleared his throat and spoke into the mic. "Breaker 1-7, this is Dutch Boy." No answer. He tried a few more times, but no one on the interstate heard him.

"Can you see how far we are off the road, honey?" Anna asked from the bed. "I remember when we came here for the concerts, there's a big meadow for parking south of the highway." She kept her eyes closed as she thought. "So at least it's flat here, and not a cliff to slide off."

David thought out loud. "The way this snow is coming

down, in a minute our tire tracks'll be obli-, obli-, what's the word?"

"Obliterated." Anna sucked in her breath. "I didn't think of them not even being able to see where we went off the road."

She heard David in the front seat, fumbling in the pockets of his old red parka, and he cursed in a way Anna had not heard since he tried to show off to his friends on the farm, when he was a new dad, with a new wife, and they were all living in his parents' basement. And, as she thought of it, also yesterday when he couldn't fix his own truck. Trying to sound like a man.

"What, honey?"

"I can't find my phone."

"Oh no! When did you last have it?"

"When I was putting the chains on," he said from the front seat.

"Do you think...?"

"Yeah, it must have fallen out again. It's probably there by the side o' the road where we stopped." He paused. "What about your phone?"

"I'll look," Anna said, taking her turn to scoot into the cab. Moments later, she looked over at him. "I found it," in a voice as small as a mouse. "It was on the floor under my purse," she said. "The screen's cracked," she checked. "And I can't even get it to turn on now."

Fresh tears squeezed out of her eyes as she slumped in her seat. "If we don't have phones, and the CB's not reaching anyone, how're we going to call for help? How're we going to tell Jessie?"

"I don't know." He tipped back his head in the driver's seat, closing his eyes. Gust after gust of impossible wind shook the cab. "Looks like we might be here for a while."

~

2:15 P.M.

"What's that movie you're always quoting lines from?" he said.

Anna looked over at David. They'd been quiet for what felt like a long time, but it might have only been a quarter of an hour. The howl of the wind made it hard to tell—she'd thought he'd dropped off to sleep. He had to be exhausted after fighting to keep the truck on the road for so long in impossible conditions. She'd dozed, but her mind was a wheel, spinning with disaster scenarios, the ones David hadn't bothered to consider when he forged ahead despite her questions. Suppose no one found them? Suppose David was wrong and the leaking fuel did cause an explosion? Suppose he was lying about stepping out on her? Suppose he was losing it—his memory, his mind—

"Anna?" he prompted.

"Um," said Anna. "I do that a lot—quote lines from movies." She rubbed her right collarbone, then stood, went to his side, and began to massage his shoulders and neck muscles.

He grasped her hand, rubbing her fingers. She laid her cheek on the top of his head. The only time she could be taller than him was when she stood next to him and he was seated like this.

"You know, the movie about the princess and the pirate?" he murmured, eyes closed.

She shook her head, and laughing, said, "You mean *The Princess Bride*? The one about the princess and a farm boy? Just like you and me, David!"

"Right, my princess. You said there's always a quote for every situation from that movie."

Anna realized he was prompting her to come up with one now. Anna was glad he'd remembered something fun that they'd shared, glad to have a glimpse of his old personality, not the new one that was so withdrawn and foggy. It was a game they used to play a lot, but on most days, he was the one to come up with the quote.

"Well," she began, "The obvious one is, 'What do we have among our assets?'" She managed a smile, though it felt forced. "In our case, what do we have, besides some smelly old blankets," she went on, "and whatever other junk you have squirreled away in the truck?"

While she spoke lightly enough, inside, she could not think straight for worrying. No one even knew where they were, or that they had gone off the road. Jessie would be expecting them later today, but she wouldn't have a reason to worry until tonight when they didn't arrive.

So they needed to keep trying the CB. They'd reach someone, eventually.

Spying the one can of soup that had flown out of the galley cupboard on the cab floor, she picked it up, holding it so David could see. "Look what we have here," she said, forcing an even tone, determined to appear calm. "Plus, we have the rest of the miserable pie." She didn't mention that all the other food they'd had was gone after she'd given the rest to Casey and the birds yesterday.

David's answering smile was so fleeting, Anna wondered if she'd imagined it. She pulled her orange beanie farther down over her ears, wondering what else they should be doing.

He tried the CB again. Nothing.

"We could take off our boots and really cuddle up," she offered.

"BRRR!" He joked. "Cold toes!"

Anna glared at him. "Do you have another idea, Mr. DeGroot?"

"I mean, good idea," he said. "One of the rules for emergencies is to stop and think before you act. Then cuddle with your lame-brained husband."

She smiled faintly. "It's a little late to stop to evaluate if the scene is safe." She unlaced her boots. "I wish we could just run out to the road and flag down a—"

"Passing car?" David's laugh was short. He dropped one of his boots. Anna noticed his white cotton tube socks on the dirty black floor as he walked back around to the bed.

"I'm glad it's still warm in here," Anna said as they settled on the bed with Casey between them. They pulled the blanket around the three of them. Casey hunkered under Anna's legs, and she petted him as she tried to settle her brain down.

The minutes .... The gusts of wind... the what ifs...

As she nestled her head against him, David began a story. *It feels like ages since he told me a story,* she thought. *But it was just two days ago.*

He began, "I heard once about a guy on a plane in the wintertime. A regular passenger, and he turned into a hero," David said. "He was on a big jet airplane flying over Colorado at night. There'd been a blizzard. There was a lot of snow on the ground like now. It must'a been cold, but it was crystal clear, pitch dark down below. There was no moon. And this guy, this passenger, sees something flashing down below on the ground, 30,000 feet below them."

"Was it a trucker?" Anna asked, looking up at him.

"No, turned out it was someone in a regular car. It's weird, huh?"

"What happened?"

"Well, the guy told the flight attendant that he'd seen these lights that looked like a dis— a dis—what's the word?"

"A distress call." Anna filled in the words David was looking for.

"Yeah. It turned out it was somebody signaling S-O-S in Morse code. You know, dot, dot, dot, dassssh, dassssh, dassssh, dot, dot, dot."

"That's incredible," she said. "But lucky for the man who was stranded. Well, that's not going to help us, is it? Not with the blizzard still blowing the way it is."

David found her gaze. "Now, listen, I'm trying to cheer you up." He pulled her into his embrace, and continuing with what Anna figured was a fairytale, he went on. "So the pilot must've radioed and got the sheriff to go check it out in whatever county it was. And it turned out to be a guy stuck in a snowdrift. He was flashing S-O-S with his headlights."

"That's a lovely story, farm boy," Anna sighed. "We better not still be stuck here when it's dark, David."

He laughed and pulled her closer. "Don't you want to spend the night with me, my princess?"

She felt a twinge from that same tight muscle in her back again. "Oh, David," she said. "Of course, I do. But not here." *Not here.*

15

———————

2:30 P.M.

David got up to try the CB again, this time sitting in the passenger seat. When he got a response, Anna sat up, feeling almost lightheaded in her relief.

"Dutch Boy," a man's voice said, "this is Scrap King. Do you copy?"

"Copy that, Scrap King. We're stuck in a ditch on La Veta Pass."

Stuck in a ditch? Anna thought. It's a little more than that, my dear husband.

"Dutch Boy, I don't know this area very well. Where's that?"

David looked at Anna for help. She told him, and he repeated it, "West of La Veta on Highway 160. East of Fort Garland. What's your 20, Scrap King?"

"I'm on the Big Road (static) Walsenburg, (static) north from New Mex (static)."

CB radio signals only work by line of sight, so Scrap King could reach them from a short section of the interstate. Anna figured the window of opportunity would close again as soon as he got farther along and the topography blocked the radio waves. She held her breath as David keyed up the mic again.

"We need help, Scrap King," he said. "Could you call in the bears or the draggin' wagon and help us get back on the road? We're in a world of hurt."

Another burst of static, then, "Come back, Dutch (static) negatory (static)." The crackling continued, but after several moments it, too, stopped. It was silent. And stayed silent.

David replaced the mic and cursed under his breath, but other than that he didn't move.

Anna let go of her breath. She started to speak, but the CB radio came alive again with another burst of static, but they could hear bits of it. "Dutch B...." It wasn't Scrap King's voice, Anna thought. "This is High.... Do you... High (static)"

David grabbed the mic. "Come back, High? You sound like a mud duck."

Crackle crackle, "High Plains Drifter. Did you say 10-34? What's your 20?"

"Affirmative." Anna listened as David again gave their location, adding, "We're off the south side of the road. Shiny side up. Send help." David was more direct now.

"Copy that, Dutch Boy. I'll see if I can send you some reinforcements. Anybody hurt?"

"Negatory. But it's getting colder by the minute. We're leaking go-juice. Not sure how long it's gonna last."

"What are you driving?"

"1997 Pete 379. All white."

High Plains Drifter tried to answer, but the earth and the driving snow absorbed the signal. A few more crackles and the radio fell silent again.

Anna wrapped up in the blanket and turned to the window, staring blank eyed at the impenetrable white world. The cab shook continuously. She shuddered at the ferocity of it, the hurricane-strength winds filled with wet snow trying to freeze them into a living ice cave. Or it would have if the engine weren't still running.

Ice and snow caked the passenger side windows already. And the front windshield was a network of fine cracks from the crash. But the north-facing driver's side and bedside windows were swept clear as they took the wind head-on.

Anna felt David's restless silence growing. Was he beating himself up for not paying attention when she'd tried to warn him not to do this? He was the one who always said there was no difference between being right and being dead. Despite his relaxed personality, the David she knew was a man who did not take risks on purpose. Unless it was to take her on a roller coaster, or make love with her in a movie theater. Just safe risks?

Until now. His moods were so erratic, and she'd seen him struggle to think of the simplest words. Maybe it wasn't an obsession with some other woman after all that was the source of the change she saw in him. But something medical ... or a breakdown of some kind. She closed her eyes, not wanting to think about it. She'd already tried to help him figure out what to do, and she'd failed.

It didn't matter if she were right, since he didn't listen to her.

She opened her eyes to find him staring at her with resolve. "What is it, David?" A wave of unease engulfed her, stronger than the storm surge that had tried to pull her and her family out to sea during Hurricane Katrina.

"I'm gonna go out there, see what shape the tractor's in," he said.

❧

2:35 P.M.

"What?" Anna gasped. "No!" She got up, and keeping the blanket wrapped around her, tried to get a closer look at him, but he wouldn't meet her eyes.

Anna tried again. "You can't go out there, David. The wind will knock you down. You'll freeze!"

"I've gotta see what's up with the fuel tank. There's a leak somewhere. I've gotta see how much diesel is missing. Or see where the leak is."

"Honey," she said gently, though inside her brain she was screaming: *Are you crazy? Do you want to die?* "You can't see fuel that's missing. You can't fix the leak, either."

He looked at her. "I can fix anything, and you know it." That flat, hard tone he'd used on her before was back and so was the flat look in his eyes. He was not the easy-going David she'd married and loved for so long. She realized with a jolt that there was a new David who had been surreptitiously taking over his familiar body in tiny, incremental steps for months now, maybe even a year. She just hadn't wanted to see, to deal with—they'd had so much other stuff to worry about.

God, something is really wrong with him.

"But you can't fix that fuel line, or anything else, *here!*" She flung her arm in a sweeping arc, encompassing the frozen, wind-ripped view. "I doubt you could even keep your balance."

"I know!" he said, punching the passenger seat.

Anna was amazed that he agreed, and when he looked up at the ceiling and repeated it, "I know that," more quietly, she saw by his softened expression that her husband was back.

He's just lost, she thought, seeing the confusion in his eyes. He's a little boy who's lost. It scared her. He'd always been her rock, her source of strength, but something inside him was wrong. He didn't feel right or look right to her. But she didn't know what she was dealing with or how to respond.

She couldn't let him go outside. For whatever reason, he couldn't see the risk, but she could. She was uncomfortable disagreeing with him and searched her mind, hunting for the right words. "Do you remember when I took the emergency preparedness class, after Katrina?" she began, and when he shook his head, she went on, even as it occurred to her they'd just been talking about that class. "Well, we learned if you're lost, you are not to leave your car if you get stuck. You should stay where you are."

"Well, yeah. That's easy for them to say when they're in a classroom."

"But the first rule of survival in a storm is not to leave the shelter you have!"

He shook his head, looking out the window, then back at her. "I'm not going anywhere, not leaving you. I'm just going out there to see what kind of mess we're in."

He sounded so sure. She set her hand on his shoulder. "It won't help anything, honey. Please stay inside."

"I can't sit here and not do anything." The flat, hard tone was back.

Anna returned to the bed. "Doing nothing except keeping warm, David. That's everything right now. Our job is to keep warm."

A stronger gust of snow-filled wind shook the cab. Casey groaned vaguely in his sleep. David put on his boots.

"Going out there is not going to help!" Anna was yelling now, an edge of something manic in her voice. She couldn't help it.

He looked at her. "Promise me you'll stay right here, Anna."

"David, they say there's no such thing as bad weather, just inadequate clothing," she attempted. "But your parka isn't waterproof. And you don't have a hat." She took a breath. "And your clothes are already wet."

"It'll be fine. I won't be out there long."

She thought how he kept using that word, "fine." But it must not have meant what he thought it meant, because their situation kept getting worse.

"Do you want my hat?" she offered, pulling it off her head.

"Nah, I'm fine." David zipped the old red parka, confirmed the earmuffs were already on his ears, and put his wet gloves back on. "I'll be back in a minute, babe," he said, and her heart almost broke on seeing his old smile. Even his eyes held a bit of the sparkle he used to have all the time.

My Dutch Boy. "Don't go out there. I need you." Her voice slipped and caught.

"Don't worry."

"I can't help it. You already said I was right about not going anywhere today, and now I'm telling you again, you should stay here."

"I love you, Anna. But I've got this. I've gotta take care of you."

Summer, 1980, Anna's kindergarten memory, Chinatown, San Francisco, California

Part 5

AT THE NOODLE SHOP, NO ONE WAS AT THE COUNTER. MAMA filled and wrapped spring rolls in the kitchen. Anna got washed up and went to work without a word. A huge plastic bag of carrots sat next to the sink, waiting for her. Mama always had a task for her to do after school.

Anna thought about Teacher while she pulled out her step stool and filled the sink with cold water. *How do I tell Mama I have to go to First Grade? She will be so angry!*

The bell tinkled as people came through the door into the front of the shop. It was quiet. After a minute, a lady called out, "Hello? Are you open?"

Mama yelled for the husband. "Customer!" but Baa didn't answer. "Oh," she reminded herself out loud. "He go to bank now."

Mama went to the counter and took their orders for spring rolls and tan tan noodles. Anna heard the familiar sound of the cash register opening to make their change, but that's when Mama made a sound Anna couldn't identify, like she wanted to shriek but had to swallow it.

"Oh, ladies. We no have any change for you. You got smaller money?"

They fussed between them for correct smaller change but didn't have enough.

"No problem. I give you discount. Go sit. I bring you food." They settled in at the table by the front window.

Mama came into the kitchen to serve up the food herself. She whispered to Anna. "Why the husband take all money to bank? He leave no money in register!"

Anna kept scrubbing carrots in the sink and rinsing them.

Mama took the food to the ladies and sat on the metal stool behind the counter until they had eaten, chatted a while, and left. Anna heard Mama open the cash register again and close it with a loud bang.

Mama ran through the kitchen and up the stairs to their room. Anna heard her open drawers, then drag a box from under the bed she shared with the husband, searching for something. She raced down the narrow steps to the kitchen, yelling, "Where the money? Where the husband take all the money?"

Anna didn't know. Her skinny legs felt weak under her.

"Where the husband? Why he not back from bank?" shouted Mama, shaking her fist in the air as Anna glanced at her and saw her flashing black eyes.

Anna thought about the three men grabbing the man and throwing him in their car. *Maybe it wasn't Baa.*

Her legs wanted to buckle. The whole earth was turning into almond jello and she couldn't stop it. She sat down on her step stool.

Mama yelled toward the ceiling. "We swim across water from Canton City! We find boat to cross ocean. We never sell enough tan tan noodles to pay the men." She paced up and down the space between the wooden and metal counters. "The men want more money all time. They don't stop. So husband put money in bank. Be safe." She took a big breath and ranted on. "But we keep little money in register for customers. So why the husband leave with all money? Why he not home now?"

Something didn't sound right to Anna. It made her wonder about what she had seen near the school. She went to Mama. "I saw Baa today. I think," she added, trembling.

Mama thundered at her. "You go to school, all day?"
Anna nodded.

"Then you no see him. He just go to bank, then come home."

Tears dribbled down Anna's chin.

Mama relented. "Where you see the husband?"

Anna took a breath. "Near my school. Some men. I think they took him..."

Mama frowned at the little girl shaking in front of her. "We run to America so we be safe and our child be smart. But now she talk like she run into ghost. Stop this crazy talk. Go finish work."

Anna climbed onto the step stool. Tears leaked out of her eyes onto the vegetables she had just washed, and she wished she hadn't said anything.

16

THURSDAY, NOVEMBER 28, 2019, 2:40 P.M., OLD LA VETA PASS, COLORADO

The wind tore the passenger door from David's grasp the moment he stepped through it. Watching from the bed, she saw when it slammed shut again, catching his leg. Hard. She heard a cry. Hers? His? She didn't know. The door closed. Climbing to the passenger seat, she peered through the window, saw him hanging on the outside handle. But suddenly, he was gone. She couldn't see anything of him, not even his head or his red parka.

"David!" Why hadn't she made him tie a rope around his waist, or something? Nothing was visible, nothing but white and more white.

It was too much. All too much. The crash. The snow. The desperation. And this feeling that even if her dear husband were with her in the cab, or even with her in Jessie's apartment, or when their house was repaired and they were home again, he would still feel so distant. She closed her eyes and pictured their warmth together in the bed this morning, and it was beautiful, but it also felt like something was changing. They were so close, but part of him was shut off from her. What part? And why?

And right now, he was out of sight, in the treacherous wind trying to move through a snowdrift. Floundering.

Tears made warm tracks down her cheeks which soon felt cold. She wiped her face and tried to peer out again, but it was pointless. "David! How is this going to turn out!" She shouted at the frosted window. "What am I supposed to do now?" The tightness in her chest hurt as she let more tears flow. "If you get hurt, I can't even lift you!" she yelled. "I am so mad at you!"

She clambered back to the bed, where Casey took up the whole middle. Anna pulled the blanket over both of them, warming herself so that when she had to go outside, she might not freeze to death as fast. The howling wind roared, seeming to get louder the longer David was out there.

"God, please help me figure out what to do," she whispered, cuddling Casey. How can I just sit here? she wondered. It felt so stupid, so useless. Like her shouting at David through the window. A fresh threat of tears narrowed her throat, and leaning back, Anna closed her eyes against them.

David was the planner in their family, despite his casual appearance. Even when she turned up at the bus station, he'd driven from his family's Nebraska farm without missing a beat. "You said you'd be here, and you're really here!" And when she told him she was pregnant, he had kissed her, walked around the park to talk, and then pulled her into the car and home to meet his parents. From there, he and his loving family had welcomed her in their own way. His parents' marriage wasn't perfect either, but they had given Anna a model of what it was like to be married and work as a team.

"I am so mad at you, David!" She yelled into the cold cab again. "We never learned how to fight with each other! We always just did things your way, because usually it didn't matter to me, and your way was fine." Screaming into the empty cab felt good. "I hardly ever had a different opinion, and when I did, I had no clue how to discuss it with you! And now look where it's gotten us!"

That's just what I did with Mama, she realized with a chill. She remembered all the times she'd gone along with Mama's opinions just to survive. She'd let her mama boss her around. *I just bailed on myself,* she thought. She didn't have a choice then, as a kid.

But David wasn't a bully. He was easy to be with and had lots of good ideas, and Anna would follow him to the ends of the earth without a second thought.

"Wait a minute, how can I be making this *my* fault!" she yelled again into the empty cab. "I did not drive us off the road!" *I can not panic. I need to think.*

She growled and swallowed, her eyes darting, focusing on nothing in particular.

But I have sure been letting us drift apart. All the conversations I never bothered to bring up, or got brave enough to deal with. Now the gap between us is filling with snow, and I can't even stop him.

She tried to peer out the window again but couldn't see anything. Couldn't see him. *How long will I sit here? How long will I let David always be the one to decide things?*

She'd gone from living with Mama to living with David and his family, where she'd once again gone along, making herself blend in, becoming the good wife, daughter-in-law, and mother they believed she already was. She thought she was, too. In all this time, she had never figured out what *she* wanted to do. Life had just kept happening to her, and while she'd been busy helping out everyone else, she'd lost herself.

"Casey," she murmured, looking down at the sleeping dog, "how did this happen? How come I didn't notice?"

He didn't do more in response than lift his head, look at her, then set his head down again.

Rising on her knees, Anna peered through the window, but the world outside was nothing more than white and shadow. And noise. The howling wind, the waves of snow sweeping across the windows. Had David made it to the back of the cab? How would she know without going out there herself? She settled back beside Casey and rubbed his sore leg gently. David had told her to stay put, and it had become her habit, doing what he said, because she usually agreed with him, anyway. "I've let him have his way on the little things for so long that when it comes to big things, like now, we have no way to deal with them!"

She brushed her hand absently over the blanket and went on talking out loud to herself in a thoughtful voice. "I don't think David and I ever saw his parents argue during the time we lived with them on the farm. They were a better example of what a loving married couple was like than Mama and Baa, but I wasn't seeing the whole story." She paused to listen, but there was no sound other than of snow and wind, her breath. She spoke aloud again, finding it eased her. "David's so easy to get along with, never asking for much, not demanding anything of me. He just wanted me and Jessie to be happy."

She growled out loud in frustration with her realization.

"I guess he assumed I was doing what I wanted to do, but all this time I've really just been following his lead and leaning on him." She pondered, trying to make the minutes go by faster. "Like my art career. He has no idea it's supposed to be a career for me, because I never told him," she told Casey. "He thinks it's just a fun hobby for me, something I do when I have nothing else to do." *But how could he know when I never said it?*

A prolonged hard gust of wind made something new vibrate on the outside of the cab, and she woke back to reality. She thought of how confused he'd become, how his memory had gaps. What could be the reason? What if it wasn't an affair at all? What if he were having strokes, or diabetes, or some other medical problem? What if he got confused outside in the storm?

She reached for her boots, knowing she'd been an idiot to let him go outside, and at the same time knowing, if she had really tried to stand in his way, he would have said, "You and what army?"

2:59 P.M.

A muffled bang hit the passenger door, and she looked up from tying the boots. "David!" Through the snow-caked passenger door window, she got a glimpse of his face, bright red with cold, before he slid out of sight again. Looking down, she saw him in the deep snow, struggling to reach up to the door handle, and she managed to crack it open from her side, both of them working against the force of the wind. He fought to free himself from the snowdrift, and the steps up to the cab were coated in ice. At last, he managed to get some traction, and pulling himself up to the upper step, he got one booted foot wedged inside the door.

The icy wind forced its way in, around David, trying to rip the door off its hinges, and simultaneously stopping David's progress. She stuck her hand down and grabbed hold of the red parka and pulled with all her might, right as he made another attempt to pull himself up.

He fell onto the seat, and she reached over him to pull the door closed. "Thank God, thank God." Tears burned her eyelids, and she blinked them away.

At first, he couldn't catch his breath. He sat on the passenger seat and beat his hands up and down his opposite forearms, shooshing out air between his teeth. Finally, he tried to talk. His voice was choked. "I almost couldn't make it."

"Oh David!" she said, her hands going to his shoulder.

"It's better in here. No wind." He shuddered and tried to wipe some slush off the side of his face with his hand.

His bare hand... "Where's your glove?" He still had on his left glove, but it was completely soaked through, and the tips of his fingers on his right hand, the bare hand, were alarmingly white and tinged with brown under the nails.

She brushed clumps of melting snow off his head, shoulders, and face, and with every gesture, every passing second, she was taking in evermore distressing details. Examining his face, she realized his cheeks were white too. It was not only his remaining glove that was wet, but all his clothes, the goose down parka with no waterproofing, his blue jeans and boots—everything he was wearing was dark with moisture. He reached to lower the coat's zipper, but his hands were too shaky from cold and exhaustion—and possible frostbite, Anna thought—to get the job done.

She knelt to help him. But should they take off the parka at all, or was it keeping him warm even though it was wet? Her brain, in its panic, couldn't locate the information she knew they had covered in the emergency class. Thoughts raced around without accomplishing anything except making her feel anxious.

"There's no way we can get out to the road," he said.

"You tried to go to the road?"

He shook his head. "No, I stayed by the truck." She tried to focus on what he said, but a buzzing sound filled her ears and brain. "But I couldn't see the road. Too much snow."

What is the right thing to do here? When he's this cold, what do I do to help him? I can't think. What did we learn in that emergency class? Don't leave your shelter, and ... I don't remember. God, please help me calm down and remember.

"We have to warm you up," she told him as she stepped back to the bed and pushed Casey off the blanket he was curled up on. She pulled the blanket over to the passenger seat, crawled up onto David's lap, and wrapped the blanket and her petite self around his whole body. She leaned closer to him, put her arms around him and pulled herself as close as she could with him still sitting in the passenger seat. It was awkward, but it felt a little warmer this way. She just needed to do something.

That's just what David had said. *Better than doing nothing.*

His teeth chattered as his body attempted to warm itself up.

The diesel engine puttered, and she turned around to increase the flow from the air vents warmed by the engine. "Could you see the diesel tank on this side at least? Is there a leak?"

He shook his head. "We're so rammed down onto the drifts, it's amazing the cab is in one piece. That front bumper must be wedged way under the engine by now. Who knows how much damage there is."

Behind the cab, Anna heard the sound of metal grinding against ice as the wind shifted something. "Was that the wind moving the trailer?"

"Could be. When I was out there, I couldn't see it. I

couldn't... couldn't... get around to see anything." His speech stuttered through his chattering teeth. "I'm g—guessing it's d—destroyed." He screwed his eyes shut, holding his mouth in a grim line. "I'm gonna have to buy a new trailer..."

She closed her eyes and hugged him closer with her whole body, grateful that eventually the warmth in the cab would help him recover. She tucked her head under his chin, her cheek against his wet shoulder, a posture which was usually so comforting to her. But now, the flesh of his neck, the wet shirt against her face—he was just so wet and cold.

Anna realized she was colder now, too. The air from the vents didn't feel as warm, and the blanket was not enough anymore to ward off the chill.

"I wish I had a hot water bottle or something," she murmured, and then, sitting upright, she said, "I've got an idea." Climbing from David's lap, she took her half-empty foam cup of cold, bitter coffee from the holder on the dashboard and put it in the microwave. "You think the truck engine will let me run the microwave?"

"Maybe," he answered.

She entered forty seconds on the keypad and pressed the start button. "Look. It's working!" She was euphoric. In all of this, it felt like a minor miracle.

The engine kept running, and so did the microwave. She now had a hot coffee cup with a lid, and tucking it into her husband's hand, she said, "Hold this close to you, honey. That's it. Try to keep it upright so it doesn't spill. Now, let's raise it up. I want you to hold it next to your throat where the big artery runs down."

She moved his hands to help him, and David did as she instructed.

Carefully, she sat on his lap again, and pressing as close

to him as possible, she managed to pull the thin blanket over both of them. But she realized that in the foam cup, the warmth would stay with the coffee, so she changed her mind and got him to take a few sips of the warm beverage, then stowed it back in the cup holder. It had been a good idea to try. *I could use some more ideas*, she told God, settling down again in David's lap, holding him as he shivered. *Remind me what I already know!* "I'm right here," she said aloud to David. "We'll wait for them to find us." Her bravado was put on, a lie. She had no idea whether anyone was coming.

"I had to try," he said.

She lifted her head from his chest. "Try?" she asked. "Try what? To get killed?" She actually said it, her worst fear out loud, and it felt good to have it out in the air between them. "Try to abandon me?" Her voice rose. "Just because you're full of testosterone and muscles does not mean you are immortal, David!"

He said it again. "I had to try."

She wanted to argue, but what good was it? "The main thing is to get you warm again," she said. "Someone will come soon. Scrap King will send help—"

Meanwhile, they had to stay put and stay warm. Or in David's case, get warm again. Thank goodness for the warmth of the truck engine. It idled in the blizzard, keeping the temperature in the cab warmer.

But then something was different. The noise of the unbelievable hurricane strength wind outside continued, but the reassuring sound of the puttering engine disappeared.

The engine had stopped. The diesel had run out.

～

3:05 P.M.

Anna's breathing stopped too, for a long moment.

The engine stopped? They couldn't get heat from the engine anymore?

She stared at David. What could he say? Her eyes watered, and she reached out for... what? David? No, he couldn't help her or himself. He was half frozen. She was the only one who could do anything. But not if she couldn't even breathe, or think.

It had to be her imagination, but it already felt colder in the cab than it had minutes ago. She reached over to turn off the vents that now only blew cold air, then as she straightened, her mama's voice came out of nowhere, out of the past, wrenching her back to the despair when she, her mama, and her teenage daughter were caught in the record-breaking hurricane storm surge, twenty-seven-feet of ocean trying to find its way onto the land.

Her mother had cried out, "Why we here? Why we didn't leave?" Jiexen had said to Anna and Jessie in her most cutting English words, when the water trapped them. "Why you not figure out what to do? What we do now? This your fault. You not smart girl." Anna was a mother herself by then, with a daughter of her own, and still she'd been forced to endure her mother's judgment, those slicing words, cutting at her since childhood.

Where had David been? Maine? Minnesota? Manitoba? It didn't matter. He sure hadn't been in Pass Christian (kris-chee-ANN), Mississippi, with her, Jessie, and Mama when the storm hit. The water from the storm surge, which hit at high tide, had crept higher and higher, pushing them first to the countertops, then to the second floor, and finally to the attic. Ripping away the structure of the building as it rose. Jessie, Anna, and the Tiger Grandma battled the fear, the ferocious putrid sea water, and each other. They finally came out alive, kicking and screaming, on the other side.

It had tested everything Anna knew of or had experienced in life back in 2005. Her faith. Her confidence. Her relationship with both her daughter and her mama, as if either of those could have been any more strained than they already were before the combined tragedy of the wind and water. How Anna wished they'd been able to evacuate ahead of the storm. Over time, she'd figured she must have done something right then. She was still here.

But now her mama's voice came again, here in the sleeper cab in the middle of a winter storm. "Why you stuck here, Anna? Why you not leave?"

The old helplessness overcame her, a noose tightening around her neck, strangling her. She wondered if this were a test from God. No, she knew it was a temptation from the enemy, the accuser, the supreme liar of the universe, trying to fill her with doubt. Trying to make her forget Who she was and Whose she was. The fear, the cold, the doubt... the enemy doesn't fight fair. He hits when you're weak.

"It's all my fault," she declared.

"What're you talking about? You didn't do this. Come 'ere." He tried to pull her back against him, but she resisted.

But then she felt the cold air seep in between them, and she pulled him closer again after all. "I should have made you stop," she said. "We should have stayed in Durango, like Lily said." The pressure of her failure kept pushing on her chest, her eyes. "Or South Fork. Or Alamosa. Or Fort Garland." The words squeezed out, louder and louder. "Why didn't I stop you?" *I could have hidden the truck keys. Too late now.*

"Keep holding onto me, babe. It's helping."

"I don't think it's gonna be enough, David." She shuddered at the realization. "I don't think we can keep this up long enough to make it." *I'm not strong enough. I can't do this alone.*

She had no sooner finished the thought when David began singing the same Scorpions song as yesterday. His voice was weak, but Anna heard the courage in it, the warmth and his strong desire to stay positive. "Wise man said ... just find your place ... in the eye of the storm..." The words, the music came haltingly from him, and they were a soft and haunting prayer.

Anna closed her eyes, and swallowing the tears in her throat, she sang with him. *That's just what I was thinking, honey. That's just what I was asking God.*

Music from heaven, even though it was hard rock music. "Here I am!" They sang the haunting tune together. "Will you send... me an angel?" Seriously, Anna thought, music could change the world, it was so full of good energy.

17

3:15 P.M.

The lyrics fired her up. "Close your eyes... and you will find... the way out of the dark." She'd heard the words so many times. She'd even thought of them when they'd been trapped during the hurricane—but during that disaster, she'd literally just closed her eyes and held on.

On the other hand, today she was taking charge, and the song was more of a prayer of thanks. That made all the difference in what the words meant. As her dear pastor, Rev. Dr. Kaylor, always said, "a text without a context is just a pretext for whatever you want it to say." This was so true, in this context, ha ha!, it made her laugh. Laugh!

David gave her a look. "What's funny?" he said through chattering teeth.

Anna already had her arms wrapped tight around him, and now she squeezed him harder for a moment. When she'd prayed to calm down, she had remembered something from that class she took.

"David, I know what we have to do," she announced. "We have to get those boots off you, my farm boy. All your wet clothes have got to go. All those wet layers are just making you colder. That's what the instructor told us." Climbing off his lap, she knelt to untie the soaked laces of his boots, then got him to stand up. He tried working the zipper of his jeans, but his hands were shaking so badly, she pushed them away. It was a struggle even for her, but finally she got the pants peeled away. She was glad she didn't have to use the knife in her purse to cut them off, but in an instantaneous flash of insight, she knew she could have done it. *What else do we have among our assets?*

Leading him to the bed, she had him sit on the edge, while she stripped him of his cotton socks, exposing feet that were too white even for a white guy. The tips of his toes looked grayish and waxy.

"Hey," he said through chattering teeth. "It's cold out here." He shivered, and his skin was paler than pale. The more of her dear husband she uncovered, the more she wanted to cover him back up and make him warm.

But everything that's wet is making him colder!

She got rid of more wet things that stole the heat from his body. The goose down parka. The long-sleeved black t-shirt. The cotton tighty-whities. All he had on was the blanket and his black earmuffs. It would've been quite a look if they hadn't been in such dire straits.

Now what?

She pushed away her mama's imagined criticisms in her head. "Mama, I'm taking charge now," she said to Jiexen in the past. "I've got to find a way to keep us warm."

Anna didn't realize she'd spoken aloud until he half grinned at her and said, "You're the one who took all my clothes."

"We have to keep our body heat in better than just with this blanket. What do we have?" She kept voicing her thoughts, and the words sounded better and more hopeful coming through the air into her ears, instead of just rattling in her head. "You don't have any spare clothes, do you? Come on, admit it. You didn't bring an overnight bag with you at all."

He shrugged like a little kid. "I guess I forgot it."

"Well, none of my clothes are big enough to fit you. So now what?" She looked around the cab. "In the class, the instructor said to improvise and overcome. Said you could use trash bags. They're an unappreciated resource." She reached into the cupboard where she'd seen the bags before and pulled one off the roll.

"What're you doing, babe?" David asked as she again knelt in front of him.

"Giving you some insulation," Anna pointed at his feet, indicating he should put them into the bag. He stood as she drew it up the length of his legs. He was so tall, it didn't reach past his thighs, so she ripped a hole in another bag to pull down over his head and torso. She layered on the sheet and thin blanket, helping as he worked to wrap the layers around himself.

She was on a roll now. "God wants me to trust him. He doesn't want this ship to go down in flames," she said with some satisfaction. "Flames!" She was almost shouting.

"Flames?" David repeated.

"Candles!" she said, grinning at him. "We need candles."

"We don't have any candles, babe," he muttered.

"Yes, we do!" she announced. She pulled her beanie down more tightly on her head, repeating it, "Yes, we do. Where is that bag?"

He didn't answer.

"David," she tried again. "Where did you put that little gray duffel bag I gave you yesterday? When we left Jessie's?"

"It was pitch dark. I don't know."

She was sure she hadn't seen it since she'd handed it to him. "Where else do you store things in here?" Not waiting for his answer, she stood up on the bed and hunted through the highest compartments she'd never looked in before, then she moved to the front of the cab, standing on the driver's seat to check above there. She crouched down and looked behind and under the driver's seat, and then behind the passenger seat.

There it was! The forgotten duffel had been right behind her since yesterday morning.

Lifting the little bag, she moved back to the sleeping area. Beside David, Casey looked on with interest. As she sang the Scorpions song again, and then hummed, she dumped out everything else from the duffel. "I've never looked at the stuff I packed since the hurricane, when I took the emergency preparedness class."

Anna's duffel bag was a treasure trove. Dry socks. An old t-shirt of David's left over from some long-ago rock concert tour. *How can it be over fifty years since the Moody Blues?* And a pair of sweatpants, which were Anna's size, but they were baggy ones, so maybe they would stretch to fit David. A flashlight, an ancient plastic bottle of water, shrunken and wrinkled with age, and two fossilized protein bars, hard as a rock. A tiny first aid kit that would help only if someone got a paper cut.

Getting David to stand up again, she shucked him out of the trash bag and began working the sweatpants over his feet, drawing them up his long legs. *I can't believe I forgot we had that bag of supplies in here somewhere.*

"Now that I think about it, we should have taken off the wet things sooner." *Give yourself a break Anna. You just forgot.*

When he sat, she said, "Stick out your foot." He obeyed

like a child and she put on a dry sock. "Now the other foot." She felt as if she were back in Jessie's childhood days. It might have been funny, but it wasn't.

Her short sweatpants left his shins exposed, and the t-shirt was short-sleeved, but at least it was dry and it fit him. She replaced both the trash bag layers. Retrieving her pajama top, she used it to dry his wet hair, muttering, "I can't believe you went out in this storm wearing just earmuffs."

He leaned against the bulkhead. "It's all I had," he mumbled, eyes closed.

She found the shirt she'd worn yesterday, which was dry, and gently wrapped it around his head and neck to keep more body heat in. Anna dropped her glance to his face, noting the white spots on his cheeks. His feet when she'd put them into the socks ... she pictured the toes ... so gray.

What was she thinking, telling him she'd thought of solutions? As the frigid gale steadily sucked the warmth out of the cab, her glimmer of hope guttered like a candle in the forceful wind of reality.

3:30 P.M.

So then, maybe it was God that prompted David to remind her to keep going. "Did you say something about a candle before?"

Hope returned. "Oh! Right!" She rummaged under the items from the bag still piled on the bed and drew out a rectangular metal can with a triumphant flourish.

"What is it?"

"A forty-eight-hour survival candle." Lighting it, she explained. "It was my birthday present from Prentice."

David groaned. "Did I miss your birthday?"

"You were on the road," she answered lightly, as if it hadn't mattered to her when it had. She'd been so mad at him; he didn't even call her. Then she caught herself just thinking it, and she said it aloud, trying to be better about communicating with him. "I was really mad at you!" It felt good, letting him know her true feelings. "You know how Prentice is, into all things survival. I'd told him about the class I'd taken, that the instructor had given us a list of what to pack. Anyway, on my birthday, when he gave it to me, I thought it was amazing. Turns out this kind of candle was on the instructor's list."

"I feel bad for forgetting. My being on the road, it's no excuse." David glanced at her. "I'm glad he did something. He's a good kid."

"Yes. He feels like we've kind of adopted him. Did you know that? It's why he wanted to give me a present." Anna watched the candle flame flicker, taking joy in it, finding renewed hope within herself, and even smiled. "This little light of mine," she sang, "I'm gonna let it shine..."

She found a large metal can that had once held peanuts and now contained random hardware and carefully dropped the lit emergency candle into it. She thought that would keep the flame from setting something on fire in the cab, and they might be able to melt snow for water to drink, if she could find another metal can. If they were here that long...

She reached for the duffel and shook it to free one more item it held. It was a package about the size of a deck of cards, wrapped in cellophane. "We even have a space blanket."

"What?" David sounded groggy now.

She was almost positive, since his fingers, toes and cheeks were an odd color, that he had some frostbite, but was he also hypothermic? She knew that was a danger, possibly the most critical concern right now. The instructions with the mylar blanket reminded her to keep a hypothermia patient awake, if possible, until their core temperature increased. Symptoms included shallow breathing, weak pulse, pale skin, and slurred speech. It also said if frostbitten body parts were likely to freeze again, not to attempt to warm them in water or rub them, because that would worsen the tissue damage.

Anna's fear wanted to make a reappearance. She spoke over it. "This blanket will help just like the trash bags are. This is made of mylar, and I'm going to wrap it around us too, to keep our body heat from leaking away so fast," she said, and going to work, she unlaced her boots and climbed in with David. She snuggled close to David, adding the insulating silver layer of Mylar first, with the smelly sheet and blanket on top, and then the trash bag, making a cocoon as best she could.

Cuddled up so close to him, with Casey as close as he could be under their legs, they didn't talk. She put as much of herself close to as much of him as she could manage, skin to skin. It was hard to move, really. Not comfortable, especially when her arm started to go numb from staying in one position too long, and it was hard to shift around much. So she shifted in small increments and kept her body touching David's in as many places as she could.

It really was warmer now, wrapped up together with more insulation. David's eyes fluttered open. "How does that feel?" she asked.

"Thanks, babe."

She found that talking was helping her think, whether David was listening or not. "When Prentice gave me the candle, I threw it in the duffel I'd begun to stock after I took the class." She hadn't finished. "It was still in my car when the fire came in August, so it's one of the few things that wasn't destroyed. I didn't even look inside it when I evacuated this summer, though, since I ended up at Jessie's and I brought a few suitcases when I left the house."

He grunted to let her know he heard her.

She was really fired up. "The one part of the duffel I actually did look into this summer after the fire was the outside pocket, for the flash drive. I've been using that to help with the insurance claims."

David was trying to follow along. A good sign. "A flash drive?"

"Yes, the instructor said to create an emergency financial first aid kit, so I saved copies of some of our important documents and passwords and phone numbers."

"Babe, I had no idea you did all that."

"Yes, I did take care of all that, so you didn't have to worry about it." A week ago, she never would have mentioned it. She hadn't told him when she'd done it for the usual reason—his need to have a relaxing home life, free of stress, superseded her need to share the burden. She wished she'd scanned copies of their photo albums onto the drive too, but it was too late now.

He said, "I've just always known you would take care of things at home, babe. But I didn't realize how much you were doing."

"Well, I didn't speak up, did I?" She took a breath, and smiling, changed the subject. "Too bad we don't have a deck of cards." She tried to joke. "You know how you always say to have cards with you when you're lost."

He didn't answer. His eyes were shut.

She touched his cheek, which was cool but not as cold as

when he got back in the truck. "Do you remember why?" she prompted.

That got a grunt. But his eyes remained shut.

She prodded his shoulder, trying to get his attention, scared to let him sleep until she knew he was warm enough. "Because as soon as you start playing solitaire," she pushed the words through her throat that felt as dry as dust, "because —" she began again — "someone will appear, completely out of nowhere, and tell you to play the black eight on the red nine!"

4:15 P.M.

Another hour passed. The lone emergency candle made a dent in the chill, but the windows were beginning to be frosted on the inside by the vapor from their breath. Anna woke without having realized she'd dozed off. Gently extricating herself from the cocoon she'd constructed around herself, David and Casey, she climbed out of the cab's sleeping area and slid her boots on. Hugging herself against the chill, she figured a way to relieve the pressure in her bladder by squatting over one of the black trash bags and then securing it in a cupboard.

Then she considered their food resources. One last can of soup and the rest of the pie, and Casey had a few more cupfuls of his food. How long until they were rescued? Staying warm and having water to drink was the key. She remembered from class that people could go a lot longer without food than without water, and her best guess was that if their CB message got through, they could be found sooner. But was "sooner" an hour from now, or a day or two?

What if they had to wait for them to plow the road? She had no way of knowing.

It's called "comfort food" for a reason, she thought. Should she ration it out between herself and David, to make it last?

Not all of it, she decided. Let's have the soup and help David really get energy to warm up. Then we'll still have the pie for tomorrow.

She got a plastic spoon out of the drawer where the sugar packets were and popped the top on the chicken noodle soup, then after setting it on the counter next to the bed with a cup of water from the container she'd filled yesterday, she grabbed Casey's bag of food, too.

"Okay, I'm going to crawl back in there with you." She slipped off her boots, pulled the blankets around their shoulders and hips, with the trash bag pulled over their feet and legs as far as it would go. The dog lay beneath their legs.

David nodded from under the blankets. "That's really good." He attempted a wink.

She laughed. "I'm glad you're in such a good mood."

She started with some sips of the water, and then she fed David half the can of cold soup, one bite at a time. He was conscious and swallowing. He started to look more human again. She ate every other bite, taking her turn while he worked to swallow his spoonful of cold soup.

The minutes went by. The wind never slowed down. But the chill in the air didn't seem quite as evil as they gathered their resources around themselves, literally.

"Remember when we first got to Colorado?" She raised the spoonful of soup and David dutifully opened his mouth. Like a baby bird, Anna thought. Like baby Jessie. "Our main objective was to be as far away from the ocean as we could get. Even my mama agreed with that part. She was already afraid of vast expanses of water, even before the hurricane."

"She was?" he asked.

"Yes, remember, they had to swim to Hong Kong so they could escape what was happening in China—the so-called Great Leap Forward, and the almighty Cultural Revolution." Anna grimaced and shook her head. "I've researched it myself since she wouldn't tell me much."

"Really? You never said—" He was trying so hard to stick with her. Anna saw it in his face.

"To get to the coastline, they went on a bus with faked travel documents. Then they swam down the river estuary at night. Can you imagine?" Anna couldn't. She offered David another spoonful of soup. "That wasn't the worst of it. But... why am I talking about this? Back to our move to Garnet after the hurricane." She knew she was babbling, but somehow the sound of her own voice kept her grounded, kept her from screaming out for help when reason said no one would hear. "I don't know how we came up with Colorado," she said. "Instead of going back to Nebraska, I mean."

"There wasn't anything left for me in Nebraska," he said. Anna paused, the spoon halfway to his mouth. He now, wonder of wonders, offered her a brief smile. "We needed a fresh start, and, you know, where the deer and antelope play, and all that."

She smiled, too, and she thought he might be warming up. She offered more soup. He swallowed it dutifully, but then mumbled something about his toes and fingers feeling numb.

Telling herself to be strong, she said, "David, I think you have a little frostbite." She paused. "And we can't do anything about it right now."

He said, "That's ridiculous. I wasn't out there that long."

She didn't answer, but it had been close to half an hour. She worried more now about him regaining his core body temperature. It helped that he was out of the wind, and was dry and bundled up close to her. She noticed his breathing seemed normal, and his words were clearer and decided to take it as a good sign.

Meanwhile, since distractions could be the best part of having a good bedside manner, she said, "Here's some dessert, honey." She opened a sugar packet, mixed it in a bit of water, and tipped it into his mouth. He slurped it up. "I'm saving the pie for later, okay?" There were three sugar packets left, along with two-thirds of the pumpkin pie. *How long will we be here?*

She kissed David and pulled the blankets up over both their heads again, making sure they exhaled their damp breath out into the cab instead of into the dry cocoon. Casey snored, having long ago settled back under their legs. David dropped off right away, and Anna tried to talk with him, but she was so tired herself, despite the concerns racing through her head. She felt her own breathing become very regular, and she felt less cold inside the blanket tent she'd created around them.

Until the dog got restless, she dozed off. She wanted him to stay right where he was with his warm mammal body, sharing his heat with them. When he stirred, she took a handful of Casey's food from the zip-lock bag on the counter next to her and fed him one piece of kibble at a time in his cave below the blankets. Casey wasn't used to being hand-fed, but he was willing to go along with it if the result was food in his mouth. It gave Anna a way to pass a few more cold, windswept minutes, and he stayed put under their legs. Soon, all three were snoring again.

Then David shifted his position, trying to get comfortable crammed next to her in the cocoon. "Do you know what time it is, babe?" David asked.

Anna shook her head to wake up. "Huh?"

"The dude on the CB said he would send help. Scrap King. Maybe they're coming soon," said David in a quiet voice. Anna thought he sounded a little more coherent, but maybe she was fooling herself. They'd lost the connection with High Plains Drifter, but Scrap King had said he'd send help hadn't he? How long ago was that?

The wind continued to howl and blow even more snow, so looking out the window by the bed didn't offer any clues as to the time of day, except that it was still light outside.

But she could see the digital clock on the microwave, since the truck's battery still had some power. "It's after four, so that was two hours ago." She tried to think about what to do next. "It'd sure be nice to warm up some water to drink. But the microwave oven uses too much power for the truck battery when the engine's off. You told me that once."

He shrugged and closed his eyes. "I dunno," he said. "Yeah, that sounds right. But we're out of fuel, so the engine's off..." he seemed to be summarizing the situation.

"Right," she said. "We're stuck between a rock and a hard place. But later, if the water jug gets empty, we could use the candle to heat some snow in a tin can."

He grunted acknowledgment.

She said, "I'm so grateful we can shelter inside the cab, instead of being out in the wind."

David said something that surprised her, especially with how forgetful he'd been lately. "They called this a bomb cyclone, right? With hurricane-force winds?"

"Yes."

"Were the winds like this when you were in the hurricane?" he asked.

"Yes," she nodded. "We haven't talked much about that time, have we?" she said.

He opened his eyes. "Nope. Not about what happened to you three when you were stuck, before I got there. When I was able to get to Mississippi with the truck and finally locate you there, it was days later, and we just focused on getting us the heck out of there, away from all the damage and the stench," said David.

"It smelled so rotten, and mildewy, and..." the decaying dead things and corpses had been the hardest to cope with. She said, "We didn't have anything to bring with us — no clothes or furniture or photos. All we owned was what was what you had stored in the cab of this truck. Everything else was washed away or soaked."

"I had this parka of my dad's with me in the truck," he said. "I wonder if he would have retired from farming by now, if he hadn't died in the tornado." He closed his eyes.

She said, "By now he would be.. let me think... about sixty-five. But you told me no one can ever really retire from farming. With your brother running the farm now, he'd probably be over there all the time."

"Yep. Wow, we've sure had a lot of natural disasters in our lives," he said.

She shook her head with the memories of the hurricane.

"But no, you never told me what it was like when you were trapped during the storm," he said, going back to the beginning.

"You didn't ask..." She paused, wondering if she wanted to get into it now, but at least it was a past storm she'd already made it through, instead of the current storm they might not survive, so she allowed her mind to go back to Katrina.

She talked with him about all of it. The fear. The evacuation order. The confusion. Why she, Jessie, and Tiger Grandma couldn't get out of Pass Christian. The ocean spilling up onto the land where it didn't belong, trapping them where they were. Sweeping cars down the street and buildings off their foundations. Sweeping animals and people out to sea...

"The storm surge must have scared the shit out of you," David said.

"It came up so fast..." Anna shuddered at the fourteen-year-old memory.

He tried to hold her closer. "Wow," was all he said. "I wish I could have helped you. I wish I'd been there."

"Me, too," she said, thinking he would never know how badly she'd wished for him to be there. But now, it was enough that he could voice his regret. It meant he was paying attention, and that had to be a good sign.

18

———

4:30 P.M.

David shifted a little on the bed next to her. He was still shivering. The instructions on the mylar blanket reminded her that shivering was good, because it meant his body was still trying to keep itself warm. If he stopped shivering, then she should be concerned. *More concerned, that is.*

"Come on David, you have work to do."

He nodded with his eyes closed. "What work?"

"You have to keep me company. I need you with me."

"How long've we been here?"

"You just asked me that, honey. It's a little after four," she said. "It looks darker out than that, though." Her ears were so tired of the blowing howling wind outside.

He pushed the blanket down so he could look out the window. Anna pulled it back up and tucked it behind them to seal the body heat tent. "Aren't we kind of running out of things to talk about?" he joked.

"No, David," she didn't want to joke around. She wanted to get to the bottom of things, whatever the truth was, so that if anything happened to him, she wouldn't be left wondering. She needed to know. "I'm worried about you. You and me."

He made another joke. "You want to talk about us? Haven't we been doing that this whole time?"

She rubbed his arm. "Honey, we have not been making the time to really communicate lately. We haven't even talked on the phone as much when you're gone." She dived in. "And also, something feels different with you, and I don't know what it is."

His reply took her off guard. "I know, Anna, you're right," he said. She thought he'd argue with her and defend himself, but he said, "I've been feeling different, too."

"Wow! What do you mean?" The tone of his answer wasn't what she expected. It was vulnerable, not defensive. *Willing to open up?*

"I'm just not at the top of my game."

She hesitated. "In what way?" She wanted to leave this open to him, to hear his ideas, not throw her preconceived notions into the conversation any more.

"My energy level's been off. My knees hurt. Stuff like that."

"Oh... Anything else?" she ventured.

"Well, yeah. It's like I can't quite remember things."

She looked at him, unbelieving he was admitting it to her that he'd forgotten important things. *Filling out the truck logbook. That Prentice was a firefighter. Packing an overnight bag. Our honeymoon. The fact that I hate coffee.*

"How long have you felt like this?"

He sighed. "I don't know. For a while."

She felt almost weak with the relief that he'd brought it up himself. "You have?"

He turned it into a joke already. "You mean, do I remember what it is I've been forgetting?"

She tried to play along, but it wasn't funny. "You mean like..." she searched for another example... "that run you almost missed last month?"

"Yeah. That was a good catch, babe." He cleared his throat. "That day you looked at me and said, 'What're you still doing home this morning? I thought you said you were heading to Nebraska today,' and I just said, 'huh?' That was a bad one. At least it was still pretty early in the morning, and I got on my way."

"Honey, I wondered if you were overtired."

"Yeah, I've been pretty worn out."

But Anna thought there was more to it than simple exhaustion. She'd noticed ... what, exactly? Spacing out more than usual. Keeping his distance from her. She'd already confronted him about there being another woman in his life and he'd denied there was anyone else. Was he lying? Sick? Living a double life? It was all so confusing and scary. She just wanted him, the marriage she believed they'd had—she wanted that back.

But now they were wedged face first into a snowdrift in the middle of a bomb cyclone.

God, thank you for giving us this shelter from the storm. Thank you for not letting the truck roll over. Thank you for letting me and David not be injured from the crash.

But David was not in any shape to solve this one.

I don't know what I'm going to do, but I have to do something. That's just what David said before he got himself soaked to the skin in a raging blizzard, she reminded herself. *I've got to think straight.*

She cuddled with him.

It would be pointless to go out there, that's for sure. She listened to the crackling of the candle and tried to count to sixty seconds. Okay, that was one minute down. How many to go? She counted to sixty again. *That's two minutes.* She sighed.

That's when she realized there was something she could do to help them survive. The air was cold, but with the candle burning... She got out of the cocoon, cranked down the passenger window a smidge, so it was open a crack. *I hate to let out any warmth, but we have to breathe, too.*

But how long is this going to take? Did the CB radio operators they talked to earlier, High Plains Drifter, or Scrap King, ever send help? Were they waiting for help that was never summoned? She had to try the radio again, and unlike the microwave or the heater, the truck battery could give the radio enough amps.

With the wind screaming past the truck, and now whistling at the slightly opened window, she picked up the mic and used the channel that might reach the interstate. Where there might be some traffic. She keyed it and asked for help, waited, tried again, waited, tried again. She switched channels and tried again. For a response, she got nothing but silence.

She got back in the cocoon, closed her eyes, and wrapped her arms around him again. His breathing was more steady, more comforting than it had been. He didn't exude heat to share with her, but at least his body didn't suck heat away from her like before.

He seems to be warming up.

She really did fall asleep. It felt so good to close her eyes and really rest. I've done all I can do. God's got this covered. It's going to be okay. But I really want to live longer before I go to meet Him.

~

4:45 P.M.

She felt Casey slide out from under their legs and jump down on the floor of the cab, yelping slightly when he landed on his sore leg.

He must have to go potty, but there's no way I'm letting him outside. He'll just have to pee in the cab like the rest of us. Anna pulled the blankets closer around her and David to keep more warmth near them as their bodies worked to generate the heat. Shame to let it escape. It was really helping.

Casey made more vocalizations, sounding kind of like Chewbacca from the Star Wars movies, but Anna kept her eyes closed while the blessing of rest relieved her foggy, tired brain again. *There's no way you can go outside right now, dear dog. I'm sorry.*

First there was an odd snuffling noise. Then a crashing sound shook her awake. Struggling to open her eyes, to make sense of the noise. At first she thought someone had come, that they were being rescued at last. She bolted upright. "David, David! Wake up. Someone's here, banging on the truck."

Flinging aside the covers, she got up from the bed. That's when she saw the true source of the racket. Casey. Casey was on the floor, and the sight that met her eyes crushed her spirit.

"Casey, No!" she yelled.

He looked up at Anna with his big brown eyes from the now empty pumpkin pie plate, then dropped his head to lick up the last few crumbs of the pie. He'd gotten the cupboard door open with his big nose. She had counted on it for one more meal, the one she thought would help them last until help came.

Their last bit of food.

And no one was coming, were they? Wasn't she just

fooling herself? She hurt inside, and she felt herself giving in to the despair that had stalked her for so long. Even if someone was attempting a rescue, what was the likelihood they would make it in time? The snow was still coming down and the wind still howled. She felt her teeth grating with anger at the horrible wind that never let up. Why wouldn't it just stop for a little while! What had she done to deserve this? Why did disasters keep following her?

She banged her hands on her thighs, on the cupboard on the counter. Why did it have to be so hard? Why did she have to keep fighting? She felt so alone.

"Don't you dare leave me, David DeGroot!" she yelled and shook him again.

"Sorry, babe. I'm so tired." His golden voice was thin.

"What if we die?" Anna couldn't help asking. The tears came spilling from her eyes and down her flat cheekbones.

"We're not gonna die," he said weakly, opening his eyes.

"I'm not worried about dying, exactly, but it's that I have so much left to do in my life! If we don't get back, we'll never get to see Jessie and Prentice's wedding, or meet our grand-kids," she sobbed.

David was trying to follow along. "What wedding? What're you talking about?" Casey hopped back on the bed and nuzzled them. David reached his arm out from under the blankets to give his ears a scratch. That was more like her own David.

"Oh, I shouldn't have said that," she said. "They're not even engaged. But they're so perfect together, aren't they? Doesn't he remind you of yourself sometimes?" She perked up with this optimistic thought, distancing her mind from the blizzard, picturing her daughter with her boyfriend, the firefighter. "He's so much shorter than you, but the way his blond hair sticks up, and the way he grins at her. And she smiles back. Prentice was a gift to our whole family."

David was quiet, looking at Anna with confusion and then un-focusing again.

She went on. "I know I'm crazy for imagining them getting married. At a time like this, when we're stranded and we don't even know if anyone's looking for us." She wrapped her arms tight across her chest as she stood. "But it gives me hope to know Jessie might have kids of her own one day, whether we make it or not."

In the bed, David pulled the blankets closer around him, his eyes wide, unfocused. In such a serious situation, she wanted him to support her, comfort her. Or make a joke. Just say something!

But what was that look on his face? Fear? Discomfort? No, it was confusion. Maybe he was having a stroke. Maybe the cold was the least of their worries. But if that was the case, she still couldn't get him medical help. Maybe she should just comfort him now.

She crawled back into the cocoon with him to share their heat again. It was all she could really do. "What is it, honey?" She wiped the tears off her cheeks with the edge of the sheet. "You know God's gonna take care of us. Whether we live or die, we will be okay, because we know where we'll end up. And so will Jessie and Prentice." She sniffed. "I'm sorry I was sounding scared. That doesn't help you at all, does it?"

"Who are you talking about?"

Anna didn't know what to say, but finally said, "Prentice. Jessie's boyfriend."

But now David shook his head and laughed softly. "Oh, right. How could I forget?"

"Honey?" she asked softly. "What's wrong with you? Is it

the cold?" *What a silly question, of course, it is. I'm cold, and I didn't even get my clothes soaked.*

"Yeah, come here," he said to her, though they were already as close as they could be. "This blizzard is for the birds. We'll get out of here soon enough. You know, when we get home, I'm gonna wrap you up right in front of the fireplace and warm you up properly. We haven't done that for ages." He smiled and his blue eyes lit up. "Why is that, I wonder?"

It was Anna's turn for a blank look. "In front of the fireplace?"

"Yeah," said David with the warmest smile. "We'll have nothing on but the blankets, and listen to the stereo, and... yeah," he said. "There's a song about that..."

"It's called, 'Nothing on But the Radio,'" She smiled weakly. "Well, that will be great, as soon as we get a fireplace."

"No kidding. As soon as we get home."

She could only stare at him. Though he was always making everything into a joke, this time he was not joking.

She said, "Jessie doesn't have a fireplace."

"Oh yeah, Jessie's apartment," he said, but his speech seemed as uncertain as his expression.

It was his mind that had already been in questionable shape before they started the trip that seemed to malfunction more and more as each hour went by. She couldn't trust anything he said. Though he was right next to her, she was so alone. How could he abandon her like this without even leaving her presence?

God, what should I do? she thought. The moments ticked by. "God, what am I supposed to do now?" she said into the chilly cab. Anna's thoughts jumped from David, to the impending darkness, to the wild screaming wind outside, to the only food they had left. Sugar packets and a small jug of water.

She talked out loud, trying to think.

"If I stay here, what good will it do?" wrapped in the blanket with her husband. Casey lay on David's legs now. She tried to warm up her own stiff fingers.

"And if I go out there in this freaking cold wind, what good will it do?"

She rubbed her clenched fists along her thighs, trying to make sense of the dwindling choices open to her.

"God, what good am I being to *anyone!?*" she said, almost yelling. "Why do I keep ending up alone in the middle of chaos?"

It was silent in the cab except for the crackling of the emergency candle. Anna took a breath and exhaled, trying to calm down and count her blessings. *Thank God for Prentice giving that candle to me. What an amazing birthday gift.*

Under the blanket, she rubbed her hand along David's arm. "Honey!?" She rolled closer to rub up and down his chest. "Please talk to me."

David's voice was so quiet. "I'm right here, my love."

Anna's sobs filled the cab, and she buried her face at the side of his jaw, covered with stubble. *Don't you dare leave me, David.*

5 P.M.

"I have no idea if help is coming. But I'm not doing you any good, either, sitting here waiting." *My knight in shining armor is the one who needs rescuing this time.*

I keep saying "I" instead of "we." But it has to be "we." I could never leave David here alone. Could I? Should I?

She tried to picture the journey out to the road in the fading light and the unforgiving wind gusts. She barely weighed a hundred pounds. She'd be lost in minutes. And there was no one out there searching for her. For them. She didn't have enough winter gear. They were miles from the closest house. *That's not the answer! That would be so stupid!*

"Come on Anna, think," she said to herself.

It was the hurricane where we needed to escape, but we couldn't get out of there. Now it's important not to get out of here, but to stay put.

"Well, then the only way to escape is to make sure help is coming," she said.

The CB radio. They'd been trying it intermittently for the last three hours, but she had to give it one more try. Just as she had this thought, a burst of static from a transmission issued forth from the CB's little speaker. *Okay, maybe someone is out there. Thank you, God!*

She kissed David, slid out of the cocoon, and pulled on all her gear, besides the orange beanie she'd kept on constantly.

She sat in the driver's seat, behind the huge steering wheel. It was the same size as the passenger seat, but it felt bigger. Surrounded by all the dials, it felt like command central. Her feet dangled above the floor.

The microphone for the radio hung from the rack next to the transceiver above her. With her hopes up again, her pulse raced.

"Breaker 1-7, this is Art Mama. Breaker 1-7 this is Art Mama. We're in a world of hurt. Who's out there on the Big Road?" She unkeyed the microphone and waited.

No one responded, so she took a breath and tried again just as a ferocious gust of wind battered the truck windows and rocked the cab.

"Breaker 1-7. Who's got their ears on? Art Mama on east side of La Veta Pass. I really need help, guys. Who is listening?"

The static was loud, but out of it a voice did take shape. She felt weak, afraid to feel relief yet, in case they lost contact again. She turned down the squelch to make it easier to hear him.

"This is Sly Fox. Go ahead, Art Mama."

Thank you God. The prayer eased through her brain. Dropping all the CB lingo, she spoke clearly. "Sly Fox, we have slid off Highway 160 at La Veta Pass. Transmitting from here is hard. Do you copy?"

A static-filled, "Affirmative, Art Mama," came the response, and Anna's hopes rose. Sly Fox continued. "I'll see if I can help. What's your 20 again?"

"Appreciate that, Sly Fox. Highway 160. On La Veta Pass. We're on the Old La Veta Pass Road, near Uptop."

"Copy that. Holy smokes, Art Mama." He repeated the location. "I'll try to get you some help from up here. What color's your rig?"

"It's white. All white." Her throat narrowed and her voice caught on the syllables. She couldn't break down, she told herself. Not now. She wouldn't think how—how anyone would ever get to where they were in the dark, through so many snowdrifts. She swallowed, and keeping her voice level, she said, "Sly Fox? Don't just try. Please. You've got to really find us some help. Please," she repeated.

"Affirmative. I hear (static)." A pause. "Is anyone hurt there, Art Mama?"

She sucked in her breath. "Affirmative, Sly Fox." It was imperative she give him the details clearly. Holding the mic in her hand activated some kind of muscle memory that turned off the panic button in her brain. "My husband is very cold, and he might have frostbite." No way to pretend anymore it was a dream.

"I'll quit jawing now, Art Mama, and send some help. The sun's gonna set soon. You sit tight. You need a meat wagon, it sounds like. Sooner than a wrecker."

Anna flinched at the term for an ambulance. "Roger, we need medical help. Send us anything. Even a donkey and a cart."

"10-4," replied Sly Fox.

"Thank you."

Stowing the mic, Anna took time for another prayer. "For He Himself is our peace..."

She meant to climb in with David again in the cocoon, but instead of finishing the prayer, she gave into a fit of anger. Not peaceful at all, just mad at the situation, she took a piece of dry kibble from Casey's bag of food and put it in her mouth. She crunched down with fury, forcing herself to chew and swallow it, and immediately she made a face. It was awful. Worse than she'd expected. It tasted like fish? Hadn't she bought chicken flavored dog food? But it almost tasted like the dried, salted fish mama had used to give her for snacks when she was little. At the time, they had been the most satisfying, crunchy snack. Over the years, Anna had stopped eating them. They were hard to find in Nebraska.

She popped another bit of the kibble into her mouth, and chewing, made another face. It was horrible. But she was cold and hungry. And in need of comfort.

And she was just plain mad. This could not possibly be what God had in store for her. There must be something more she could do, knowing that help really was on the way now. It prompted her to turn and look back at the dashboard. The lights, she thought. The Pete's headlights and trailer lights ... if the battery still had power, would they work?

Returning to the driver's seat, she sat down and scanned the dashboard, hunting for the light controls. She flicked them on and off and was heartened when she peered through the snow-covered windshield. She could see a glow appear and disappear at her command. While the headlights were blocked by the snow, some light still escaped, making a glow that might be visible. And the parking/clearance lights would show a line of lights along the top and back edges of the trailer. If anyone were searching for them now, they might be seen from the highway.

Remembering the story David had just told her, she began to operate the lights in a sequence: dot, dot, dot, dassssh, dassssh, dassssh, dot, dot, dot.

S - O - S.

19

6 P.M.

No more than an hour went by, but sunset comes quickly in the mountains, especially when there's a snowstorm. The warmth from the sun fighting through the snow disappeared. And though the candle helped make the cab less cold, the temperature in the cab was definitely dropping as night fell.

Meanwhile, the bomb cyclone continued with ridiculous, inconceivable persistence.

Through the darkness, Anna heard something. It wasn't the wind, though that was the loudest. Unlike before, when she was tricked by the metallic sound of the pie plate on the floor, this really did sound like an engine, up at the highway. Casey heard it too and jumped off the bed and onto the passenger seat, barking his head off. His leg didn't seem too bad.

A narrow beam of light swept across the snowdrifts, focusing on the truck, joined by steadier, stronger beams of light, like headlights pointed off the road toward them.

Anna took her hand off the headlight knob and the tension inside her melted, leaving her weak. If she hadn't been sitting down, she would have collapsed with relief. Sly Fox had made it happen! He'd gotten word to the officials about their location and now someone had found them.

"David!" she cried. "They found us!" She went back to kiss him on the forehead and on the mouth. He opened his eyes, and she leaned down to hug him, wrapping her arms behind his shoulders and burying her nose in his neck. "Wake up! Get up!"

She went back to the seat, checked the zipper on her parka, snugged down her orange beanie, and patted her mittens together.

The noises outside came closer, and she saw the beam of a flashlight shine through the whirling snow and land on the passenger door, illuminating the window. She knelt on the seat and waved. "We're here!" she said. Anna braced herself for the freezing wind and held on tight to the interior handle as she opened the door a crack.

She saw at least three search and rescue volunteers down there in red and white parkas and red helmets. They had a long orange sled. It seemed like they all wore snowshoes.

Standing on the sled, one of them took off his snowshoes and approached the door. He climbed inside wearing his backpack full of supplies and closed the door, and Anna stepped back to make room for him on the seat, at the same time grabbing Casey's collar to stop him from smothering the man with doggie kisses.

"Thank you! Thank you! I was so scared!" she said.

"You're welcome. Ma'am, I'm with Huerfano County Search and Rescue. We're here to help."

She wanted to hug him but restrained herself. "Oh, thank you so much! I'm really okay, but my husband's so cold. I'm afraid he has frostbite, and maybe hypothermia."

"Yes ma'am. What we'd like to do is ferry both of you across the snow back up to the highway, one at a time, on that sled down there. You'll go first while I check on your husband. And we'll get you checked out more thoroughly once you're up to our volunteers in the 4x4. Sound about right?"

"Can't you take him first? He's so cold, he needs more help than I do. But..." she stopped. "Do you have any extra clothes for him? I took his off since they were wet and..."

"Good move, ma'am. That was the right choice. I can help him. What's his name?" As she answered his questions about how long they'd been stuck and what had happened, the man got to work. "That's all I need from you." Just as he said this, another rescuer climbed into the cab, and the first man gave him a thumbs-up signal. "Let's get you out there on the sled. They're going to use a pulley system to zip you right up there to the vehicles. Sound good?"

She hesitated and said, "Can our dog go on the sled too?" The man nodded and motioned to one of the other volunteers, then attended to David. Anna was guided out into the storm and into a prone position on her back in the sled, where they secured her with Velcro straps and the rope and pulley system winched her up the hill. More rescuers wearing parkas, heavy gloves, and red helmets with lights on them efficiently got her out and into one of several vehicles parked along the highway to get further help.

The wait was over. Time started again.

6:30 P.M.

The snowplow driver wore a rugged jacket and a warm hat with the flaps pulled down over his ears. Anna had just moved from the rescuer 4x4 into the passenger seat of the snowplow's cab while they got David out of the Pete.

"Want some coffee?" he asked her.

She wrinkled her nose, reached across the computer console between them, and took the thermos cup from him in her damp mittens. "Thank you. Thank you again." The coffee smelled horribly bitter. She sipped it anyway.

"Don't mention it," he said. Reaching behind the seat and rummaging around, he extricated a wrinkled mylar blanket. It had been carefully folded after its last use and slipped in a plastic bag, and as he pulled it out, it crackled when he drew it out and tucked it around her shoulders, leaving a space for her to hold the coffee. Meeting her glance, he said, "We're glad we found you two."

She could only nod. Her eyes were wet again.

He watched her closely. "Lots of people were looking for you and your husband, Art Mama." Lights flashed and reflected on the blowing snow that slid across the windshield. "Art Mama. That's the name the CB radio operator gave the state patrol when he called them and told them you and your husband needed help."

Her eyes blinked with tears, but they were happy ones. "His name is Sly Fox."

Lights from the jeeps lit up the darkening view in front of the plow, which was parked pointing west in the eastbound lane. One jeep faced east, its headlights shone into the cab. The other one, with the pulley system attached to the winch on the front, faced the marooned semi-trailer off the highway.

"As soon as the volunteers get your husband and your dog out of the truck on the rescue litter, we'll switch you over to the jeep so you can ride with them to Walsenburg."

"Oh, thank you so much. I wish I could have stayed with

him, but...." That didn't make sense. There was only room for one in the sled. "My name's Anna."

"Hi Anna. I'm really glad to meet you." The snowplow driver shifted in his seat. The coffee was gone, so she handed the cup back to him and tucked her arm back in under the flimsy mylar, which made a remarkable difference in the temperature. They just waited. He adjusted the flow of warm air from the vents and reached over to tuck the space blanket more tightly behind her shoulders. Anna didn't move. Her mind was numb.

"And, like I said, your CB emergency call did the trick. That radio guy notified emergency dispatch, and that's how I knew to watch for you as I worked this highway. The 4x4 guys were right behind me, since they coordinate their missions with the sheriff's office. You know."

Anna finally processed some of what he had been saying. "No. I didn't know," she said quietly. "And they're all volunteers? How far away did they come from? Do you know?"

The man shrugged. "This search and rescue team is volunteers from the whole county, but with the weather like this, I don't know."

"It was a miracle," she said. "Thank you. What's your name?"

"Ben."

"Thank you, Ben." The minutes ticked by, and Anna felt her hands and feet tingle as she warmed up, ever so slowly. She wished she could see how they were helping David.

Another vehicle drove up behind the others in front of them, lights reflecting off the mirrors and making shadows. "That's probably the sheriff's deputy," said Ben.

A commotion happened outside, and Ben pulled down

the earflaps and put on gloves to go out and check. "I'll be right back," he said. "Stay here."

He appeared on her side of the snowplow and knocked on the glass before opening her door, filling the truck with snow and cold air. He opened her door to let the dog in the cab.

"Casey!" Anna exclaimed, pushing aside the thermal blanket and reaching for the dog as the very snowy yellow lab jumped into the snowplow cab and between her legs. "Casey!" She rubbed his snow-covered head with her mittens and found it helped her hands feel less bad, even though he was so cold and wet.

Ben closed the door carefully so Casey's tail would not get crimped. Anna rubbed the fur on his head and ears and chest and he licked her face all over, slobbery, warm wet dog kisses. "Oh, Casey!" He leaned sideways to soak up the warmth from her legs.

Ben climbed back in the driver's side and said, "He looks glad to be with you."

Anna buried her face in his wet dog fur on top of his head.

"Oh, just a sec." Ben went back outside into the storm again and was back in another minute.

"Anna, I think they're close to getting your husband loaded in the 4x4. I see them unhooking the rescue litter from the pulley system."

"Oh thank God," she said. "Can I go over there now? You said I could ride with him?"

Ben said, "There's not much room in there, so let's give them some time to stabilize him as much as they can, and when they're ready, you can get in too."

She started to cry.

"What is it, Anna? You're all in good hands now..." he

began. "And he's okay. And your dog's here..." Ben was at a loss but wanted to help.

"I just realized...." She sucked air into her throat, "This is so stupid, but ... my purse is still down there, in our truck, I mean." It might as well have been a hundred miles away through deep snow. A fresh burst of sobs shook her body. "And I'm sure David's wallet is in the console, too."

Ben searched his pockets and finally scrounged up a fast food napkin she could use as a tissue. "You know, Art Mama, I bet one of those volunteers would get those for you. They still have the winch and pulley system connected from the 4x4 down the hill."

Her mouth opened with surprise. "They would do that? Would they?"

"Sure, I'll go ask them." Ben pulled down his earflaps and went to talk with the search and rescue leader near one of the 4x4s.

She rallied herself to climb out of the snowplow. But then it felt like a new wave of tears might overtake her right as Ben came back and sat in his seat but didn't close the door all the way.

"What is it?" he asked, seeing her continued distress. "You're in no rush. It's okay. I'm here to help you."

"And Ben? I should try to call my daughter. But even if they bring my purse, my phone's in there, but it's broken, so I still can't..." she was on the verge of more tears.

"Oh," he said with relief, "I can help with that. Do you want to borrow my phone?"

She shook her head, then nodded. "I...yes, that would be great."

Ben watched the volunteers outside as he shook his head. "Or, how about, can I call her for you? It looks like they're getting ready over there to load you up, and I've gotta keep my phone with me. I'm still working."

She nodded and finally could speak. "Yes. Yes. I need to tell her what's going on. I don't even know —" she paused for air "— what to tell her. Where are they going to take us?"

"Give me her number, and as soon as I confirm where they're taking you, I'll tell her where to find you both. I mean, you three," he glanced at Casey, standing wedged between Anna's legs. "Okay?" Fierce wind pushed through the crack in the door and tried to rip off his heavy cap as he riffled through his coat pocket for a pen and some paper.

Anna tried to think of Jessie's cell phone number, but she couldn't come up with it. *Come on Anna. You can do this. Oh, I know!* What finally worked was recalling how Jessie's voicemail message recited her own phone number. Anna had listened to it so many times. "Got it!" She wrote it down.

"Why don't you give me your number too, ma'am, okay? So I can tell her the message is from you?"

Anna added that to the scribbled note, nodded her thanks, and climbed down out of the snowplow.

The search and rescue guy in a tough red and white parka approached Anna and took her elbow, helping her step over the uneven ruts in the snow from all the vehicles. Despite his sore leg, Casey followed Anna eagerly over the piles of freezing snow to the volunteer's jeep where David was. Another volunteer, a lady in her sixties, wore the same serious red and white parka, red helmet over a winter hat, and heavy gloves. She handed Anna's purse and David's wallet to her.

"This was so kind of you. You didn't have to do this," she said to the woman.

She smiled. "We're here to help people. That's what we love to do."

They found us.
We're safe.

Thursday, November 28, 2019, 6:40 p.m.

Pioneersburg, Colorado

Darkness had fallen now in Pioneersburg, too. Jessie was in the bathroom when Prentice hollered down the hall from the living room. "Hey, Jessie. Your phone is pinging again."

"Oh, thank God!" she said from behind the door.

He added, "But it's not that whistling song from the movie, so it must not be your mom."

"What does it say?" she called from the bathroom.

"Just a sec, lemme check," said Prentice.

By then, she'd washed up and stood next to Prentice in the living room. He held her phone in his hand and shook his head.

She took the phone and read the screen as it chimed again with a second message. "This is from a number I don't know. Weird area code, too." She felt herself want to run away from what it might say. She looked at Prentice instead of reading the message.

"I think that area code's from southern Colorado," Prentice said.

"Huh? Okay. Oh gee…" She forced herself to read it.

It said, *For Jessie via Ben from mother Anna, Art Mama.*

She kept reading. *I M Ben Wester. CDOT snowplow driver. Highway 160. Your parents are on the way to hospital after accident in snow. Art Mama asked me to contact you.*

Jessie typed a message back. *R they OK?*

Ben wrote, *They went with 4x4 rescue just now.*

Instead of texting him back, Jessie pushed the button to

call him. A young man picked up immediately. "Is this Jessie?" he said.

"Yes. Who are you?"

"Ben Wester. I work for the department of transportation. I found your mom after the state patrol got a distress call about them from a CB radio guy."

Jessie gasped. "You *found* my mom?"

He said, "Yeah."

Jessie sputtered. "But why did she need finding? Hold on a minute. What is your name again? Who are you, really? This is not funny."

"No, ma'am," said the young man's voice. "I'm not kidding. Your mom gave me your number."

"But..."

"She warmed up in my plow truck while they got your dad out of the rig."

"Oh, my gosh. Is he OK? You haven't said...."

"I really don't know more than that. The search and rescue team is taking them to the Walsenburg Health Center. Your mom asked me to call you. She lost her phone."

"Oh, my gosh. I wish I could have talked to her."

The young man said, "She was pretty cold. I wrapped her in a space blanket. Then the search and rescue volunteer team took her and your dad in the jeep."

"Thank you so much. I can't believe this." She glanced at Prentice. "We need to go!"

"Wait! Jessie?" Ben's voice came from the phone. "One more thing, your dog. Your dog is safe too. He's with your mom."

"Oh, thank you so much," she mumbled. "I forgot to even ask about Casey."

The young man laughed softly. "He's a good pup, but he

shook off inside my cab and the whole place smells like Wet Dog now."

"Oh, my God. This is unreal... Thank you. Thank you, Ben."

Jessie disconnected the call and put her phone on the dining room table, collapsing onto a wooden chair and crossing her arms on the table to make a pillow for her face.

"Jessie? Was it about your mom and dad?"

Her head, still pillowed in her arms on the table, nodded up and down. She told him about the news.

He said, "Let's call that hospital and make sure we're heading to the right place."

They both turned to look at the sliding door as icy snow pelted the glass in a big burst. The vertical window shades even moved inside the door, as freezing cold air found its way inside the apartment through leaks in the frame. It was dark out there now, but the wind was not slowing down at all.

She squared her shoulders and took a breath. "Right. I'll call them. Right now." A few minutes of waiting on hold and then two separate conversations, and Jessie had good news to share with Prentice.

He sat with her at the table. "Remember, I'm your space ranger. So, what did they say?"

"Well," Jessie said in a more official voice, one that helped her focus, "I found the right hospital. They let me talk to Mom, and she asked if we could get down there."

"Are they in Walsenburg, I'm guessing?"

"Oh," Jessie said. "Yes. Walsenburg. I'm not communicating very well, am I?"

He nodded. "Straight south on the interstate, in good weather, it would take less than two hours."

Jessie was on her feet in a second.

Prentice didn't move. "But tonight..." he continued, "we could try to get down there, but hold on." He put his hand up to make his point. "The smart question is, when should we go?"

"Well, right now! Let's go! I'll get my coat."

He smiled his cute, crooked smile at her and cocked his head, but he still didn't move from the dining room chair.

Jessie stood in front of him and reached down to run her hand through his rumpled blond hair, and then bent to give him a hug. "Thank you, Prentice." She kissed him. "You're a trained first responder, so thank you for not letting me make a colossal mistake. Mr. Keene. I don't know how I would be doing all this without you."

He laughed and hugged her waist. "I know you want to rush down and see them, but it would, indeed, as you have surmised, be really stupid to jump in the truck and head into a raging blizzard right now."

Outside, a particularly ferocious gust of wind rattled the dark windows again.

"Even if my mom and dad are in trouble," she sighed. "I mean, they are in the hospital already, after all. I wonder how long the storm will last."

They both looked at the dark, rattling patio door for a minute.

"Jessie, could you let me use your computer? It'll be easier than doing this on my phone." She looked curious, brought her laptop to the dining room table, and logged him on. He started clicking the keys as soon as she had it ready. "Lemme check the department of transportation website." He shook his head. "Nope. The interstate is shut down from the Wyoming state line to the New Mexico state line. We can't get to Walsenburg right now at all. The only reason they made it to the hospital was because of the trained 4x4 rescuers escorted by a state snowplow, so…"

"So now what?" she exclaimed, despite her intention to stay rational. "We just sit here and keep checking this website every half hour all night until the road opens and we can leave?"

"Nah," he shook his head. "This is cool. Check it out. If we go to the COtrip.org website, we can create a unique route and get the website to send us messages when something changes on that route we want to take." He waited for her to realize how this would help them.

"So, it would tell you when the interstate opens again between Pioneersburg and southern Colorado?"

He smiled that charming smile and looked sideways at Jessie. "Yep. And that way, we could actually get some sleep tonight and not leave until we can actually get somewhere more safely, okay?"

"Oh, thank you, Prentice." She hugged him. "Thanks for using your brain. I'm just not thinking straight right now."

"Nope, you're not. But I'm selfish. I really don't want to sleep in a cold truck in a snowbank if I have other options that are warmer and make more sense. Like your sofa." He laughed with Jessie, who actually did insist he sleep on her sofa. "Anyway, stick with me." He hugged her. Tight. And she hugged him back as some tears leaked down onto his shoulder.

"We can't go to sleep right away though," she said after a minute.

"Oh?" He took a step back from her, put his hands on her shoulders, and dipped his chin to look into her eyes. "Whaddaya have in mind?" His hazel eyes twinkled at her.

In spite of the worry that clenched in her stomach, she laughed, and it felt good to release some of the tension. "Oh, you are terrible! But seriously, we need to pack up the rest of the food we cooked for today and put it away."

"Let's bring some of it with us too," he said. "Nothing like eating cranberry salad in a snowstorm to keep you warm."

She ignored his joke. "Okay, let's make a plan before we try to get a little sleep. Like you said, it would take two hours to drive there if the roads were clear, but even when they open them, whenever it is, we'll have to take our time."

He added a Tupperware of cooked wontons to a cloth grocery bag full of fruit and canned soup and smiled his engaging crooked smile. "I've got a good blizzard kit in my truck: clothes, hat, gloves, candle, and some granola bars. I've even got one sleeping bag, just in case, but if you have another sleeping bag for you, in case we run into trouble, it would be great."

"Yes, I'll go get it. But I hope once we do leave, when the interstate is opened, we can just get down there without any delays or having to sleep in your truck."

"Agreed," he said. "That's why we're not leaving right now, so we don't get stranded in the middle of the night somewhere between here and Walsenburg."

She hugged him again. "Thank you for helping me think, Prentice."

"No worries, Jessie. This is a lot to deal with." He added, "And how about some dry socks? Let's start out with dry socks right now, just to be on the right foot," he chuckled.

Jessie said, "Sure, dry socks! Coming right up. Start out with warm, dry clothes while we have the chance."

They got everything packed and stashed by the door, then Prentice turned up the sound on his phone so he would hear the message sent by the department of transportation when the interstate was open.

In the middle of the night, Jessie heard a noise and got

up. Prentice was gone. She got dressed and followed him outside. The blinding snow had stopped, and the world was muffled in deep white drifts. "The road's open now, Jessie," he said. "We need to dig my truck out, and then we can go."

She said, "I guess we should have shoveled it out earlier."

He laughed, "No, the wind was still drifting everything earlier, and our work would have been wasted." He pulled his winter hat lower over his ears. "Ready to get to work?"

He dug in, and with an attitude of gratitude, Jessie picked up Prentice's folding emergency shovel off the snow and helped dig his truck out of the surrounding drifts. Around them, the pitch dark night was quieter than it had been for hours.

In less than an hour, they hit the road heading south.

2 0

FRIDAY, NOVEMBER 29, 2019, 7 A.M., WALSENBURG, COLORADO

Anna didn't know how much time went by until it started getting light outside. The diffuse light through the clouds touched her face but didn't feel warm. She didn't understand how sunlight could feel cold. She reclined in a hospital bed, covered with several white blankets. *Maybe that's a heating pad on my belly.* She considered looking at it but decided not to try to move. *I'm too tired. And it's warm here.*

She heard the door open, and she made her eyes look toward the sound. Jessie came in, followed by Prentice carrying a cloth bag bulging with containers.

"Jessie! And Prentice!"

"Mom, I'm here." Jessie leaned over and hugged her through the blankets.

Anna roused herself enough to get her arms free and sit up to give her daughter a better hug. "I'm so glad you're here, my sweet girl. Thank you for coming."

Prentice took a step closer to her and offered her a hug, which she gratefully received.

"It's so good to see you both," Anna said.

266

Casey came out from under Anna's bed, stretched his long upward-facing-dog stretch, shook all over, and trotted to Jessie.

"Oh Casey, you smell like a Wet Dog." Jessie ruffled the dog's soft ears as she said. "He's allowed in the hospital?"

Anna laughed, "No, not really. But what choice did they have when the search and rescue volunteers brought us here in the middle of a blizzard?" She followed Jessie's glance over to David's bed, closer to the door. His eyes were closed, as they had been almost every time she'd checked on him during the night. He looked peaceful. He was dead to the world. But he was alive, just disguised under all the blankets and equipment. "Go ahead," she said to Jessie.

Jessie went to him, touched her dad's chest gently and put her hand to her lips. She .put a kiss on her fingers, touched her hand to his chest again, then backed up a step and turned to her mom.

"Jessie, where are we?" Anna asked once she'd regained her composure. "I'm not even sure."

"We're in Walsenburg. This is the health center, right off the interstate."

That made sense to Anna. She was still trying to get her bearings and lifted her blankets to look down at what she might be wearing. Turned out it was a hospital gown and those socks with non-skid rubber patterns on them, with heated blankets on her belly. It felt like a year since she'd put on her leggings and work out top Thursday morning at the motel in Durango.

"How long did it take you to get down here?" she asked.

Jessie thought for a second. "I'm not sure. Longer than it should have, but the interstate was okay. We didn't even leave Pioneersburg until the interstate was open. That was about four a.m."

Anna shook her head. "Oh, you two are amazing. Waiting till the road was open. Good idea." She shook her head slowly from side to side. "So you haven't had much sleep?"

"Some. We slept until we knew we could dig out Prentice's truck and leave." Jessie turned to look at her dad again. He breathed softly. Jessie looked back at her mom.

Anna cleared her throat. "Jessie, Prentice, I need to tell you about what happened. I need to tell you, so you'll understand."

But any explanation was interrupted by a nurse who acknowledged them all with a smile but then turned to check David's vitals. He roused briefly as she recorded her observations on his chart and replaced the heated blankets with warmer ones.

"How is he?" Anna asked.

"He's making good progress, Mrs. DeGroot," the nurse replied as she checked the sterile dressings on his frost-bitten toes and fingers.

"Thank you," Anna said. "Is it okay that he keeps sleeping so hard?"

"Yes, but I'm sure you'll have more questions for Dr. Carson and she'll be in sometime around midday. Meanwhile, Mrs. DeGroot, may I check your vitals, too, even though you have company?" Anna nodded, and the nurse approached her bed. Prentice and Jessie moved to the window.

Watching them, Anna thought what a good team they made.

"You're in pretty good shape for the shape you're in, Mrs. DeGroot." The nurse grinned at her joke, making Anna laugh. "Is there anything else you need right now?"

"Would it be possible to get another cup of hot tea?" she

asked. "And possibly some plain yogurt for Casey. He's been through a lot and yogurt is a treat to him."

"Yes, I'll send some up," the nurse answered.

"Thank you," Anna said. She glanced down at Casey, who was now stretched out with his back against the legs of two of the chairs.

The nurse promised to be back soon to check on them again. "It's been a quiet night at the Walsenburg Health Center. I'm glad you're here, but I'm sorry you need to be here," she smiled.

"Thank you for all your help," Anna said, then motioned to Jessie and Prentice to pull the chairs by the window closer to the bed. But when it came time to explain, she didn't know how to start.

"So, you had an accident..." Jessie encouraged her.

Anna swallowed. "Yes. We had an accident," Anna began. "The truck went off the road in the storm yesterday... I think it was yesterday..."

"Yes, it was Thanksgiving. Yesterday." Jessie took her hand, and it gave Anna the strength to explain. "We'd heard about the bomb cyclone in the weather forecast on Wednesday when we were almost in Walsenburg. I'm so glad you kept texting me, Jessie," she said. "David kept saying we'd be back home before the storm hit on Thursday, and who was I to say no at that point," Anna said. "But we had a delay getting to Durango on Wednesday, when the air lines broke, and that night I found out he had scheduled another truck run for Friday, to Pittsburgh, or Peoria, or Pensacola. That's why he was in such a rush to get back." She paused. "Oh no, today's Friday. I have no idea what to do about the long-haul dispatcher..."

Prentice spoke up. "Oh, I can try to reach them and tell them what's happened."

Anna relaxed. "Yes, that would be great. Thanks." As he stepped out of the room with his phone, Anna continued with Jessie. "The forecast kept getting worse. I kept telling your dad we should wait it out in Durango, or stop at a lodge that was open, or even pull over in a parking lot after the weather really hit."

Jessie nodded for her to go on.

"But he just said he could do it and that he had to get back so he could leave again, and I didn't know how to stop him." She looked at Jessie. "The other scary part was the way he kept making mistakes and forgetting things. Important things..." she trailed off, not wanting Jessie to shoulder that all at once. "Then he finally stopped to put chains on, but by then, the storm was on top of us. He lost his phone then, we realized later. We got going again, and that's when the truck veered off the highway and we plowed into a drift on La Veta Pass. David went outside to check the damage, and he got all wet..."

"Oh mom, you must have been so scared." They sat in silence, and Anna squeezed Jessie's hand.

Prentice returned and gave Anna a thumbs up. "I reached his dispatcher, Anna. They'll take care of it."

"Thank you for solving that, Prentice." She stopped to think. "So then he was shivering, he was so cold. He said we would have enough fuel to keep the engine running and the cab warm, but the tanks had a leak somewhere, and the engine stopped. I couldn't think what to do at first." Then she explained the next steps she had taken to warm him up. "That emergency candle you gave me for my birthday saved our lives," she told Prentice.

"It sounds like you did a lot of things to save your lives, Anna," he answered. "You got David's wet clothes off and kept him warm. And you kept calling on the CB until you got someone's attention."

"Yeah, Mom, if you hadn't done that, um…"

No one spoke. None of them had the courage to say it, Anna thought, that without her getting through to Sly Fox, one or all of us might be dead. Jessie gently rubbed Anna's hand. The silence grew.

Anna found the energy to speak after a minute. "They've been so good to me here. Checked me out from head to toe, but no lasting damage somehow. I'm finally starting to feel warm again." Anna's red-rimmed black eyes filled with tears. "Casey was so cold and snowy when he jumped into the snowplow, even though his leg was sore." She pursed her lips and looked up at the ceiling. "He sat between my legs and put his big doggie head on my knee. The snow melted off him onto my leggings. Everything was soaked from the snow…" A raw sob escaped her throat with the fresh recollection.

Casey must have heard his name and perked up. He rested his big head on the mattress, where both Anna and Jessie could rub his soft ears.

"You're safe now. You're safe now. And don't worry, Mom. Casey's fine. Prentice will take him outside in a minute."

"I wonder if he'll ever want to play in the snow again after today," Anna worried.

Jessie tried to make a joke in this desperate moment, "He generally likes summer sports more than snow sports."

"Huh?" *I don't get it.* "Oh. I meant Casey."

Jessie didn't push it.

"Anyway, we were both so cold. David was going into hypothermia. I think he had some frostbite. You saw the bandages?"

Prentice piped up. "Those are sterile dressings, not bandages."

"Okay. Sterile dressings," said Anna, with a vague smile. They all looked over at David, asleep again in the other bed. They could not see much of him because of the blankets, but he breathed regularly, and the nurse said reassuring things each time she checked in. "You know, his color's closer to the healthy pale faced look of a Dutch guy than the death-warmed-over white he was yesterday afternoon."

"Oh, mom." Jessie rubbed her mom's shoulder. "I'm so glad you're all safe."

Anna cleared her throat again and asked for a tissue, blowing her nose loudly. Her eyes focused on Jessie, and she said, in a sharp voice edged with tears, "I am so mad at your dad."

Again, the three of them turned to look at David, right there next to them. "He can't even defend himself, and here I am dumping on him," said Anna to Jessie. "I love him so much, but these last few days have been a horrible roller coaster ride."

Jessie said, "Mom, let's wait to talk about this. Just rest now, okay?"

Anna said to Jessie, "Yes. That's a good idea, sweet girl," and then to Prentice. "I really hate roller coasters now."

Prentice nodded. Jessie moved her chair in between the two beds and rested her hand on his chest. Everyone settled in to rest and wait. Anna slept fitfully. She sensed Casey leaving and coming back, with Prentice speaking softly to him as they went.

IO A.M.

Someone knocked on the door and came in. A tall, trim, fifty-something man with a friendly smile and a bald head joined them with eager purpose. He wore a dark shirt with a white clerical collar, a dark blazer, and dark pants, and he carried a shoe box and set it on the chair. He said, "Mrs. DeGroot. Hello, I'm Bob, the hospital chaplain. I don't know if you remember, but we met last night."

Anna looked at him. She had no idea. So many people had helped her.

"Is this your daughter?" He stuck out his hand to shake Jessie's. "You told me about her last night," he said to Anna.

"Oh, did I?" said Anna.

"Yes, I am," said Jessie to the chaplain. "And this is Prentice."

"I'm glad to meet you and know you're here for your mom and dad. But I'm here to help all of you. And with that..." With a proud flourish and a grin, he opened the shoebox and brought out an iPod and a tiny speaker. "I have a surprise to share with you and your husband." He nodded at David, who still slept hard, but it didn't faze the chaplain.

No one said a word while he connected the devices, set them on the narrow table next to Anna's bed. Before he switched on the player, he said, "According to what I learned from you last night, both you and your husband will like this." Then a tinny version of a classic rock song belted out of the little speaker. It was the long version of the band Boston's "It's Been Such a Long Time," with the psychedelic electric keyboard and bass guitar intro called "Foreplay."

Anna looked shocked, then delighted. She smiled so hard she thought her face would split, and after a minute, she started doing air guitar with the bass part. Jessie laughed and bobbed her head with the music.

Chaplain Bob grinned, nodding his head along with the

boom-boom-boom-boom. When the song transitioned into the more melodious part with the lead guitar, David's face relaxed and he might have been hearing the music. The four others sat and listened, tapping a foot or a hand, or mouthing the words, till the nine-minute song was over.

"Oh, Bob, how did you know that's what we needed?" asked Anna.

"Last night when the volunteers brought you in, I got to talk with you," he said in a pleasant, gravelly voice. "And it's my job to show God's love in creative ways."

Anna shook her head with wonder.

"This little health center's staff checked you out but wanted to focus their energy on David," he said. "I was snowed in here already, so I was assigned to keep you company and get you to stay awake while you had something to eat and started to warm up. And then I could alert them if you had any trouble."

Anna shook her head in wonder. "I'm sorry I don't remember. It was such a blur."

"Well," said the chaplain, "You were pretty scared and cold." He nodded at each of them in turn. "I was here for an hour or two."

"It was all such a blur," said Anna again.

"I took the dog outside twice, and I just asked you some basic questions, and it was clear to me that your life has a classic rock soundtrack."

Anna looked surprised. "How about that?"

"Yes," he paused. "You hummed a song by Boston when you started to feel better, after we'd gotten you feeling safer."

Anna smiled. *I kind of remember that. It was "Higher Power."*

Prentice said, "The music is great, and it helps mask the

beeping sounds from the machines, too. Do you think we could borrow your iPod until we leave?"

Bob nodded and smiled. "Of course. I'll pick it up tomorrow when I come back here. And for now, I wondered if you would like me to say a prayer for your dad, and for all of you, now that you're all here together."

"Thank you, Chaplain," said Jessie.

Jessie, Prentice, and Chaplain Bob moved to stand between David's and Anna's beds, took each other's hands and bowed their heads with thanksgiving. He prayed that they'd remember God was with them all the time, especially during adversity. "Truly, He is my rock and my salvation. He is my fortress. I will not be shaken," he quoted. "Amen."

After Chaplain Bob left, Anna got out of bed and hugged Jessie, then got down on the floor in her flimsy hospital gown and buried her face in Casey's fur, until he'd had enough and shook his body from head to foot. Fur flew into the air and was caught in the isolated beam of sunlight that had found its way through the thin place in a cloud.

"Look, Mom, it's not quite as cloudy now."

"I don't think I've ever been so thankful on Thanksgiving before."

Jessie teased her, "Or on the day after Thanksgiving, either."

12:01 P.M.

She smelled delicious food and opened her eyes from another morning nap to find Prentice and Jessie arranging plates full of homemade wontons, cranberry salad, turkey, and other treats on her hospital table. She wanted to cry, she was so touched.

"It's okay, Mom," Jessie said softly. "You're safe now. We're here for you and Dad."

Prentice added, "Anna, it's lunch time. Are you hungry now? I made these for you," setting a wonton on a little paper plate and sliding it toward her.

Glancing at the window, where the sun made the white sky glow, she sat up in bed, put a whole wonton in her mouth and chewed it up. "Prentice, these are great." Knowing that Prentice, who had very little cooking experience, had learned to make them for her, made the whole tragedy real. She couldn't pretend any longer that it had all been a horrible dream if she was getting such acts of kindness from Jessie's boyfriend of only a few months.

"So, you're mad at Dad, huh?" Jessie finished off her dumpling and wiped her hands on her napkin. "You want to talk about it now?"

Anna nodded even though David was sleeping right next to them. She would talk with him directly when he had his strength back.

"I'm upset with him, too, Mom, but you go first." With a kind smile, she added, "Goodness knows we've done enough Twelve-Step sharing to start our own recovery tradition."

She loved how her own daughter encouraged her, and everyone she met, to be transparent. Anna nodded again. "Those accountability and support groups have made so much difference. For you, first when you were in college, and then I finally caught on when I saw how much happier you were." She sighed. "I wish I'd known those things when Mama was alive. What a storm cloud she was."

Prentice said, "Anna, did you know, I've been studying the steps too? It's helped me a lot. The one that hits me most says, 'We have an overdeveloped sense of responsibility and it is easier for us to be concerned with others rather than ourselves.' That's me, to a T!" He smiled.

Jessie said, "It's awesome that you can smile when you say that. It shows how far you've come!" She thought for a moment. "The one that applied most to me was 'We get guilt feelings when we stand up for ourselves instead of giving in to others.' It still does, but identifying that trait helps me see it."

In turn, Anna looked right at Jessie and Prentice. "I can quote one for you. 'We are dependent personalities who are terrified of abandonment and will do anything to hold on to a relationship in order not to experience painful abandonment feelings, which we received from living with sick people who were never there emotionally for us.'"

Jessie said, "But now you're finally getting to the flip side of that step, Mom. That one says, 'We grow in independence and are no longer terrified of abandonment.' It takes longer than we want it to, huh?"

Anna looked at the ceiling in acknowledgment. This was not a new conversation for her and Jessie, but looking at how it played out in real life, with a flawed husband in a real blizzard, took time to comprehend.

Prentice peeled an orange, and Anna relished the citrus-sweet scent that filled the room, disguising the antiseptic smell. He distributed the sections on another round of paper napkins, and sitting down again, popped two pieces into his own mouth. David stirred but his eyes stayed closed.

"I tried to get David to stop," Anna said, darting a glance at him. "I did try, but he insisted we could beat the storm. And I..." she choked up, "I just haven't ever learned how to disagree with him, you know?"

Jessie nodded for her to keep talking.

"But," Anna took a breath, "Usually we see eye to eye,

anyway. It's always been so easy. And he's been my rock. And I'm the water that just flows around him."

Jessie took her hand.

"But it's been different recently with him. His stories used to be funny, but ... have you noticed him being really out of it?"

"Yes," Jessie said. "This week when he got lost coming home. And there were some odd things back in August when he and I spent time in Maryland." Jessie reflected. "That was a serendipitous visit," she began. "We had fun!"

"But?"

"Well, there were a couple of times he'd lose his train of thought. Or just forget what we had just planned to do that day. And he kept misplacing things."

"Really?"

"Yes. Especially on the day we went hiking. I noticed it when we got to talk more than we have in a long time."

"And?" asked Anna.

Jessie thought about it. "I didn't make a list or anything, but when I brought up a fun memory, like the time for my birthday party when he borrowed someone's old suit coat and tie and pretended to be a waiter, it didn't seem like he remembered it."

"He didn't?" Anna looked into the middle distance. "That was when you turned six, I think. It was the year we moved to Mississippi, and he started the dry van trucking."

"Yes," said Jessie. "Kinda memorable. My truck driver dad in a black suit jacket and red tie serving bowls of melted ice cream to a bunch of little girls." They both smiled.

"Wish I could have been there." Prentice grinned.

Anna said, "My mama hadn't moved in with us yet. That time was like our last moment of family freewheeling before the hammer came down, huh?"

"Was she really that difficult?" Prentice asked.

"Mom had no idea what it would be like with her there," Jessie answered.

"Oh, I should have. I grew up with her," said Anna. "How could I expect her to change? You know the story about the scorpion who asked the frog to give him a ride across the river on his back... But she needed a place to go, and we thought we needed her help. We thought it was a great solution."

"Didn't turn out that way, I guess," Prentice said.

Jessie helped her mom climb out of that emotional hole by changing the subject from scorpion grandmas back to David. "I thought the weird things I saw meant Dad was tired, or not paying attention."

"Well," said Anna, "I've wondered if it was more, like, at times I've thought—" she broke off unsure if she wanted to share the notion. "It seems pretty ridiculous now, but I thought he'd met someone else."

"No way." Jessie rubbed Anna's forearm. "Do you still think—?"

Anna pulled herself upright, adjusting the pillow at her back. "No. All his bad decisions, the things he's forgotten... it's... it isn't simply that he's distracted like a man would be if he were ... you know? He's forgotten things he never would have in the past. I mean, stopping at the grocery store is one of his rituals before he goes on a run, but he told us he'd pick up things for us, then forgot to go to the store, forgot where we lived, and forgot to tell us he had a run the next day at all."

"Yes," mused Jessie, as they all looked at David.

"His logbook was full of gaps. That's an expensive mistake. And — have you seen the inside of the cab?"

"Not since August. It was not great then, I must say."

"It's a mess. That isn't like your dad. He used to keep his truck spotless. It's his second home." She had to take a breath, wondering if he would ever see that wrecked truck again at all. But that was something to solve tomorrow, Anna decided. "And then—then yesterday, get this—he got me a cup of coffee."

"Are you serious?"

"Yes," said Anna. "Like the Valley Girls used to say, 'gag me with a spoon.' But it's no joke, and I'm sorry we've landed in the hospital, but maybe if we're surrounded by doctors, we'll be able to get him checked out."

A muffled voice spoke from the other bed. "Get who checked out?" David asked from under the blankets. "Me?"

1 P.M.

Dr. Gayle Carson joined the family as they gathered around David's bedside. Anna's eyes met the doctor's, making sure it was okay to try to talk to him now.

"David, you're really awake!" said Anna, rubbing his chest with one hand. She still wore her hospital gown and tried to hold it closed in the back with her other hand. "You've been sleeping so hard!"

Jessie stood between his bed and the wall and rubbed his shoulder again. "Dad, it's me, Jessie. I'm so glad you woke up!" Prentice hung back and stayed in his chair by the window, letting the family welcome him back to consciousness.

David tried to talk, but his throat was dry. Jessie got him a cup of water with a straw. That helped. "Wow," he said. "What's goin' on?" He looked around the room. "Are we in the hospital?" Anna and Jessie both nodded.

"Yes, David," said Anna. "We're safe. We're in good hands."

The doctor stood next to Anna between the two beds.

She came across as a well-experienced doctor with a direct but caring demeanor.

"First, Mr. DeGroot, I need to introduce myself to you, now that you're really awake, though I've been examining and treating you since you got here." She gave him a gentle but official pat on the forearm instead of trying to shake his bandaged hand.

"Thank you for helping me, Doc," David said with a raspy voice. "We were in dire straits, weren't we, Anna?"

Anna nodded, smiled, and looked at Dr. Carson.

"Yes, well... I want to give you some good news. All of you." She looked at Anna. "First of all, Mrs. DeGroot, you are coming along very well. Your core temperature is fine, and you have not suffered any frostbite. I think we can discharge you now. One of the orderlies will bring your clothes back, now that they're dry."

"Thank you," Anna said. "I feel so much better. But how is David?"

"When I palpated your neck, I noticed there's some enlargement in the thyroid gland. I want to check on that," Dr. Carson said. "You will need follow-up care for the extremities injured by frostbite. That can take weeks or months to heal, as much as the skin can when it's been injured. You'll be on a course of antibiotics," she said to David. "The good news is you have a relatively minor case of frostbite. You might lose the tip of a toe or finger, but we'll have to wait and see. You will do follow-ups with your primary care doctor regularly."

"Oh, shoot. That's gonna impact my modeling career," joked David. "But I'll be able to get back to trucking, right?"

At that, Anna spoke up. "Just a minute." She looked at him, then at the doctor. "Since he's brought it up already, there's another question we wondered if you could answer," said Anna. "We've been noticing some unusual behavior..."

Anna looked at David, not for permission, but to let him know it was time for this talk. She made sure their eyes connected.

"Go on," said Dr. Carson. "Who has been noticing this?"

"I have, and so has Jessie," said Anna. "It's been a gradual change..." she trailed off. "I don't want to hurt your feelings, David, but something is different about you." She bit her lip.

Jessie picked up the story, but she directed her comments at her dad. "What Mom means is, it seemed like you've been super forgetful lately. You have just not been yourself. We thought you were overworked or distracted by something."

Dr. Carson asked, "Mr. DeGroot, do you agree with these observations?"

Anna noticed that David looked off to one side but didn't respond.

"For example? I need specifics," said Dr. Carson, addressing Anna and Jessie again.

"Well, he told stories about how he'd totally forgotten his destination while driving his rig down the highway," said Jessie.

"He's also put things away in the wrong place. I found the shampoo in the mini fridge in the cab for instance." Anna backed up so she could sit on the edge of her own bed and still be close to David.

The doctor took notes as the two explained things to her.

Jessie said, "Dad lost his keys while we were together in Maryland. He always puts them in his pocket. We searched and searched. Finally, I found them laying on the catwalk behind the cab."

They shared a list of more examples. David listened without interrupting until he caught sight of Prentice sitting on the other side of the room. "What are you doing here? I remember you from before..."

Jessie said, "Dad, that's Prentice! My boyfriend!"

"Oh, right," David muttered.

Anna had to stand up and hold David's arm again to comfort him. "Honey, we're not doing this to embarrass you. But since you don't seem to remember what you have forgotten, we need to tell the doctor about it. Maybe she can help explain it." Clearing her throat, Anna continued, "I've been wondering if David should even go back to truck driving."

Jessie had a thought. "Dad's under a lot of stress too, since they're not even living in their own house. They moved in with me after the fire in Garnet this summer. Is that important?" she asked.

The doctor nodded and asked more questions. "I can see now why you had additional concerns, Mrs. DeGroot. Jessie. You have a lot going on in your lives. You realize I can't make a real diagnosis just by talking with you, but your descriptions, combined with the physical examination results, have made me wonder about a possibility..." Neither one said a word.

The doctor looked thoughtful and turned to David. "Mr. DeGroot, have you been getting your annual primary care provider checkups?"

Everyone looked at David again, wearing the cotton gown in the hospital bed. *He looks like a little kid right now,* thought Anna, still holding his arm.

He answered in his still-raspy voice. "Well, whaddaya

mean? I've gone to urgent care a few times when I thought I had the flu, or once when I got a big chunk of something in my eye."

Dr. Carson shook her head. "No, I mean annual physicals. Where they check your blood pressure, like that, and draw blood and do a chemistry panel?"

David wobbled his head noncommittally. "I have to go every two years for a DOT health exam. To renew my commercial driver's license." He closed his eyes to think. "I know they check for diabetes. And color blindness, vision, and hearing. I thought that was enough." He looked at her. "I don't know, Anna. Do you remember if I did?"

She shook her head. "No, that's something you always have done on your own. I really don't know, honey."

"Mr. DeGroot, can you tell me the name of your primary care provider?" He shook his head.

Dr. Carson shook her head back at him, but she looked right into David's eyes, so he didn't miss her words. "Have you been avoiding your regular checkups? Big tough guy, doesn't like needles, right?" She didn't wait for him to answer. "Well, a lot of those annual blood tests are to screen out known risks and catch things before they get out of hand. Let me ask you," she said to him. "Have you noticed the slight swelling in your neck or this puffiness in your face?"

He looked surprised and shook his head again. "No. I dunno. I grew a beard so I wouldn't have to worry about what my face looks like," he joked.

Anna said, "Oh, I noticed it this week for the first time. Is it important?"

Dr. Carson surprised them all with her next question to David. "Mr. DeGroot, did either of your parents have a history of dementia? Or thyroid problems?"

David said, "No. But they died kind of young, so we wouldn't have known." He looked worried.

~

1:30 P.M.

Anna continued rubbing his arm and wishing they could stop the line of questioning. But it was important to get all the facts out in the open. So Anna took up the story. "A tornado destroyed their farm in Nebraska, and they were both killed before they were fifty. David's brother had to take over what was left of the dairy operation." She looked at Prentice, still in his safe spot in the corner chair. "We were in Mississippi by then."

David grew agitated. "Hey, are you saying I have dementia?"

"No, Mr. DeGroot. I'm trying to follow a line of questioning." Dr. Carson tapped her pen on her chin as she considered this new data. "So there's no way to verify that part of your parents' health history," she pondered. "But based on your anecdotal evidence, it sounds like his symptoms could be consistent with ... let me see... there are several possibilities to consider."

She wrote more notes and turned to David again. "There are other possibilities besides dementia. So, tell me, have you been feeling cold a lot?" That sincere question made everyone laugh, in spite of themselves, despite the horrible experience of the last two days. Of course he'd been cold! The doctor laughed even as she apologized. "I mean," she said, "in the last year or so, not just yesterday. Have you had trouble keeping warm?"

Anna found David's gaze. "You did—you kept the heat on really high in the cab on this trip," she said gently.

Turning to the doctor, she said, "He runs hot. Usually, he chooses to keep the temperature lower than I do."

"What does it mean, Doc? Old people lose their minds. They get cold, too." David looked stricken. "But I'm not old!" Anna touched his cheek. She was frightened, too.

"Hm," said Dr. Carson as she thought. "And, I need to ask, have you had any trouble in the, well, in the bedroom department?" the doctor asked, looking intently at David, meaning he was the only one who could answer. Not Anna, who was still right next to him, wishing desperately they could just be out of this uncomfortable situation. However, if the doctor had asked Anna about her point of view, her answer would have been yes.

He said, "Yeah, I s'pose." The only sound then was Casey's loud snoring, where he was racked out under Anna's hospital bed. No one said a word until David asked, "What's wrong with me, Doc?"

"There are several possibilities, ranging from chemical imbalances to... more serious problems. We'll run some tests, do bloodwork for a start."

"Can we do that here?" asked Jessie.

"Yes. I'll order the bloodwork now."

"What are you thinking, though?" Anna asked anxiously. "You mentioned dementia, but David's so young. Are there other things, less serious—" She stopped, afraid she would cry.

"Let's not get ahead of ourselves." The doctor switched her glance to David. "It could be as simple as a thyroid issue. The thyroid gland in your neck might be a clue of something. Hypothyroidism, for instance, can run in a family and would explain your symptoms, and the good news is that it's treatable."

Looking at David, Anna tried a smile. "I never thought

I'd find myself wishing for you to have a disease, but that sounds preferential to—"

"Losing my mind?" David grinned shortly. "Yeah, I have to agree."

"It's not something you would suspect. Especially not if the family history didn't provide a clue or warning." She looked out the side of her eyes at David. "Or, if you weren't getting thorough annual physicals, which would have spotted it." She shrugged. "It sounds like you've missed one or two of those."

Anna said, "So this week, when he didn't know what the date was, and all the really bad decisions he made..." She burst into tears. "There really was something wrong. I should have talked sense into him! I should have stopped him..."

"Mrs. DeGroot, please don't blame yourself," the doctor said. "You have experienced an awful lot of chaos lately, from what I can tell." Prentice and Jessie mumbled agreement from the peanut gallery.

"You realize this is all conjecture, but it's true that stress, or a total disruption of routine, can aggravate symptoms that might not have been noticeable before, for any one of the conditions I'm considering. We need to do some more testing and data gathering."

Anna, Jessie, and Prentice processed this new information in light of what had happened during this truck run leading up to the blizzard. David just looked bewildered and tired.

The doctor left the room. Soon, a nurse wheeled a cart into the room, followed by Dr. Carson again. The nurse uncovered David's arm, swabbed it with alcohol, and drew several small vials of blood. She applied a band-aid, attached the labels to the containers, and pushed the cart back out into the hall.

"You know," Dr. Carson said to Anna, Jessie, and David. "His core temperature is normal. His circulation is good again, except for the frostbitten areas. Like I said, he will need to get those treated over the next weeks and months."

"That long?" asked David.

"But otherwise…?" asked Jessie.

"Well, as soon as those blood tests come back, we'll know if one of my theories is correct, and then I can send you home to follow up with your primary care physician." She paused, adding, "Mrs. DeGroot, I'm assigning that responsibility to you. Mr. DeGroot, you have a loving wife here and I'm asking you to follow her instructions until we get this figured out, all right?"

David said, "Yeah, she's a keeper." He asked, "But what about my job? I'm self-employed."

"In my professional opinion, you must take some time off, whether you have sick days or not. Just the frostbite is enough to make me say that, but these additional symptoms need to be explained before you get behind the wheel of a big rig again. Or even a car," she added.

Anna reached down to David and gently slid her arms behind his shoulders to squeeze him and give him a kiss, a good, warm one. He kissed her back, though he couldn't put his arms around her and rub her back like he usually would have because of the dressings on his hands.

I think that knot behind my shoulder blade is gone, she realized. And she kissed David again.

FRIDAY, DECEMBER 6, 2019, 12:30 P.M.

Pioneersburg, Colorado

A week later, Anna pushed David in a wheelchair out of the medical center complex in Pioneersburg. The pavement near the handicap parking was clear of snow, making it easier to get to her car than it had the last two times they'd been here this week. She rolled him next to her little sedan, locked the brakes, helped him in. Then she loaded the borrowed wheelchair in her car, with great difficulty. She took her time and made every movement carefully, making sure she didn't hurt herself.

It was all because of the tissue damage to David's toes from the frostbite. The doctor wanted David to stay off his feet and not use his bandaged hands for anything while his body worked to heal. Time, and a series of additional doctor visits, would tell them over the next weeks and months how deep the tissue damage went. They both hoped he would not need surgery to remove any appendages, but it was early in the process. Meanwhile, Anna got the privilege of using a temporary handicap tag when she brought David to his appointments.

She sat down in the driver's seat and stopped to say a prayer of gratitude for David's healing and health.

He interrupted her prayer, then joked with her about their terrifically exciting plans for the day. "For a change, let's go home and watch some TV. We haven't done that enough yet this week."

"That sounds fabulous, farm boy," she said. "Let's go to the drive-through on the way and pick up some vittles. I don't want to cook. I'm worn out."

"You're full of creative ideas, my sweet bride," said David.

She said, "We'll need to go to the pharmacy again tomorrow to get your new thyroid prescription, so I'll do the grocery shopping then."

"The doctor said we might have to mess around with that thyroid medicine to get it right, didn't she?" he said.

"Yes. But I'm glad you have hypothyroidism, David," Anna said with a serious expression.

"Gee, thanks babe," he said.

"No, I mean, I'm glad you have a condition that explains all the scary, ridiculous stuff you did."

"Yeah, I'm glad to be feeling more like my old self already," he said. "At least mentally. But I'm tired of these bandages on my hands and feet. I feel like an invalid."

"Well, you're in my total control for now!" With a playful grin, Anna did an amazing impression of Vincent Price's maniacal horror movie laughter. "Ha ha ha!... So you just follow the instructions so you can get better faster."

In an equally bad monster movie accent, David joked, "Yes, master."

"But you know," she added, "I'm grateful you have something like an under-active thyroid, because it's easy for them to treat. You just have to keep taking your medication and checking in with the doctor so she can monitor your metabolism."

"Yes, ma'am," he said gently.

"What she told us today was surprising, don't you think?"

He thought. "Which part?"

"When she said all things being equal, if you have an underlying medical condition like hypothyroidism, you're more likely to get frostbite than if you didn't have it."

"I missed that part. She told us a lot," he said.

"The point is, I don't want you to go plowing around in any more snowdrifts ever again, David," she said firmly.

He closed his eyes, relaxed his head against the headrest, and smiled. "As you wish, my princess bride," he said.

"I love you too, David."

~

Saturday, June 13, 2020, 9 a.m.
Garnet, Colorado

Anna sat in a colorful lawn chair on her new front porch, soaking up the spring sunshine. She and David were finally back home, living in their little mountain town house again. They were some of the first people to move back into historic Garnet's downtown. Their home had escaped the worst of the fire and the punishing flood waters, but wildfire smoke damage had required ripping the walls down to the studs and working out from there.

She was so thankful she'd finished navigating the maze of work with the insurance company and the builders. The house was dried-in, and they had electricity, water, and natural gas service again. As soon as the contractor installed flooring she could walk on in her bare feet, they moved out of Jessie's apartment and into the bare-bones house.

The white walls begged for colorful paint.

From the porch, she looked at the empty lot across the street that used to be her friend Michelle's house. Now, after all these months, the burned structure had been removed, but no other progress was happening. It was a mud pit. She didn't know if Michelle could come back.

Other houses had been rebuilt. But when a house had a mortgage on it, even if it was a charred, uninhabitable ruin, residents still had to make monthly payments to the bank while living somewhere else. And some people had no homeowner's insurance to help them.

Anna reflected on more changes. Most years, the land in Garnet turned green in the springtime. New grass and wildflowers on the hillsides joined the dark green pines, with the wind blowing through the distinctive fascicles of three needles each collected together to make a towering Ponderosa.

This year was different. This was the first spring since the fires, and soot black and muddy brown painted large swaths of the mountainside, the plains, and the town. The fire had cleaned out acres of overcrowded trees. And then the flash flooding in the wake of the fires had caused even more damage, swooshing down the burn scars, across roads, and into town.

I'm so grateful to have a home to come home to, Anna thought.

She sipped a cup of English breakfast tea with hot milk as she relaxed in the lawn chair. It was an old aluminum frame chair with faded and missing straps that she'd found at a garage sale in Pioneersburg a few weeks ago. She'd spruced it up by weaving a new seat out of colorful craft cord in the bright colors of the desert and a pattern reminiscent of the West.

It was one of the few pieces of furniture they owned, and it was light enough to carry around the house to wherever she needed a chair. The only other furniture they'd bought so far was a bed, a recliner for David, a picnic table and benches for the dining room, and supplies she needed for her expanded art studio. *We'll get there. We're already better off than I could have imagined.* She smiled with gratitude.

Just as she picked up her knitting, her cell phone rang in her over-sized art smock's pocket. Jessie's photo showed on the screen. Anna picked up. "Hi, my sweet girl. What're you up to?"

"I just called to check on you, Mom. I miss having you

and Dad here all the time. Mostly," she added, teasing. They both laughed.

"Aren't you and Prentice off doing something fun?"

Jessie said, "No, he's on shift today in Garnet. If you miss him so much, he's right down the road from you. Maybe you could call 9-1-1," she said with a weak laugh.

"Er... nah. That's okay." The attempt at a joke didn't work for either of them. Too much 9-1-1 in their lives since last summer.

"Mom, despite everything, all the disasters this year, I'm so grateful we're such a close family," she said. "And that dad's healthy again and you're both able to spread your wings in new ways."

"For sure. God pretty much had to kick me right in the hinder to get me to start some new habits," she said. "Hinder" rhymed with finder and was an anatomy word she picked up from David's mom on the farm. It always made her laugh, though she missed David's mom. "By the way, I memorized a new verse to share with you."

"Okay, I'm curious!"

"It's from Habakkuk, in the Hebrew Bible. It says, 'Look among the nations, and see; wonder and be astounded. For I am doing a work in your days that you would not believe if told...' Doesn't that hit home?"

"God works in mysterious ways, for sure."

Anna agreed. "That's right, sweet girl."

Jessie moved onto a more down-to-earth subject. "Are you teaching your Saturday class today, Mom?"

Anna smiled into the phone. "I sure am. My students will be here soon."

As soon as they moved back into the house, she'd set up her art studio with purpose, and she had new paintings already placed in two local galleries and a commission in the works for a client who wanted a mural painted in her stairwell. She'd also reached out to a new gallery in Pass Christian, Mississippi that had opened years after Hurricane Katrina as the town was slowly rebuilding.

But she also wanted to share her energy and creativity. She asked the local high school how she could help students who needed a fresh start with school. She'd told David, "They don't do their homework, even though they have the skills. I think it's just a symptom of their uncertainty about their value in the world, and I can help with that."

So, she had reached into her heart and arranged it with the school for some students to work at her house on Saturdays instead of going to Saturday detention. They did homework first, with her help if needed, and then it was fun art lessons in the afternoon. Hanging around together and talking. They enjoyed being with her. She let them call her Art Mama as long as they were respectful about it.

And their parents. They were willing to pay for the opportunity for their children to have this new kind of support and accountability. They were caring people trying to bond with their children but not realizing they were asking their teenagers the wrong questions. She hoped to connect with their parents soon to share her ideas about communicating with their kids. It was no fun trying to talk to a brick wall. She hoped that eventually even the parents might take her art classes. Why, she could even offer family art classes!

Jessie brought Anna out of her reverie. "So, Mom, what's your plan for your students today?"

"Well, we've done enough with line drawing and cartoon drawing, and now we're moving on to tattoo drawing."

"Tattoo drawing!" Jessie laughed. "I bet that'll get their attention."

"It's a sneaky way to get them to be patient and precise and still be creative," said Anna.

"Yes, it's relaxing to focus on just one thing and block out all the noise. I bet it's helping them deal with all of this year's disasters, one day at a time."

Anna agreed. "They've all been through the fires, and then the blizzard. It's affected everyone differently. But I'm positive every one of them had communication issues in their families before any of those things happened."

"You're so good for them."

"I hope so. I feel like they need me right now, and I love it."

"I need you, too, Mom!" Jessie laughed.

"I know, honey, but not like these kids. They have such big holes in their lives, and I'm just asking questions and showing them how I'm living an imperfect but happy life." She pondered. "We process life together, as Mike Donahue says."

"He's a great motivator for teens. And like him, you're honest with them, and they trust you," Jessie said. "They know what you've been through."

Anna said, "We have some things in common."

"Yes, and besides that, it's a welcoming place for them. You've transformed the house, and it has good space for them in the studio," said Jessie. "Benches and long tables and shelves full of paper and paint and everything."

"Well, they don't know this yet, and neither does David, but next month I'm going to ask them to design and paint a mural for me on the back wall in the living room."

"That's cool," said Jessie. "I wish you could have done something like this a long time ago."

"Hm... Painting a mural?" she laughed. "You mean teaching?"

"It feels like you held yourself back." Jessie paused. "No, that's not it exactly. More like, you spent so much energy putting me and Dad first, and Tiger Grandma too. You didn't have anything left for yourself."

"I didn't mean to, and I know better than that now, but it's hard to analyze your own life from the middle of the storm."

"We've learned that the hard way, too," Jessie agreed. "I better get going. Time for yoga. It's good to check in with you, Mom. Love you."

"Thanks for calling... I love you too." She pushed the red button to disconnect and sipped some more of her tea.

David was gone today, even though it was a Saturday. His new job as a truck yard "dispatch" had regular hours, but that didn't mean someone didn't have to work on the weekend, and he was still the new guy on the totem pole. Her phone rang, and it was David, even though he had just left for work a few hours ago.

Anna rejoiced that the accidental snowdrift had melted, and they talked all the time again.

"Hi, honey," she said. "How are things at the yard today?"

He switched into his vaguely British pirate accent from the *Princess Bride* fairytale. "Once word leaks out that a pirate has gone soft, people begin to disobey you, and then it's nothing but work, work, work all the time," he joked.

"David, I'm so glad you're on the road to being healthy again."

He laughed at her seriousness. "I'm hardly on the road at all now, just here in the office. And I'm pretty healthy, but I can't count to ten on my toes anymore, since one toe is missing." He added, "but it is sweet to sleep at home with you every night."

"It's a dream come true," she said. "And so is having you back to your lovable self again, David. Thanks for following the doctor's advice and taking your meds like you're supposed to."

"As you wish, my princess."

She smiled. "So, what do you need today, my farm boy?"

"I just called to hear your voice," he said. "Communication is a wonderful thing."

The End

AUTHOR'S NOTE

Why did I write this novel?

In March 2019, I and everyone living in the U.S. West and Midwest experienced an unprecedented blizzard. Despite all the warnings that it would be as strong as a Category 2 hurricane, people were still caught off guard by the "bomb cyclone." In Colorado, many thousands of motorists popped outside for one more quick errand and ended up sleeping in their cars overnight after getting stranded on major highways and smaller roads. Even snowplows could not work due to the horrible conditions. So:

• Do you have a blizzard kit in your vehicle? See https://community.fema.gov/ProtectiveActions/s/article/Winter-Storm-Supplies for ideas, and customize your kit for what you and your family will need when it's all you have.

• Prepare to find shelter from a storm. See www.ready.gov/sites/default/files/2020-11/winter-storm_information-sheet.pdf.

• Prepare and store your emergency financial first aid kit, like Anna did. See www.fema.gov/emergency-financial-first-aid-kit.

• Take a Red Cross CPR and First Aid class. See www.heart.org/en/courses/heartsaver-first-aid-cpr-aed-course-options.

How can we pretend a disaster is never going to affect us?

It might be a bomb cyclone. Or it might be an annual checkup that was skipped or a medical diagnosis that was ignored. Help keep each other accountable. Look for people in your life who would like to get all this done but need help. Today. Denial is disastrous.

Share this novel with friends, family, and your local emergency responders so they can tell others about it. It can be a tool to save lives, relationships, and property. It's true, as my husband Mark says: Communication is a wonderful thing.

Write a review of *To Melt A Snowdrift* on the site where you bought this book or www.goodreads.com/book/show/195233885-to-melt-a-snowdrift so it will get noticed.

See LisaHatfieldWriter.com to sign up for my intermittent newsletter and receive a free short story. My website also has resources for book clubs who wish to study wildfire or blizzard preparedness together. **Tell me about your experiences and successes!**

ACKNOWLEDGMENTS

Thanks to:

Tony A., "The Laundry List." adultchildren.org/litera ture/laundry-list/

Robin Adair, Pikes Peak Regional Office of Emergency Management and Community Emergency Response Team. admin.elpasoco.com/pproem/cert/

Marge Bardeen

Natalie Barszcz, *Our Community News*

Christy Bilbrey, over-the-road trucker, & her beloved cat Lily (2005-2022)

'Boston,' the band

Don Corgi, "17 Different Types of Drawing Styles Every Artist Should Try." doncorgi.com

Den Kwai Ying

Depeche Mode

Mike Donahue, *Talking to Brick Walls.* value-up.org

Electric Light Orchestra (ELO)

Dan Ellis, *Katrina Survival and Revival: A Pass Christian MS Story*

El Paso County Search & Rescue. Epcsar.org

Deb Geolat

Shelby, host of "Happiness by the Mile" YouTube channel

Pamela Hart, author of *Beauty from Ashes* and *City of a Thousand Tears*

Eric Hartman, over-the-road trucker

Mark Hatfield, husband, gentleman, and geographer

Doug Higgins, Northwoods Equipment & Transport LLC

Jennifer Sue Horsey

Dr. Gayle Humm, M.D.

Bill Kappel, President/Chief Meteorologist, Applied Weather Associates

Katrina.passchristian.net/stories.htm

Rev. Dr. Robert Kaylor, "Wednesdays with Wesley" podcast

Carley Lehman

Nancy Kaplan Marshall

C. W. McCall

Doug Meikle, Community Emergency Response Team

Ross Meyer

S. Morgenstern, *The Princess Bride*

André Mouton, Community Emergency Response Team

Finn Murphy, *The Long Haul*

Matthew Nelson, City Arborist & eternal optimist

Steve Pate, *Our Community News*

Randy Petrick, author of *The Soul Repair Manual* and creator of www.wordsofabundance.com.

The Police

Scott Rand, Medical Reserve Corps of El Paso County

Rush, the band. www.rush.com

Dr. Gordon Saunders, Mastermind group and author of The Verdura series and The Young America series. gordon-saunders-writer.com

The Scorpions, www.the-scorpions.com.

Julie Shook

Barbara Sissel, Reedsy Developmental Editor

Linda van Noordt and The Leddies

Blair Walker, host of "Better Preparedness" YouTube channel

Michael Weinfeld, *Our Community News*

Ben Wester, Black Forest Together

Joyce Witte, WoTLM Tri-Lakes Monument Radio Association

Kent Wong, *Swimming to Freedom: My Escape from China and the Cultural Revolution*

Margie Wood, Mastermind Group and author of The Rose Haven Journals. margiewoodwrites.com

Jack Zenger, "The Confidence Gap In Men And Women: Why It Matters And How To Overcome It." Forbes.com, April 8, 2018

ABOUT THE AUTHOR

Lisa Hatfield shares emergency preparedness ideas so people will be more ready for natural and family disasters.

As they say in her Community Emergency Response Team (CERT), "We want you to be able to help yourself and others in the middle of chaos... when 9-1-1 isn't coming."

To Starve an Ember and *To Melt a Snowdrift* are the first two novels in Lisa's **Ready to Go?** series. The next novel will go back in time to Hurricane Katrina, where Jessie, Anna, and Tiger Grandma, Jiexen, fight to survive the storm in Mississippi while wrestling with their own demons.

Stay tuned at LisaHatfieldWriter.com where you can see updates, get book club resources, or sign up for my occasional newsletter.